ADVANCED
PHYSICAL
CHEMISTRY

Also by Susannah Nix

I and Love and You: A Romantic Short Story Collection

Chemistry Lessons Series:

Remedial Rocket Science

Intermediate Thermodynamics

ADVANCED PHYSICAL CHEMISTRY

SUSANNAH NIX

Haver Street Press

FIRST EDITION: March 2018

ISBN: 978-0-9990948-3-9

Haver Street Press | 448 W. 19th St., Suite 407 | Houston, TX 77008

Edited by Julia Ganis, www.juliaedits.com

Ebook & Print Cover Design by www.ebooklaunch.com

For the Ladies' Lifting Club

Chapter One

ell, frak, Penny Popplestone thought as she stared at the couple who'd just sauntered past the window of the coffee shop. *Why does this keep happening to me?*

She couldn't believe it—and yet at the same time, she could absolutely believe it, because apparently she was forever doomed to date unfaithful men.

She had discovered her last boyfriend was cheating on her only a month after she'd picked up her entire life in Washington, DC, and moved across the country for him. And before that, she'd been cheated on by both her college boyfriend and her high school boyfriend. She'd had four whole boyfriends in her life, and as of this moment, every single one of them had turned out to be unfaithful. A perfect 0-4 record.

She must be cursed. There was no other explanation for it.

The bell on the front door of the shop jangled as Kenneth, her current—soon to be ex—boyfriend, strolled in. The very same Kenneth who had canceled their plans for tonight because he had to go out of town for work. And who, instead of being out of town, was in Penny's favorite coffee shop with his arm around another woman.

The gall. The absolute gall.

She'd call it almighty stupidity on his part, except she wasn't supposed to be here tonight either. Her knitting group usually met here Monday nights, which Kenneth knew very well. But this Monday one of the members had an art show, which Kenneth also knew, because he had declined Penny's invitation to be her plus-one. What he didn't know was that Penny had called the group at the last minute and asked if they wanted to meet tonight instead.

There was no reason for him to suspect Penny would be at Antidote on a Friday night. And yet, here she was. Witnessing his indiscretion with her own eyes. Like fate had set her up for a punking.

Fortunately, Kenneth's attention was so wholly consumed by the woman with him that he hadn't even noticed Penny sitting with her friends at the big orange couch in the far back corner. He was too busy nuzzling his nose into his date's silky blonde hair as his hand stroked her tiny, taut butt through her skintight dress while they waited in line.

He'd never behaved that way in public with Penny. Not that she would have wanted him to—public displays of affection were bad manners. But it might be nice if he'd at least tried. Of course, Penny's butt was neither taut nor tiny, and she certainly didn't own any skintight dresses. Not with her size sixteen figure.

Kenneth had always claimed to like her curves, but he'd never liked them enough to feel them up in public the way he was doing with his skinny blonde date.

The baby hat Penny had been knitting for her cousin lay forgotten in her lap as she reached up to touch her coarse red hair. Every morning she spent thirty minutes attacking it with blow dryers and flat irons to torture the curl out of it, but she could never get it as smooth and shiny as the blonde's hair looked. She'd never been that skinny either, even during her years of chasing fad diets and exercise crazes.

Penny's friends continued to chat and knit around her, as

oblivious to Kenneth's presence as he was to theirs. Cynthia, the one having the art show Monday, was venting about the challenges of managing caterers and publicity for her show, and the others' attention was focused on her. It was just as well. If they knew, one of them might decide to confront him, and Penny didn't want a scene.

What she wanted was to not have this happening to her *here* of all places, in front of her friends. Antidote was *her* place. She lived just a few blocks away and worked out of her apartment, so she walked here almost every weekday for her morning coffee break. Which Kenneth also knew, because this was where they'd first met.

She'd been sitting at her usual stool at the counter two months ago, enjoying her usual midmorning nonfat latte, when he'd come in for a triple espresso and asked if the seat beside her was taken. They'd chatted for almost half an hour, and she'd been thoroughly dazzled by his British accent and charming manners by the time he went back to work. Every day for a week after that, he came into Antidote at the same time to see her again. On the fifth day, he asked her out to dinner, and they'd been together ever since.

It had all seemed so romantic. So perfect. Except for the fact that Kenneth worked late a lot and traveled out of town nearly every other week. Which, in retrospect, probably should have clued her in.

Penny was definitely cursed. Either that or deeply stupid, to keep falling for one cheating man after another.

Her throat tightened as she watched Kenneth lean over to whisper something in his date's ear. Whatever he said made the blonde blush and giggle. His hand curled protectively around her waist, and she leaned into him, resting her head on his shoulder.

Penny blinked as her throat burned. She was about five seconds from crying, and she needed to get somewhere private before that happened. Calmly, so as not to arouse any suspicion, she set aside her knitting, excused herself, and hurried to the bathroom.

There were two stalls in the ladies' room and fortunately both were empty. Penny chose the larger one and slid the bolt home as tears welled in her eyes. Her vision blurred as she peered at the lidless toilet seat. Whatever. She could cry just as well standing up.

Kenneth had *lied* to her. How long had it been going on? How many times had he lied to her before this? Had he *ever* gone out of town for work, or had it all been an elaborate ruse? One that she'd fallen for hook, line, and sinker. She felt like such a chump.

For all she knew, he'd been seeing this woman for a long time. Maybe even before he'd asked Penny out.

Oh, God. What if he was cheating on this other woman with *Penny*?

A moan escaped her lips at the thought. How could she have been so dumb? So trusting? You'd think she would have learned to be more cautious after the last time—the last *three* times. To recognize the signs. But apparently not.

She heard the creak of the bathroom door opening and clapped her hand over her mouth to stifle her sobs. She was almost positive Kenneth hadn't seen her, and she didn't think any of her friends had noticed anything wrong. Hopefully it was just some stranger coming in to pee.

"Hello?" said a male voice that definitely did not belong to Kenneth. It took her a moment to place it.

"Caleb?" He was one of the baristas who worked there—and not just any barista, but the superhumanly hot barista she'd had a shallow crush on for months.

"Yeah."

What was he *doing* in here? She sniffled and scrubbed at her eyes. "This is the *women's* restroom."

"I saw you get up when Kenneth came in with that woman."

Wonderful. Now Hottie Barista knew what a pathetic chump

she was. Perfect. Of all the people who could have witnessed her indignity, it had to be him. She tore off a strip of toilet paper and blew her nose.

"You okay in there?" Caleb asked, sounding uncomfortable. Which made two of them.

"Of course I'm not okay. My boyfriend is a cheating creep."

"I'm sorry."

The pity in his voice filled her with anger. As if it wasn't bad enough that Kenneth had cheated on her and lied to her, he had to make her humiliation public by parading that woman around in front of people who knew her. Penny's throat closed up in panic as she wondered how many times he'd done it before. Maybe he brought women here all the time. Maybe *all* the employees knew her boyfriend had been making a fool of her.

"Did you know?" she choked out.

There was a long pause. "Yes."

"I can't believe it," Penny moaned. Her wad of tissue was soaked through already. She dropped it into the toilet and tore off another length. "I'm such an idiot. Did they come in here all the time? Did everyone know but me?"

"I don't think so. I only saw them once before. Malik was working that night too, but he was in the back when they came in."

Well, that was something. At least she'd be able to look the rest of the staff in the eye. It was only Caleb who'd known and done nothing to warn her. Which wasn't all that surprising. He'd always acted distant and a little aloof. She was shocked he'd even bothered to check on her.

"How long ago?" she asked him.

She heard his feet shuffle on the tile floor, but he didn't answer.

"How long?"

"About a month ago," Caleb mumbled.

A month? A choking sob bubbled up from Penny's throat, and she bit down on her lip.

"Penny?"

"*What?*" She felt trapped, like the walls were closing in on her. She needed Hottie Barista to leave. She needed to not be having a breakdown in a public bathroom stall. But mostly, she needed Kenneth to not be a lying, cheating scumbag. Or else she needed to go back in time and never agree to go out with him in the first place. That would be okay too.

"Can I do anything?" Caleb asked.

"You can leave me alone to cry in private, thank you very much."

"Okay," he said. "Sorry."

Penny heard the bathroom door close and buried her face in her hands, sobbing even harder than before.

Too late, she realized she should have asked Hottie Barista if Kenneth was still out there. She had no idea how long she needed to keep hiding in here. Maybe she could slip out the back door. She could make up an excuse and text the knitting group, apologizing for running out. She could say she'd gotten sick—no, they might think it was the cookies she'd brought. She could say she'd left the oven on. That would do it.

She was already fumbling her phone out of her purse when the bathroom door opened again.

"Penny?" her best friend Olivia said. "Are you okay?"

"Yes, I'm fine." She tried not to sound like she'd been crying, but the fact that her voice came out like a drowning frog sort of gave her away.

"Open the stall."

Penny slid the latch back and pulled the door open a crack. She could tell by the look on Olivia's face that she knew. "Did you see him? With that *woman?*"

Olivia shook her head, her ash-blonde hair falling across her face as she dug around in her big black purse for a packet of

Kleenex. "Hottie Barista came and told me," she said, handing Penny a fresh tissue.

"Awesome." After months of basically ignoring her, why had he picked tonight of all nights to suddenly take an interest in her? Penny blew her nose and Olivia handed her another tissue.

"I'm sorry your boyfriend's a dickless weasel."

Olivia had been the best thing about moving to Los Angeles. The two of them had been friends online for six years before they'd wound up living in the same city. They'd both been obsessed with the TV show *Sherlock* in college, and had spent hours on Tumblr picking apart the episodes, reading fan fiction, and swooning over Benedict Cumberbatch. That two-year hiatus after the cliffhanger ending of "The Reichenbach Fall" had been agony, but it had cemented their friendship. Their *Sherlock* obsessions had faded in the intervening years, but they'd remained friends as they each moved on to other interests—although they hadn't met in person until Penny moved to LA a year ago. She never would have survived her first few miserable months here if it hadn't been for Olivia.

"Are they still out there?" Penny asked.

"No, they got their coffee to go and left."

Thank goodness for small favors. At least she wouldn't have to hide in the bathroom all night while Kenneth and his other woman lingered over their drinks and gazed lovingly at each other.

"Why does this always happen to me?" Penny asked, dabbing at her eyes. "What's wrong with me?"

"Nothing's wrong with you. You're awesome."

"Well, something about me sure seems to make men want to cheat on me, because it keeps happening over and over again. Do I give off some kind of pheromone that says *please cheat on me?*"

Olivia tried to push the door open wider, and it bounced off Penny's arm. "Come out and wash your face."

Penny shook her head. "I don't want to. I want to stay here and be miserable."

"I know you do, but it's a toilet, Pen. It's gross in here. Come out and be miserable around people who love you. Cynthia's getting a bottle of your favorite wine for the table and I'll buy you a chocolate cupcake."

"I can't eat a cupcake, I already had a cookie."

Penny was strict about her sugar intake and the Antidote cupcakes were humongous. One of them was like a week's worth of sugar.

"You just found out your boyfriend is a cheating asshole. You can make an exception this once and eat a damn cupcake. You know you want to."

She did want to. Even though she knew it would just make her feel even worse later. Part of her wanted to feel bad though. A gluten stomachache would really drive home just how miserable her life was.

Penny came out of the toilet stall and washed her face at the sink. The crying had left her pale skin bright pink, which brought out the green in her hazel eyes. Her mascara had smeared, making her look like the Winter Soldier, but Olivia produced a makeup remover wipe from her purse and helped her clean it up. Olivia's purse was like a mini Rite Aid. She always seemed to have whatever anyone needed at any given moment: ibuprofen, lip balm, concealer, antacids, a granola bar. If you needed it, it was probably in Olivia's purse.

Once she was presentable again, Penny followed Olivia out of the ladies' room and back to the orange couch. Everyone had put their knitting away, and Cynthia was at the register talking to Roxanne, the manager. Caleb was at the espresso machine making a drink. His eyes flicked to Penny when she came out and then away again quickly.

"Honey, come here," Vilma said, opening her arms. Olivia squeezed Penny's arm and went to join Cynthia at the register.

Penny sank down on the couch and crumpled into Vilma's embrace. She was the oldest member of the knitting group, a middle-aged schoolteacher with two teenage sons, and she gave excellent, motherly hugs.

"What an asshole." Esther scowled under her thick brown bangs as she leaned back in her chair across from the couch. "Bringing that woman here when he knows you come here all the time. He deserves a kick in the balls."

Esther had never been shy about expressing her opinions or standing up for herself. Penny wished she could be more like her. She never would have let a guy like Kenneth make a fool of her.

"It was like he wanted to get caught." Esther's best friend Jinny shook her head, tossing her dark straight hair over her shoulder. "Maybe he did. Maybe the guilt was eating him alive and he was hoping you'd see him and put him out of his misery."

Jinny sat in a big green armchair that was nearly twice her size. Like Penny, she was an optimist who always tried to see the best in everyone. Despite the fact that she was petite and beautiful, she'd been cheated on by her last boyfriend too. Maybe the problem wasn't Penny. Maybe the problem was men.

Except Jinny had a new boyfriend who was sweet and perfect and would probably never cheat on her. Esther had a boyfriend too, and Penny couldn't imagine anyone daring to cheat on her. And Vilma and Cynthia were both happily married. The only single woman in the knitting group was Olivia—and Penny would be joining her in spinsterdom as soon as she had a chance to dump Kenneth.

"Or maybe he's just an arrogant prick who thinks he can get away with anything and never suffer any consequences," Esther suggested, leaning forward for one of the cookies Penny had brought.

Penny always baked homemade treats for knitting. She loved to bake, but she only allowed herself one sweet treat per day, so she gave away the spoils of her labors. Technically, you weren't supposed to bring food into Antidote since they sold pastries sourced from a local bakery, but Penny had special dispensation since she was friendly with the manager and always brought extras for the employees.

"Wine's on the way," Cynthia announced, coming back with six wineglasses. She looked like one of the Dora Milaje from *Black Panther* with her close-cropped hair and tall, slender figure. Except Cynthia was a children's illustrator who mostly wore long dresses instead of Wakandan armor.

"And one chocolate cupcake." Olivia set it on the table and sat down on Penny's other side, passing out forks and small plates so they could all share.

Penny sniffled and pushed herself upright. "Thank you." The cupcake looked magnificent. Three inches of moist chocolate cake topped with generous swirls of silky buttercream icing and dark chocolate shavings. It was almost too pretty to eat.

"You're drooling." Cynthia flicked her skirt aside as she lowered herself into the empty chair on Esther's other side. "Don't just stare at it. Dig in."

Penny cut the cupcake into six pieces and dished them out to everyone, keeping the smallest piece for herself.

"What are you going to do about Kenneth?" Jinny asked, digging in her purse for a Lactaid.

"I'm going to break up with him. Duh." Penny scooped a bite of chocolate cupcake into her mouth. It tasted just as heavenly as it looked.

"Yeah, but how?" Esther asked. "Like, in person or over the phone?"

"You want us to go with you?" Vilma said. "For solidarity."

It was tempting, but Penny couldn't imagine trooping over to Kenneth's apartment with her entire knitting group in tow just to break up with him. "I'll probably just call him."

"Screw that, send him a text," Cynthia said. "He's not even worth the time it would take to tell him you're dumping his sorry ass."

Penny stabbed another bite of cupcake. "I think I need more closure than a text."

"Closure's overrated," Jinny said around a mouthful of icing. "Remember when Stuart cheated on me? He kept calling, begging me to take him back for weeks—and I almost did it. Take my advice and block Kenneth's number as soon as you dump him."

"When are you going to do it?" Esther asked.

"If you call tonight you might catch him in the middle of sexy-times with his lady friend," Jinny pointed out, wrinkling her nose.

"Do it tonight." Esther bobbed her head eagerly. "Cockblock that motherfucker if you can."

"One bottle of New Zealand sauv," Roxanne announced, pulling a corkscrew out of her back pocket as she arrived at their table. She wore a sleeveless black T-shirt that showed off her tattooed arms and pulled tight across her pregnant belly.

Before she'd gotten pregnant, she'd been a regular on a local roller derby team and still looked like she could break a man across her thighs. Penny had once heard her threaten to kick a customer's teeth through his skull for making a lewd comment about her ass.

She cast a sympathetic look at Penny as she stooped to fill their glasses. "Sorry about your boyfriend, sweetie."

"Did you know?" Penny asked. It was one thing for Caleb not to tell her—he'd never really acted like he wanted to be her friend —but Roxanne was different. Penny *liked* Roxanne. She was halfway through knitting a blanket for her baby. If she'd been protecting Kenneth too...

Roxanne shook her head. "I didn't. I swear. They never came in when I was working."

"Would you have told me if you knew?"

"Hell yeah, I would have. Solidarity, sister." She extended a fist and Penny gave it a half-hearted bump. "Besides, you're a way better customer than he is."

"No wine for me," Olivia said when Roxanne got to her glass.

"I'm on call again tonight." Olivia was a systems analyst for a power company and spent a lot of nights on call in case any of her systems went offline.

Roxanne obligingly poured Olivia's portion into Penny's glass and took the empty bottle with her back to the counter.

"A toast," Esther said, and everyone raised their drinks. "Good riddance to bad rubbish."

"Here here," they all said as they clinked their glasses against Penny's. She tried to smile, but couldn't quite pull it off, so she took a big gulp of wine instead. Followed by another.

Jinny set her glass down and picked up her knitting. "He did you a favor, you know."

Penny squinted at her over the top of her wineglass. "By cheating on me?"

"By getting caught so early in the relationship."

"It's true," Olivia said, leaning back on the couch. "Can you imagine if you hadn't been here tonight? Who knows how long you might have gone on dating him, totally unaware that he was a chickenshit dickweed."

Penny shuddered at the thought. She'd actually thought Kenneth might be the one. They hadn't exchanged *I love you*s yet, but she'd assumed they would soon. Even though it was only April, she'd already been planning to take him home to meet her family at Thanksgiving and fantasizing about a trip to England to meet his parents over Christmas. She'd figured sometime next year they'd probably get engaged. Plan a June wedding for the following year. Start trying for a family after their first anniversary. She'd be able to stay home and keep working, and maybe by then his company's IPO would have gone though, so they could afford to buy a house in a neighborhood with good schools.

It was possible she'd gotten a little ahead of herself.

"I'm going to be honest," Esther said, picking up her knitting again. "I never liked that guy."

"Me neither," Vilma said.

Jinny tilted her head. "He did seem kind of...snotty."

"Yes! Exactly!" Vilma pointed with the hand holding her wineglass. "Did you ever notice how he talked to service employees?"

Cynthia pursed her lips without looking up from her knitting needles. "Like they were the help?"

"That was just his Britishness," Penny said.

"He never looked me in the eye." Cynthia shook her head slowly. "There was definitely something weaselly about him."

"You are incredibly tall," Penny pointed out. "And he's incredibly not." She wasn't sure why she was defending him. Habit, maybe.

Cynthia sniffed. "He could have tilted his head a little. It's not that hard."

Jinny twisted her lips to one side. "Cynthia's right. He never gave anyone the time of day unless he was trying to get something from them."

"I thought he was charming when I first met him," Penny said. If there was one thing Kenneth had going for him, it was charm.

Esther snorted. "Yeah. Because he wanted something from you."

Penny frowned at her in confusion. "What?"

"Sex."

Penny wasn't so sure about that. "To be honest, he never seemed that enthusiastic about it." She grimaced. "I guess now I know why."

"Mmmm, that doesn't surprise me one bit." Vilma looked up from her needles with an evil grin. "The way his hair's thinning? Low testosterone."

Penny let out a giggle that quickly turned teary, thanks to the wine coursing through her system. "Thanks for being here tonight, you guys." Vilma patted her knee and pushed her share of the cupcake onto Penny's plate.

Cynthia directed an expressive look in Penny's direction. "You know we'd do anything for you, right?"

Esther nodded her agreement. "If you want us to go over to his apartment and kick his ass, all you have to do is say the word. We'll totally do it."

Penny shook her head, smiling at the image. "Thank you, but I don't think that's necessary. I'm actually feeling better about the whole situation already."

"How about instead we get another bottle of wine?" Jinny said, getting to her feet.

Cynthia held up her half-empty glass. "Make it two bottles."

Penny glanced toward the counter and caught Caleb watching them. As soon as their eyes met he turned away. She knocked back the rest of her wine and tried not to care.

Chapter Two

*B*y the end of the evening, their table had gone through four bottles of wine—although Penny suspected she'd consumed at least one and a half of them all on her own. She didn't usually drink more than a single glass at a time, and she was definitely feeling the effects when Olivia drove her home.

It felt good though. The fuzziness helped dull some of her rage and humiliation.

"You want me to come up?" Olivia asked as she stopped in front of Penny's Culver City apartment building. "I think I saw a space back there."

"Not necessary," Penny said, fumbling with the door handle. "Thanks though."

"You sure? We could get in our pajamas and watch TV. Anything you want."

Penny yawned and shook her head. "I appreciate the offer, but I'm just going to fall into bed and go straight to sleep."

"Drink some water," Olivia instructed as Penny hauled herself out of the car. "And call me tomorrow."

Penny waved goodbye and headed inside.

The walk upstairs in the cold night air woke her back up, so she didn't feel as sleepy by the time she let herself into her apartment. It also reawakened her anger. She gazed around the cozy two-bedroom space she'd decorated with cheerful floral patterns and overstuffed cushions, unsure what to do with herself.

Kenneth had never liked spending time at her apartment. He'd said it was too girly, and complained about all her throw pillows. They'd spent most of their time together either out at bars or at his place. Penny didn't like bars particularly, but Kenneth did, so to bars they went. She'd spend the whole evening standing awkwardly at a high-top, nursing a fifteen-dollar glass of ten-bucks-a-bottle wine and being jostled by passersby as she tried to have a shouted conversation with Kenneth over the music. Then they'd go back to his place, have very brief sex, and fall asleep immediately afterward. And in the morning, Penny would make him breakfast.

She always wound up cooking for the men she dated, because the only other alternative was eating out, and it was difficult to eat healthy when you ate out all the time. Also because she liked cooking. At home, her mother was always in the kitchen making something delicious, so that was what home meant to Penny. But had a man she was dating ever offered to help her cook? No. They were so used to being waited on by their mothers and their girl-friends that they pleaded helplessness in the kitchen and let her do all the work. As if they were incapable of learning how to chop an onion or dice a tomato.

Just thinking about all the omelets she'd cooked Kenneth made her blood boil. Anyone could learn to make an omelet! All you had to do was watch a three-minute YouTube video! It wasn't like it was hard. But he'd never bothered, because it hadn't even occurred to him.

Penny had cooked for him and then she'd done the dishes and cleaned up his kitchen afterward. She'd even folded a load of his laundry once, because it was just sitting there in the basket getting all wrinkled, and the sight of unfolded laundry made her twitchy.

She was getting angrier by the second. Suddenly, more than anything, she wanted Kenneth out of her life. Right. That. Second.

She pulled out her phone, her veins coursing with righteous indignation and liquid courage. When she pulled up her Favorites she felt even more rage, because what was Kenneth even doing in the number one spot? Above her parents and her best friend? He'd never been worthy of that kind of honor. She angrily smashed her index finger into his face, wishing it was his real face instead of just a picture.

He answered on the second ring. "Hello, darling. You're up late."

"What's her name?" Penny said, trying to keep the tremble out of her voice.

There was a pause. "What?" he said, choosing to play dumb. "Whose name?"

"The woman you were with tonight at Antidote."

"I don't know what you're talking about, love. I'm in Portland." He was a smooth liar, but then he'd have to be. Otherwise he would have gotten caught much sooner. "Did someone tell you—"

"I saw you, Kenneth. I was there when you came in."

Another pause. "Shit."

"Yeah," Penny agreed. "That about sums it up." She almost never swore, but she was tempted tonight.

"Listen, darling—"

"No, don't you darling me. Who is she?"

"She's no one. Just a coworker. That's all."

Penny snorted in disbelief. If tonight's display was an example of how he behaved with his coworkers, his office must be a hotbed of sexual harassment.

"Look," Kenneth said, at least having the decency to drop the *darling*, "the truth is my trip got canceled at the last minute.

Things have blown up with this project and we've got a real disaster on our hands. I didn't tell you because I knew I'd be burning the midnight oil all weekend and wouldn't be able to see you."

"Unbelievable," Penny said. "You're still lying." He really thought he could talk his way out of this. That he'd feed her some story and she'd believe him, despite the evidence of her own eyes. How pathetic he must think she was.

"I don't know what you think you saw, but I can assure you—"

"*Stop it,*" she shouted before he could gaslight her any further, the repulsive slug. "You know what, Kenneth? I'm not interested in anything you have to say. Now or ever again. You don't have to lie about going out of town anymore. From now on, you're free to see whomever you want—other than me, because we're through."

"Penny, please. Let me—"

She disconnected the call before he could finish the sentence.

Her phone started ringing again almost immediately. Remembering Jinny's advice, she blocked his number and went to bed.

THE NEXT MORNING, Penny's alarm went off at eight a.m., just like it did every Saturday. Her yoga class started in an hour, and she liked to get up and fix herself a light breakfast well before she started exercising.

Instead of popping out of bed with her usual enthusiasm, she rolled over and groaned. Her head was pounding, both from all the wine she'd consumed last night and all the crying she'd done in the bathroom at Antidote.

She definitely should have drunk more water before bed. In fact, she should get up and drink some right now.

Instead, Penny lay on her back staring up at the textured plaster ceiling without moving. A faded yellow water stain shaped like a snowman stared back at her.

Her limbs felt heavy, like they'd been encased in cement. The thought of doing anything made them feel even heavier.

Go on, get up. Have a glass of water and an Advil. Maybe a banana too. Then get dressed and go to yoga.

It would make her feel better. She knew it would. But she didn't actually want to feel better. She wanted to wallow. Just for today. She was entitled, wasn't she? She'd just broken up with her cheating boyfriend. If anything entitled you to wallowing, it ought to be that.

She typed out a text to her friend Melody.

I think I'm coming down with something. Not going to make to yoga today.

Penny tossed her phone down and went back to sleep.

She slept until noon, which she hadn't done in months. Not since her last breakup. She stayed in her pajamas and watched a *House Hunters* marathon on HGTV all day, directing all her residual anger at the insufferable, underemployed couples on the screen who felt they should be able to afford a chef's kitchen and whirlpool tub with the money their rich parents had gifted them for a down payment.

She didn't even feel like knitting, that was how bad things were. Roxanne's half-finished baby blanket taunted her from the coffee table. If there'd been any junk food in the apartment, Penny definitely would have eaten all of it. Instead, she had to content herself with toast. But she put butter and sugar and cinnamon on it so it'd feel like dessert. So there.

Olivia called in the afternoon to check on her. "Did you talk to Kenneth yet?"

"Yeah, I called him last night," Penny said, pushing herself upright on the couch.

"How'd it go?"

"About how you'd expect. He tried to deny it, and then he tried to make excuses. So I told him to stuff it."

"Good for you," Olivia said. "Are you okay?"

"I'm fine." Penny brushed bread crumbs and sugar granules off her chest. She was on her fourth piece of cinnamon toast.

"Do you want me to come over? We could watch TV and order pizza."

Penny didn't want company. Having company might interfere with her plans to feel sorry for herself. "Thanks, but I think I'm going to call it an early night. Yoga really kicked my butt today."

"You went to yoga this morning?"

"Yep." Guilt burned in the pit of Penny's stomach. She knew it was wrong to lie, but she wanted to be by herself. If Olivia knew she'd skipped yoga to stay home and wallow, she'd insist on coming over.

"That's good. You're really doing okay?"

"Sure," Penny said, trying to sound like she meant it. "I mean, I'm bummed, obviously, but I'm better off without him, right?"

"You definitely, definitely are."

"There you go. I just have to repeat that a few hundred more times, and by Monday I'll have forgotten him altogether."

"If you change your mind and want company, give me a call."

"I will, thanks."

When she got off the phone with Olivia, Penny called the nursing home where she volunteered on Sundays and canceled her shift. She could already tell she wasn't going to feel like leaving her apartment tomorrow.

She was taking the whole weekend off. From everything.

ON MONDAY MORNING, Penny lay in bed trying to convince herself to go to her spin class. Her limbs still had that encased-in-cement feeling, and she was completely drained of both energy and motivation. This was what she got for spending the entire weekend alone eating badly and wallowing in self-pity.

She knew better. She had her routines for a reason.

When Penny first moved to Los Angeles, after she discovered

the boyfriend she'd left her perfectly happy life in Washington, DC, for was cheating on her, she'd fallen into a little bit of a depression.

Her degree was in chemical engineering, but she worked as an examiner for the US Patent Office and had applied for a telecommuting position so she could follow that rat Brendon to the West Coast. There she'd been, all alone in a strange new city with a broken heart and a job that didn't require her to leave her apartment.

The thing Penny hadn't realized until *after* she locked herself into a work-from-home position was that she needed a routine and regular social interaction in her life. She was a people person, and she didn't do well cooped up in an apartment all day with no one but herself to talk to.

So she'd joined a gym. And a knitting group. And a book club. Signed up for a yoga class and a spin class and a weight training class. Started volunteering at a nursing home on Sundays and as a Planned Parenthood escort one or two Saturdays a month. And she made herself a rule that every single morning she had to shower, put on real clothes and makeup, and leave the house at least once. Which was when she'd incorporated the daily coffee breaks at Antidote into her routine.

Penny's Monday spin class started in half an hour. She just had to brush her teeth, change into workout clothes, and get in her car. Once she got to the gym, it would get easier. Her competitive instincts would kick in as soon as she got on the bike, and there'd be music to cheer her up. The exercise would make her feel better about herself, and that would make her feel better about everything else.

With a bone-deep sigh, she threw back the covers and pushed herself to her feet.

An hour later, sweaty and humming a Jackson Five song, she let herself back into her apartment feeling at least fifty percent better. It had been Motown day, which was always a guaranteed mood elevator. Plus, she'd beaten her previous energy output record and helped her team take first place. So far, her plan was going well.

After a shower and a breakfast of yogurt and fresh fruit, she sat down at the computer in her home office and opened a new patent application. This one was for a composite shoe insole, and after familiarizing herself with the specification, she spent the morning scouring government databases for older patents and scientific journal articles pertinent to the technology.

When her usual break time rolled around, she was still in a pretty good mood, even after three straight hours researching methods of curing composite materials for use in orthotic insoles. But as she logged out and stretched her legs, a tremor of unease ran through her at the thought of going to Antidote.

It was the site of her humiliation. Hottie Barista would probably be there, and for once, she didn't look forward to seeing his devastatingly handsome face. She still resented that he'd known her boyfriend was cheating on her and said nothing. He'd just let her go on seeing Kenneth, knowing she was going to get hurt.

Hottie Barista was kind of a jerk, as it turned out.

Far worse was the very real possibility she'd see Kenneth there. His office was just down the street, and he knew what time she went for coffee every day. If he wanted to force a conversation, Antidote would be a convenient place to do it. She'd half expected him to show up at her apartment over the weekend, but he might be waiting for today so he could ambush her in public, knowing she wouldn't want to make a scene. That would be just like him.

She pondered skipping the trip to Antidote this morning. It wasn't like she *had* to go out for coffee. She owned a perfectly good coffeemaker. She could take her break here at home. Surf the internet or watch some TV for an hour.

Bad idea.

Once Penny gave herself permission to sit around watching TV in the middle of the day, it would be difficult to go back to work afterward. She needed to leave her apartment and be around people for a while.

Fine. What if she went somewhere other than Antidote? There was a Coffee Bean not far away. She could go there instead.

But she didn't want to change coffee shops. She loved Antidote. It was her *Cheers*, where everybody knew her name. Kenneth shouldn't get to take that away from her. How was that fair when he was the villain? He should have to find a new favorite coffee place, not her.

To heck with Kenneth. And to heck with Hottie Barista too. Penny was sick and tired of rearranging her life to accommodate men. She was going to Antidote.

It was a beautiful April day when she stepped out of her apartment. The marine layer had burned off leaving behind a glistening blue sky and a crisp breeze. The walk to Antidote only took ten minutes. Her stride started out brisk and confident, but grew slower the closer she got to her destination. By the time she drew within sight of the building, she was dragging her feet like a recalcitrant toddler.

No one had seen her yet—it wasn't too late to fake her own death and start over with an alias in a new city. Or maybe just find another coffee shop to hang out in.

Her mother's voice popped into her head, telling her that was coward talk.

Penny wasn't a coward. She straightened her spine and pulled open the door, determined to face both Kenneth and Hottie Barista with her head held high.

After all that, there was no sign of either of them. Instead of Hottie Barista, the new girl, Elyse, stood alone behind the counter, looking overwhelmed. Penny let out a relieved breath and got in line.

Elyse was small framed with short hair and big round eyes set in a heart-shaped face, giving her a pixie-ish appearance. "Did you want any syrup in your skinny vanilla latte?" she asked the woman in front of Penny.

"Vanilla...?" the woman replied, sounding confused.

Elyse had only started working at Antidote last week. She was young—a sophomore in college—and her only prior experience had been at the coffee stand on campus, which had apparently not offered a broad selection of authentic espresso drinks.

Penny was only twenty-five herself, but college students looked positively fetal to her these days. All shiny and new, untarnished by the pressures of adult life. It felt like a hundred years ago to her instead of only three.

It took Elyse nearly five minutes to make the poor woman's skinny vanilla. She had to throw the first one out and start over when she forgot to use the sugar-free syrup. Penny waited patiently until it was her turn to order, in no hurry.

Elyse finally greeted her without enthusiasm. "Morning. What can I get you?"

"She always gets the same thing," Caleb said, coming out of the kitchen with a tray of clean dishes. "Regular nonfat latte. Ring her up and I'll make it."

Penny froze at the sight of him. Six gorgeous feet of tanned skin and muscles topped by thick golden hair and a face so beautifully symmetrical it stopped you right in your tracks. Perfectly proportioned nose. Strong chin. Granite jaw. And then there was the matter of his eyes, which were a gold-tinged brown so striking it felt like they were looking straight into your soul.

There was a reason Penny's knitting group called him Hottie Barista. The man was supernaturally handsome. He looked like he should be followed around by a key light and a menagerie of cartoon animals.

The first time Penny had seen him he'd rendered her so tongue-tied and breathless, it had been all she could do to blurt out her coffee order. But over the intervening months, she'd gotten more used to looking at him. She still deeply appreciated the view, but he didn't steal the air from her lungs anymore. He was a part of the scenery now, like a majestic vista she was lucky enough to gaze upon every day.

His eyes sought hers, which in and of itself was unusual. He almost never made eye contact. Or smiled. Or made conversation. It was part of his mystique.

Penny was a naturally friendly person. Her open, sympathetic demeanor invited confidences wherever she went. She couldn't get on an airplane or sit in a waiting room without hearing the life story of the person next to her, which was fine with her because she loved talking to people. She'd never met a stranger she couldn't befriend—until Caleb.

Apparently, he was too cool to make small talk with her. All she'd ever gotten out of him was disinterested monosyllables and shrugs. It wasn't like she'd been flirting with him either. She was aware that her chances with a man of his physical perfection were approximately infinity to one.

She liked to think of herself as pleasingly plump, like Nancy Drew's best friend Bess, even though she knew there wasn't any such thing as "pleasingly" plump as far as most people were concerned. Especially not in LA, where almost everyone walked around looking like runway models.

Penny had been fat all her life, and she'd tried everything to lose weight. Any fad diet or exercise craze you could name, she'd tried it, even though she knew better. She was a scientist; she knew bad data and specious claims when she saw them. But she'd been so desperate to look like everyone else, she'd ignored her own better judgment in her quest to be thin.

Until one fad diet too many had left her with a vitamin deficiency and borderline blood glucose levels that had caused a scary fainting incident and landed her in the emergency room her sophomore year of college. A very nice female doctor had sat her down and explained that she was doing more harm to her body than good, and she would be much better off eating a well-balanced diet and throwing her scale in the dumpster.

Ever since, Penny had been rigorous about eating healthy —*actually* healthy, not fad diet healthy. Once she stopped torturing her body with juice cleanses and extreme diets, her weight stabilized at her current size sixteen. This was the size her body naturally seemed to want to be, and Penny had made her peace with that.

Mostly.

The whole body positivity thing was still a work in progress. Moving to the land of free-range size 00 actresses had certainly put it to the test, but she felt like she was doing pretty well, considering. Penny was a big believer in the "fake it till you make it" theory. Pretend you have self-esteem long enough, and eventually you'll actually *have* self-esteem.

Regardless, she had no illusions about her chances with a man like Caleb, so she was always careful to keep her overtures polite and platonic. She didn't want him to think she was like all the other women who came into Antidote and tried to flirt with him— women whose overtures he ignored just as determinedly as he ignored Penny's, no matter how attractive they were.

Maybe he was gay. Or had a girlfriend. Still, it had always bothered her that he was so determined not to talk to her. She was delightful, darn it. Everyone else wanted to talk to her. But no matter how many times she came in here, how unfailingly polite she was or how well she tipped, she'd always gotten the same bland indifference from him as everyone else.

Until he'd come into the bathroom to check on her Friday night. And now he was staring directly at her with those piercing eyes and his forehead all creased in concern. Like he was looking at someone who'd received a terminal diagnosis.

Penny felt the blood rushing to her cheeks and tore her gaze away, fumbling with her wallet. She could still feel his eyes on her as Elyse rang her up. Why was he just standing there? Wasn't he going to make her drink?

"Your name's Penelope Popplestone?" Elyse said, squinting at Penny's credit card. "For real?"

Penny smiled reflexively and nodded. "For real."

"Badass. That sounds like a character in a children's book."

It took Elyse three tries to swipe Penny's card, and Caleb stood there the whole time. Just staring at her. It was unsettling. Finally, Elyse mastered the credit card machine and it spit out a receipt.

"Tables need busing," Caleb told Elyse as she shoved Penny's card and receipt at her. Elyse nodded and grabbed a rag, leaving Penny and Caleb alone at the counter.

Penny cleared her throat. "Can I have a pen?" Elyse had forgotten to give her one.

Caleb grabbed a ballpoint from the cup behind the register and held it out to her. He had neatly trimmed nails and callused fingers, like a man who knew how to use his hands.

Penny swallowed and took the pen from him, her heart thudding painfully in her chest as their fingers touched.

Stop it, she told herself as she clenched the pen. *He's just a pretty jerk.* She scrawled the tip and her signature and thrust the receipt back across the counter.

"How are you?" Caleb asked before Penny could make her escape.

"I'm fine," she replied without meeting his eye. Why did he have to suddenly be friendly today? She'd spent months fruitlessly trying to make small talk with him, but it wasn't until she'd been rendered pathetic and pitiable that he was finally interested in having a conversation. Figured.

"I'm sorry I didn't tell you what Kenneth was up to."

Penny shrugged like she wasn't still bitter about it. "It's not your job to police my boyfriends for me."

It's your job to make my coffee order, she thought silently, wishing he would go and do it. He was the next to last person in the world she wanted to talk to right now—the absolute last being Kenneth.

"I could have warned you though."

She forced a smile. "It's fine." She tried to imbue the words with sincerity so he'd stop looking at her like she was dying of a brain tumor, but they came out sounding flat.

"I didn't think it was any of my business."

"You're right. It's not." She meant it to sound nicer than it came out. Really, she did. But at least it got her out of that awkward conversation, because Caleb finally headed for the espresso machine to start making her latte.

Penny moved down the counter to claim her usual spot toward the back. She would have preferred to sit at one of the tables on the other side of the room today, as far away from Caleb as possible, but she refused to give him the satisfaction of thinking he was important enough to make her uncomfortable. If she wasn't willing to change her routine to avoid Kenneth, she definitely wasn't changing it because of some barista she hardly knew.

"Morning, Penny!" Charlotte called out from the orange couch in the corner.

Penny swiveled on her stool, brightening. "Good morning!"

Charlotte was a regular at Antidote like Penny. She was a philosophy grad student with a wispy beard and a bright green streak in her blonde hair. Today she was wearing a polka dot dress with bright pink tights and green high-top sneakers, and she was surrounded by stacks of papers and books.

"Sorry to hear about your boyfriend."

Penny groaned. "Does *everybody* know already?"

"Roxanne told me. You could do so much better than that guy. I always thought so."

"Thank you," Penny said. "I guess." It wasn't like there was a line around the block of disappointed lovers she'd rejected in favor of cheating jerks. The cheating jerks were the only options presenting themselves.

Charlotte seemed like she had a lot of work to do, so Penny turned back around and got out her phone. She'd sit here for fifteen minutes and drink her coffee, then she could go. That would be enough time to prove she wasn't afraid to show her face.

Caleb brought her latte over a few minutes later and retreated without a word. Good, he was back to ignoring her. That was exactly what she wanted. For things to go back to normal.

He'd made a heart-shaped flower design in the foam today instead of his usual leaf, but she chose not to read anything into it. Hearts were a common theme in latte art. They were probably the easiest shape to make. Still, it was pretty. She swiped to the camera app on her phone to take a picture—but only because it would look good on her Instagram. Not because she was at all charmed or impressed by Caleb's latte art.

As she was deliberating over the best photo filter, she heard the bell on the shop door ring.

"Penny, thank God," Kenneth said behind her. "I've been trying to call you all weekend."

Chapter Three

---

*P*enny continued swiping through Instagram filters without looking up at Kenneth. "I don't have anything to say to you."

He was close enough she could smell his Armani cologne. She should have known better than to date a man who wore cologne.

"Please, darling, let me explain." He slid onto the nearest stool, brushing his leg up against hers.

She shifted her leg away, still refusing to look at him. "There's nothing to explain. You wanted to see other women without telling me about it. I understand the situation perfectly."

His hand closed on her forearm. "I'm so sorry. I messed up. It was a terrible mistake. Give me a chance to make it up to you."

She pulled out of his grasp. "I'm not interested in dating someone who would lie to me. Now please go away."

"You're being unfair. At least give me a chance to explain."

"Can I help you?" Caleb asked, looming over Kenneth. He held a freshly made iced coffee, and though his tone was neutral, his nearness and physical mass carried an implicit threat.

Kenneth gave him an irritated glance. "No, mate. I'm trying to have a private conversation, if you don't mind."

Caleb didn't move. "It sounds like she doesn't want to talk to you."

Kenneth got to his feet, jutting out his chin like a terrier with an unfortunate underbite. "I don't see how it's any of your damned business." Caleb had a good four inches on him and at least thirty pounds of muscle mass, which didn't help Kenneth look any less ludicrous.

"It's my business to make sure no one's harassing any of our customers," Caleb said calmly. "You're not doing that, are you?"

"The only one being is harassed is me, while I'm having a simple conversation with my girlfriend."

"*Ex*-girlfriend," Penny muttered through clenched teeth.

Had Kenneth always been this petulant? She was finding it difficult to remember what she'd ever liked about him in the first place. Had she just been dazzled by his British accent?

"I think you should probably leave now," Caleb said.

"Are you threatening me?" Kenneth attempted to puff out his chest, which only made him look punier and more ridiculous. "I think you should step back, friend."

Caleb took a slow, exaggerated step back and gestured toward the door with his free hand.

Kenneth's nostrils flared. For a moment it looked as if he might try to stand his ground, but he finally seemed to realize the odds weren't in his favor. He threw a scowl in Penny's direction and shouldered his way past Caleb, even though he had plenty of room to get by. It was a petty move, and it backfired wonderfully. As he jostled Caleb's arm, the iced coffee tipped, drenching the front of Kenneth's green polo shirt and dress khakis.

"Son of a bitch!" he shouted, recoiling as the cold coffee soaked through his clothes.

"Sorry," Caleb said. "You bumped into me."

"*You bloody did that on purpose!*"

"Is there a problem here?" Roxanne asked, coming out of the

back office. She stuck her pregnant belly between the two men and turned her formidable glare on Kenneth.

He took a half step back, his eyes dropping uneasily to Roxanne's protruding stomach. "Yeah, your man here tried to threaten me and then dumped coffee all over me."

"No one threatened anyone," Penny said. "And Kenneth's the one who bumped into Caleb."

"It's true," Charlotte said from the couch. "I saw the whole thing."

Kenneth's mouth twisted into a sneer. "That's how it's going to be, is it? All of you ganging up on me? Well, you can be sure the owner of this dump will be hearing about this. You've just lost yourselves a paying customer."

"That's fine." Roxanne rested her hands on her hips. "You can get your coffee somewhere else from now on, friend-o. You're not welcome here anymore."

"Assholes," Kenneth muttered on his way out the door. "The whole lot of you are bloody assholes."

Roxanne watched him stalk past the window before turning to Penny. "You okay, sweetie?"

Penny nodded. "I'm fine. Thank you." Her heart was still racing and she wanted to crawl into a hole and die of embarrassment, but otherwise she was just great. "Sorry about that."

"Hey, anytime. We've got a zero tolerance policy for jerks in here."

Elyse brought out the mop and rolling bucket. "That was pretty exciting," she said as she cleaned up the puddle of spilled coffee on the floor.

Well, at least Penny's disastrous love life had brightened Elyse's day. Swell.

"You think he'll make a stink to Reema?" Caleb asked, stepping out of the way of the mop. Reema owned Antidote, as well as another bar in the neighborhood, which was where she spent most of her time.

Roxanne smirked. "Let him try. All I have to do is tell her he was harassing a female customer and tried to start a fight when you asked him to leave."

"Which was exactly what happened," Penny said.

"She'll probably give you a medal." Roxanne grimaced, stretching her back as she rubbed the underside of her stomach. "Whose coffee was that, anyway? Better make 'em a new one."

"It was mine," Caleb said. "I'll pay for it."

"Don't worry about it." Roxanne clapped him on the shoulder, smirking. "Good job." She set out the *Caution: Wet Floor* sign and took the mop bucket from Elyse. "I'll put this away. You man the register for a while."

Caleb started to follow Elyse behind the counter, but Penny touched his arm to stop him. "You did that on purpose!" she whispered when Roxanne was out of earshot. "You made that drink with the intention of spilling it on him, didn't you?"

The corner of Caleb's mouth twitched. "I *wanted* to dump it over his head, but I thought better of it."

"Thank you," Penny said. "That's the sweetest thing anyone's done for me in a long time."

He lifted an eyebrow. "Dumping a drink on a guy?"

"It was *really* satisfying. You have no idea." If only she'd thought to record it with her phone. *That* would have made a great Instagram. No filter required.

The bell on the shop door jingled again. "What happened?" asked the elderly man who came in, gesturing at the wet floor sign. He was one of Penny's favorite regulars, a retired cinematographer by the name of George Simkin.

"Roxanne threw Penny's boyfriend out," Charlotte announced from the couch.

"*Ex*-boyfriend," Penny said.

"Caleb dumped an iced coffee all over him," Charlotte added. "It was awesome."

"I miss all the fun," George said.

"Ring up a brewed coffee for George," Caleb told Elyse. His hand landed on Penny's shoulder, squeezing briefly before he walked away, and her stomach did a traitorous flip-flop.

Stop it, she told her stomach firmly. *He's only being nice because he thinks you're pathetic.*

"And a cherry Danish," George called out as he slid onto his usual stool, two down from Penny's. He stopped in almost every day for his plain black coffee and cherry Danish. Penny suspected he was lonely; his wife had died a few years ago and his son lived in San Jose.

She reached for her latte, which had gotten cold. Great. Stupid Kenneth, ruining everything. She pushed the mug away glumly. Her shoulder was still tingling where Caleb's hand had been, and she reached up to massage it, trying to rub away the sensation.

George leaned toward her, running a hand through his wispy white hair. "What do we think of the new girl?" he whispered.

"Her name's Elyse," Penny whispered back. "She's a sophomore at Loyola Marymount and she seems very nice."

"Yesterday she tried to upsell me one of those fancy coffee drinks that are nothing but foam and sugar." George shook his head and pushed his glasses up the bridge of his nose. "Don't know why anyone bothers with those things."

"I happen to like my fancy coffee drinks," Penny said. "You don't have to get them with syrup if you don't want."

"Can't beat a bottomless cup of good old-fashioned joe. Best value on the menu. They didn't used to have coffee this good when I was young, you know. Only coffee you could get back then tasted like bilge water. Course, it only cost you a nickel. Can't buy a damn thing for a nickel these days."

Penny admired George's dedication to perpetual crankiness, which reminded her of her own grandfather. She came from a large, close-knit family, but they were all back in Virginia. Her weekly video chats with her mother didn't do enough to assuage the homesickness she felt being so far away from them.

George peered at her over the top of his glasses, which had slipped down his nose again. "So what'd Kenny boy do to get himself dumped?"

"It turned out he was cheating on me," Penny said, scraping at a chip in her Tiffany blue nail polish.

"Really?" George's bushy eyebrows lifted in poorly feigned surprise. "That's just terrible."

She narrowed her eyes at him. "You knew too, didn't you?"

He spread his hands, shrugging.

"Did *everyone* know?"

"I only knew because Caleb told me."

Exactly how many people had Caleb told who weren't her? And why was he talking about her at all? He couldn't be bothered to talk *to* her, but he talked *about* her when she wasn't around?

"Why didn't he tell *me*?" Penny asked George. "Why didn't *you* tell me?"

George shot a glance at the pastry case where Caleb was plating his Danish, then leaned toward Penny again, lowering his voice. "It's not the kid's fault. I told him not to tell you."

"Why would you do that?"

"Some people don't want to hear a thing like that. They'd rather live in their happy little bubble than have their world turned on its ear."

"Well, not me. You officially have my permission to tell me the next time you know my boyfriend is cheating on me." She raised her voice loud enough to carry all the way to Caleb at the pastry case. "You hear that, everyone? From now on, *please tell me* if you know my boyfriend is a cheating cheater who is cheating on me."

"You got it," Charlotte said from the couch.

Penny swiveled on her stool and shared an air high five with her. Caleb ignored them all, pretending not to hear.

"I'm sorry," George said. "You're a nice girl. You deserve better than some schmuck who cheats on you."

Penny sighed. "People keep telling me that, and yet it keeps happening. I'm beginning to think the problem is me."

Maybe she was *too* nice. Maybe it was her niceness that made men think she was a doormat. Or maybe it was a turnoff, and that was why they always ended up looking for more exciting pastures to sow their oats in.

Caleb dropped off George's black coffee and Danish, studiously avoiding Penny's eyes as he slunk back to the espresso machine.

"Thanks, kid." George picked up his coffee cup, blew on it, and took a sip. He set it down again, grimacing at the temperature. As he tore off a chunk of his Danish, he directed a thoughtful glance at Penny. "You know, my neighbor's son is a very nice-looking banker."

Penny held up a hand to stop him. "Thank you, but no."

"Steady income, good manners..."

She shook her head. "I think I'm done dating for a while."

"Suit yourself. But lemme tell you, being alone isn't all it's cracked up to be."

Penny's heart squeezed in sympathy. George and his wife had been married for forty years before she died. She couldn't even imagine what it must be like to build a whole life with someone and then have to go on without them. And here she was feeling sorry for herself over a man she'd only known for a couple months. A man she hadn't even really liked that much, as it turned out.

Caleb came back and set a fresh latte in front of Penny.

"What's this?" she asked, surprised.

He leaned his hip against the counter and crossed his arms. "Lavender latte. Something new I'm playing around with. Tell me what you think."

"But I don't—"

"There's no syrup," he said, anticipating her objection. "I steeped dried lavender in the milk to flavor it."

Penny lifted the cup and sniffed it, a little dubious of lavender-flavored coffee. She took a tentative sip, and was surprised to discover it was delicious.

"What do you think?" Caleb asked, watching her.

"It's wonderful! How did you ever come up with it?" She sniffed it again, appreciating the subtle lavender aroma.

"There's a place over by my house that serves them. I thought I could improve on it by cutting out the syrup."

"You should get Reema to add this to the menu."

The old familiar indifference clicked back into place and he shrugged like it wasn't worth his time. "Maybe."

Penny watched him walk away, confused by his behavior. He'd been awfully nice for a minute there, before he'd slipped back into old habits. He was probably just doing it because he felt sorry for her. But still.

He'd chased Kenneth off for her. And apparently he'd been talking to George about her. And now he'd made her a special drink as a peace offering.

She smiled as she took another sip of her lavender latte. Maybe Hottie Barista wasn't such a jerk after all.

CYNTHIA'S ART show was that night at a warehouse space in the Fashion District. There were a lot of cool-looking LA people there in addition to the people Penny knew. Cynthia and her husband were there, of course, although her attention was in such high demand she didn't have time to do much more than thank Penny for coming. Vilma and her husband Emilio were there too, and Penny chatted with them for a few minutes before she spied Esther standing alone by the hors d'oeuvres.

"Make me stop eating cheese," Esther said, looking relieved to see Penny.

Penny linked her arm through Esther's and led her away from the cheese tray. "Where's Jonathan?"

"TA'ing a night class."

Esther's boyfriend was in the graduate screenwriting program at UCLA. He only had a few months left before he finished his degree, and he'd already landed an agent after one of his scripts made the finals in a big screenwriting competition.

"That's too bad." Penny liked Jonathan. He was a little awkward, but in a sweet way. He made a good match for Esther because they were both awkward in social situations, but in totally different ways. Left to her own devices, Esther defaulted to lurking alone near the food, whereas Jonathan had a tendency to talk too much when he was uncomfortable—mostly about himself. But when they were together, they brought out the best in each other. Jonathan gave Esther a reason to join the party, and Esther relaxed Jonathan enough that he didn't slip into lecture mode—or if he did, she gave him a sharp nudge in the ribs to make him cut it out.

It was the kind of relationship Penny had always wanted. One based on give and take. Two mismatched pieces fitting together to make a whole.

Instead, Penny always seemed to be the one doing the giving, and her boyfriends did all the taking. She hadn't yet figured out the secret to achieving the right balance.

"Is it me, or is Cynthia's stuff way better than everything else here?" Esther whispered.

"It's not you." Penny squinted at an installation in the middle of the floor. "Is this part of the show, or did someone leave a ladder sitting out?"

Esther tilted her head. "I think it's supposed to be art?"

"It's a ladder."

"I don't know what to tell you. I'm not really an art person."

"Me neither." Literature Penny could do, but the subtleties of the visual arts were a mystery to her.

"I'm gonna need more wine for this," Esther said, and they detoured past the bar to snag two glasses of white before continuing their circuit around the gallery. "So how are you doing with the breakup thing?" she asked as they stopped in front of a photograph of an old tire.

Penny studied the tire, trying to figure out what was special about it. "I'm fine."

Esther cocked an eyebrow at her.

"Seriously." They strolled to the next display on the wall. "I mean, sure, I was upset at first. But mostly I feel stupid that I didn't realize what kind of guy he was."

"I'm not sure how you're supposed to know in advance that a guy is a cheater," Esther said.

"Beats me. They should have to wear a sign." Penny stared at the painting on the wall in front of them. It looked like someone had spilled blue paint across a canvas. How was that art?

"We should be able to clip their ears like feral cats," Esther said with a smirk. "That way everyone knows what they're getting into. 'Warning: this guy's a cheater. Fuck at your own risk.'"

Penny snorted at the image of Kenneth trying to pick up women with one of his ears clipped. "Yeah, so...I think I've had it with dating."

Esther's eyebrows shot up. "Permanently?"

"Probably not."

They stopped in front of one of Cynthia's paintings. This one, Penny could appreciate. It was a watercolor portrait of a weathered old black woman with haunting eyes. Penny thought it might be Cynthia's grandmother.

"For the immediate future anyway," she said to Esther. "I'm just tired of dealing with it. I don't need that kind of trouble in my life."

Esther nodded. "I don't blame you."

"Really?" Penny looked at her in surprise. "Aren't you going to try to talk me out of it?" She'd expected more resistance from someone in a happy relationship. People in relationships always seemed to want everyone else to be in relationships too.

"Why would I?" Esther shrugged. "I think you should take as much time as you need."

"Thank you," Penny said. That was exactly what she wanted to hear.

"You don't need a man in your life to be happy."

"Exactly."

"Most of them are more trouble than they're worth."

"It's true!"

Esther paused. "Although—"

"No! Don't *although*. I liked everything you said before the although. Don't ruin it."

"I was just going to say that as a reformed nonbeliever in romance, when you find the right guy, it's totally worth it."

"Well sure. But how do you find the right one? How many frogs am I expected to kiss before one of them turns into a prince?"

Esther brushed her long hair off her shoulder. "Maybe you should stop kissing frogs and start kissing—I don't know—chipmunks or raccoons or something. Maybe the frogs are the problem."

Penny made a face as she sipped her wine. "Raccoons are vermin."

"Okay, then otters or sloths or whatever you want. I'm just saying, maybe try casting your net a little wider instead of shutting yourself off to the possibility of love, is all."

"Is that a *ladder* over there?" Jinny whispered, coming up to them.

Esther shrugged. "I don't know, man. Art."

Jinny looked skeptical. "Is it, though?"

"Penny's sworn off men," Esther said.

Jinny's eyes widened. "For good?"

"No," Penny said. "Just for a while."

"Feeling gun-shy," Jinny said with a knowing nod.

"A little," Penny admitted. "This just keeps happening to me, you know? I feel like it must have something to do with me."

Jinny punched her in the arm. It was shockingly painful, given her diminutive size. "Shut up! That's not true! You're beautiful and lovely!"

Penny rubbed her arm. "Thank you, but...I think part of the problem is that I'm the kind of girl guys think they're supposed to marry. They look at me and see their mothers."

Esther's lip curled. "Ew."

"I can see it though." Jinny nodded over the top of her wineglass. "You are really into taking care of people and organizing things."

"Right? They look at me and see someone who's going to take care of them and cook for them and iron their shirts."

Esther looked horrified. "You don't iron their shirts, do you?"

"No!" Only the once. And only because they'd been running late for a wedding. It wasn't like she made a habit of it. "But they look at me and see someone who might. I'm a *nice* girl. The kind you can take home to your parents. And that's what they *think* they want—but what they actually want is a *not* nice girl."

Jinny pursed her lips, nodding. "A dirty girl."

"Exactly!" In her vehemence, Penny sloshed some of the wine out of her glass and onto her chest.

Jinny used the sleeve of her cardigan to blot Penny's boobs dry. "Most men want a little of both."

Esther shook her head. "Most men don't know what they want."

"I think that's why they end up cheating on me," Penny said, trying to fan her chest dry. "After a while they start to resent the same qualities that drew them to me in the first place. And then they get restless and start to feel trapped, so they go looking for something more exciting. That's my latest theory, anyway."

"Hey," Olivia said, coming up to them. "Is that a fucking

ladder?" With her pale skin, thick black eyeliner, and dark lipstick, she fit in perfectly with the art crowd.

Jinny lifted her wineglass. "That's exactly what I said."

"Where's Yemi and Jonathan?" Olivia asked.

"Night class," Esther said.

"Yemi's over there." Jinny pointed to the other side of the gallery, where her Nigerian boyfriend was deep in conversation with Vilma's pot-bellied husband. "Talking to Emilio about tabletop war games. He's such a dork. I love him."

Jinny was also in a perfect relationship with a perfect boyfriend. Penny was surrounded by nauseatingly happy couples. On the one hand, it gave her hope that maybe one day she'd find her perfect match too. But on the other, it highlighted how much of a failure she was in the relationship department.

"Can you guys keep a secret?" Jinny asked, leaning in close and lowering her voice.

"Of course." Penny loved secrets.

"Yemi's going to propose."

Olivia's mouth fell open. "What?"

"Shut the front door!" Penny said, spilling her wine again. "Are you serious?"

They'd only been dating for six months, which seemed a little fast. Jinny and Yemi both came from conservative Catholic families, so they might be feeling added pressure to hurry up and tie the knot. Or maybe they just knew they were ready.

Sometimes it happened that way, right? Two people met and fell in love, and they were so confident in each other they didn't need to wait to start the rest of their lives together. Not that Penny would know anything about that.

Esther smirked as Olivia handed Penny a tissue. "He asked me for ring advice at work today." Esther and Jinny and Jinny's boyfriend all worked for the same company, but Jinny worked in a different department than Esther and Yemi. "He tried to be sly and couch it like a hypothetical question, but it was definitely not hypothetical. And then he swore me to secrecy. Obviously, I told Jinny immediately."

"Obviously," Olivia said.

Jinny gave Esther a fist bump. "Hos before bros."

"No idea on the timeframe," Esther said. "He's still in the early stages of the process, so it might be a while yet."

"But it's happening!" Jinny cast a look in Yemi's direction to make sure he wasn't watching them before bouncing and waving her hands excitedly.

"I'm so happy for you!" Penny said. Yemi seemed genuinely wonderful and he treated Jinny much better than any of her previous boyfriends had. They deserved to be happy together.

It was just...hard not to feel even worse about her own disastrous love life when everyone around her was so blissfully coupled up. She was starting to think she was never going to be anyone's first choice.

That was fine though. Penny was capable of being happy for her friends and feeling sorry for herself at the same time. It was practically her second career at this point.

Chapter Four

"*H*ow come you guys didn't come in last night?" Caleb asked when he rang up Penny's coffee order on Tuesday.

She looked up, startled. He never initiated conversation with her, and now he'd done it two days in a row. Three, if you counted Friday night in the bathroom.

"My friend Cynthia had an art show," she said. "That's why we were here Friday night when...well, you know." Penny had seen her boyfriend with another woman and fled to the bathroom to cry. Fun times.

Caleb's mouth pressed into a pained line, like he regretted asking the question, and he retreated to make her nonfat latte without another word.

Penny figured that would be the end of his conversational overtures. He'd attempted small talk, and it had been awkward. He'd probably never bother again.

But when he brought her latte to her, instead of dropping it off and hurrying away like he usually did, he lingered at the counter where she sat. Weird.

She thought he might be looking for validation, so she took a sip of her latte, which had another heart flower in the foam. "It's good," she said, nodding at him. "Thank you."

Instead of accepting this as permission to flee her company, he continued to hover nearby, shifting his weight from one foot to the other. It would be one thing if he were actually *doing* something, like wiping down the counter, but he was just watching her. Staring, really.

Penny refused to look at him, because she was certain if she did, she'd see pity in his face again. He must think she was still distraught over Kenneth's infidelity, and that was why he was hovering like she was some kind of wounded bird.

She wasn't. She was fine. *Really* fine. She'd moved efficiently through all seven stages of grief over the last few days and was now comfortably sitting pretty in acceptance.

In fact, she was glad it had happened. Jinny was right. Kenneth had done her a favor by getting caught before she'd had time to develop a strong attachment to him. And this time, she was going to learn from her mistake. No more Doormat Penny. From now on, she was putting herself first.

Well, except for her family. They were important. And her friends, of course. Friends were also important. And people in need. You should always put the needs of those less fortunate ahead of your own.

But other than *that*, Penny was putting herself first.

Caleb was still hovering, but she refused to let him get to her. For months, she'd tried to be friendly and gotten clear signals that he wasn't interested in talking to her. If he wanted something from her now, he was going to have to spit it out.

Old Penny would have felt the need to fill the silence with conversation, but New Improved Penny was done groveling for the attention of people who weren't interested in her. Just because he was standing nearby didn't obligate her to talk to him.

She pulled out her phone and opened up the *X-Files* fan fiction she'd been reading last night. Surely that would send a strong enough *you don't have to talk to me* vibe. He'd see that she was reading, realize he was off the hook, and leave her alone.

Nope. Still standing there. Still not saying anything.

Fine, whatever. Two could play this game. He had no idea what he was up against. She could ignore him for as long as he could stand there without saying anything.

"What are you reading?" he asked.

Well, darn.

It was a fanfic reader's most dreaded question. On the one hand, there was no reason to be ashamed of reading fan fiction, so she shouldn't have to lie about it. But on the other...she really didn't want to field the ignorant questions and disdainful comments that usually came next. Plus, he'd probably assume she was reading smut—not that there was anything wrong with smut. But she didn't want him thinking she was sitting here reading it while he was standing two feet away from her, because *that* would be weird. She happened to be reading a plotty amnesia fic with only a moderate amount of smut in it. And she wasn't on one of the smutty chapters right now. So there.

"A book," she said without looking up. It was the path of least resistance and technically not a lie, since the fic was over one hundred thousand words.

She saw Caleb nod out of the corner of her eye and braced herself for further interrogation. After another moment, he heaved himself off the counter he'd been leaning on and wandered off.

Penny blew out a relieved breath and went back to reading her fic.

CALEB WAS OFF ON WEDNESDAY, but Thursday morning he was at it again.

"Got any plans this weekend?" he asked when he brought her latte to her.

Never once had he inquired about her plans before, on the weekend or otherwise. Never. Once.

Penny had asked him that exact same question many times, trying to initiate conversation, and never received anything more than a vague shrug and mumbled "Not really" before he made his escape from her presence.

"Not really," she said, and shrugged.

Caleb continued to hover. Was he expecting her to make conversation? Because if so, he'd be waiting a long time. She was done with that. From now on, she was giving him what he'd always seemed to want: silence.

Malik was working today instead of Elyse, and Penny stared at the back of his dreadlocked head while he pulled shots of espresso. He had on an acid-washed denim vest that looked like something Penny's mother might have owned in high school. A few stools down the counter, a man in a plaid shirt stood up from his laptop and paced nervously back and forth. He wore a headset, and from his occasional exclamations and muttered curses, she presumed he was on some sort of conference call that was going badly.

Penny took a sip of her latte and thought about getting out her phone.

Caleb cleared his throat. "One of my roommates wants me to go see the new *Transformers* movie with him, but I don't know if I want to."

What? Was happening? Was this the same Hottie Barista who had previously resisted her every attempt to coax him into conversation? After nearly a year of hitting a brick wall, she hardly knew what to do with this wealth of volunteered biographical information. He had roommates, apparently. One of whom liked *Transformers* movies. Which Caleb himself was ambivalent about. Would wonders never cease?

Something in her expression made him flinch. "What?"

"Nothing," she said, taking another sip of her latte. "I've just never heard you talk this much before."

"Oh." He looked embarrassed.

She set down her cup. "Why are you acting so weird all of a sudden?"

"I'm not." This was a blatant lie, and he knew it. She could see it in his face.

"You don't have to feel sorry for me, you know. I'm fine. I don't need pity."

"I'm not—that's not it." He grimaced at the floor like this was the most painful conversation he'd ever had. It was certainly in Penny's top ten.

She waited.

He glanced up without quite meeting her eye. "I feel bad for not telling you what Kenneth was up to."

Ah. Guilt. That was almost as bad as pity. Well, he was in luck, because she was more than happy to let him off the hook if it meant things could go back to normal.

"You don't have to feel bad. Like I said, it's not your job or your business."

Instead of looking relieved, he nodded sullenly at the floor. Whatever he'd been hoping she'd say, that was apparently not it.

Penny had no idea what he wanted from her. She'd offered him absolution. What else was she supposed to do?

He started to walk off, then stopped and turned back. "It seems like you're mad at me, is all."

Penny's mouth formed a silent *oh.* She supposed she had been more short with him than usual, but she was honestly surprised he'd even noticed—or minded. She'd assumed he preferred being treated that way, since it was the way he'd always treated her. Was it possible he'd actually *enjoyed* her attempts at conversation all this time?

She really did not understand him at all.

"I'm not mad," she said. "I'm sorry if it seemed like I was. I guess I was just embarrassed."

His brow furrowed as his eyes met hers finally, causing her stomach to give a little lurch. "You don't have anything to be embarrassed about."

"Thank you," she said, feeling her cheeks heat at his unexpected earnestness.

He nodded and left her alone.

"WHY NOT TRY SOMETHING DIFFERENT TODAY?" Caleb suggested when Penny ordered her usual on Friday. "Be adventurous."

Something had definitely changed between them. It was like the ice had broken, and suddenly he didn't mind talking to her so much anymore. Evidently, the key to making friends with him was abject humiliation and a little crying. *Neat.*

"Like what?" she asked, curious to see what he would recommend.

"The Mexican mocha with cinnamon and cayenne is my favorite."

Penny tucked this information away in the ever-expanding mental folio file with Caleb's name on it. Favorite coffee beverage: Mexican mocha. Check.

"Too much sugar," she said, shaking her head. "One of my uncles lost a foot to diabetes. Do you want me to lose a foot?"

Caleb's eyes sparked with amusement and her mouth fell open in shock. He should have a license for those eyes. At the very least, he should have to issue a warning before he let them twinkle at anyone like that.

"The usual it is," he said, and went to go make her nonfat latte.

"You're looking chipper this morning," George observed as Penny took her usual perch two seats down from him. He was reading the newspaper, and there was a stack of discarded classifieds on the stool between them.

"I'm *feeling* chipper this morning, thank you for noticing." She certainly was now, after that eye twinkle Caleb had given her. She might be able to get used to this new normal between them.

As Penny watched Caleb work the espresso machine, she wondered if he'd been smiling at her with his eyes all along and she'd just never noticed. She usually tried to avoid looking directly into his eyes because they were too dazzling. She had a tendency to get hypnotized by them and lose her train of thought. It was much easier to play it cool around him when she didn't focus on his uncannily gorgeous face.

Maybe his eyes had been twinkling at her all along and she'd completely missed it. Was it possible she'd been misreading him all this time? Or was the eye twinkling new behavior, like his sudden interest in talking to her?

When he pulled a mug out of the warming rack, she caught a glimpse of the tattoo on his right biceps peeking out from the sleeve of his T-shirt. It was some sort of writing, but she'd never been able to see enough of it to decipher it. She thought it might start with a T. Or maybe an I. Possibly an L?

It could be a girlfriend's name, or maybe his mother's. Or the name of a deceased friend who died tragically and too young. Or perhaps a favorite childhood pet. That would be sweet. It could also be a bible verse or line of poetry. Or a song lyric. She tried to imagine what sort of lyric Caleb might choose to tattoo into his skin. Was he a Beatles guy or would he choose something more contemporary?

Penny considered asking him about it, since they were being all chummy now. But she feared it might be too personal. They'd only just begun their expedition into the world of small talk. Inquiring about the body art lurking under his clothes felt like an abrupt escalation.

She leaned forward as Caleb poured the milk into her latte,

fascinated by the way he could create pictures out of surface tension and fluid dynamics.

"How did you learn to do that?" she asked.

He didn't look up as he concentrated on his design. "Practice."

His distraction allowed her to brazenly appreciate his physical perfection. He wasn't just a pretty face—although his face was certainly one of the top three pretty things about him. Penny was also a huge fan of his arms. Particularly his thick biceps, which flexed appealingly as he worked. And then there was the way his chunky Timex watch drew the eye to his exquisite forearms. She'd never paid much attention to men's forearms before she started patronizing Antidote. But now, thanks to Caleb, she considered herself a connoisseur.

When he was done, he set the frothing pitcher down and brought her latte over to her.

"A bear!" Penny exclaimed, delighted. It had a big round snout and two cute little round ears. "I love it!"

The corner of Caleb's mouth twitched, which was as close as she'd ever gotten to a smile out of him. "It'd be cuter if you let me dot the eyes with chocolate syrup."

"All right, fine." Penny pushed the latte toward him. A tiny bit of syrup wouldn't hurt. "Just a dot though."

Caleb grabbed the squeeze bottle of chocolate syrup and bent over her cup. "You want him to be a one-eyed bear?"

"That would be tragic. Permission to use two dots."

He made the eyes and straightened, looking pleased with himself.

"He's perfect," Penny said, opening her camera app to take a picture. "I love him so much, it almost seems a shame to drink him."

Caleb arched an eyebrow. "Almost?"

She finished snapping the photo and picked up her drink. "He's a latte bear. It's his life's purpose to be enjoyed." She pursed her lips as she blew gently across the top. "I wouldn't want to deny him his life's purpose."

Caleb's mouth twitched again. "Glad you like it."

He was being so convivial, she decided to test the limits of their new friendship. "You know, it's funny," she said. "We see each other almost every day, but I don't know anything about you."

He frowned. "What do you mean?"

Penny took another sip of her latte. "I know more about everyone else here than I do about you. I know Roxanne skates with the LA Derby Dolls, her wife is a chef, and they're going to name their baby girl Julia after Julia Child. I know Malik plays bass, his band is named Savage Oxide, and his mother lives in Atlanta. Elyse has only been here a week and I already know she's an accounting major with a roommate named Gwen. But I know literally nothing about you. Isn't that weird?"

Caleb shifted uncomfortably. "Is it?" George's newspaper crinkled loudly as he unfolded it and turned the page.

"Yes!" Penny said. "I know all about George's family too."

"What?" George said, peering over the top of his newspaper. "I wasn't listening."

"I was just telling Caleb how weird it is that he never talks about himself."

"Ah." George disappeared behind his paper again.

"What do you want to know?" Caleb asked, rubbing his hands on his thighs. He looked wary, but he hadn't run away yet.

"I don't know. Anything." Penny cracked her mental knuckles, considering her opening gambit. "Are you from Los Angeles originally?"

He leaned back against the opposite counter, and Penny tried not stare at the way his jeans hugged his hips—and other parts of him. "I'm an army brat, so I'm from all over. But most recently Fort Irwin, out past Barstow."

Ah ha! A military upbringing could explain his reluctance to make friends. His detachment and unsociable behavior could be a defense mechanism from moving around so much during his formative years.

"Is that where your parents are now?"

He crossed his arms across his chest, which did amazing things for his already impressive biceps. "My dad's a doctor at the hospital there."

"What about your mom?" Penny asked, trying not to stare at his arms.

"She's a professional officer's wife."

"What does that mean?"

He uncrossed his arms and rubbed his thumb over his palm. "It means she does a lot of volunteering and organizing social activities on post." His voice sounded tight and his entire posture radiated unhappiness. This was clearly torture for him. But he hadn't bailed yet.

"Brothers and sisters?" Penny asked.

"Two younger brothers. One in college and one in high school." His jaw tightened. "Both headed into the army like our dad."

"But not you? You didn't want to go into the army?"

He made a face like he'd drunk sour milk. "No."

"You really hate talking about yourself, don't you?"

"I just don't like talking about this."

"I'm sorry." Penny made a mental note that said *family issues* and tucked it away in his file.

He shrugged. "It's okay. It's just...my dad wasn't too happy when I didn't go into ROTC."

ROTC meant he'd gone to college, but before she could ask him where, a new customer came in and Caleb escaped the rest of her interrogation by going to take his order.

That was all right. Penny's file on him had already expanded by leaps and bounds. She was pleased with the progress.

"Ask him about something besides his folks," George said quietly from behind his newspaper.

"Why?" Penny asked.

"His father's a real piece of work. It's a sore subject."

Penny folded down the corner of George's newspaper so she could look at him. "How do you know that?"

George shrugged. "We talk sometimes."

Interesting.

So she'd been right about the family issues. Good to know. Next time she'd steer clear of his home life, and maybe he'd loosen up a little more.

She was looking forward to adding more pieces to the Caleb puzzle.

SATURDAY MORNING PENNY went back to yoga class, because routine was good. Routine was better than a boyfriend because it never let you down.

"Are you feeling better?" her friend Melody asked as they laid out their mats in their usual spots at the back of the room.

They'd met last year through their Great Books group. They were the only two people in the group under the age of forty, and after they'd bonded over their shared love of Marvel movies and fan fiction, Melody had turned Penny on to this yoga studio.

Penny bent to adjust her mat so it was more perfectly parallel to the floorboards. "Tons better."

"We missed you last week," the instructor, Tessa, said, laying a hand on Penny's back as she glided past. Tessa had long blonde hair and a gentle, calm demeanor that effortlessly commanded attention. Despite her youth, she reminded Penny a little of her mother, with her teacher's knack for inspiring respect without ever raising her voice.

Conversation quieted automatically as Tessa reached the front of the room. She greeted the class, started up a playlist of meditative music, and began leading them through the warm-up sequence.

Penny had only moved up to the advanced class a few months ago. She'd been intimidated to the point of nausea when Tessa had first suggested it. All the advanced women were slender and athletic. They looked like they could have played the Amazon warriors in *Wonder Woman*, and for all Penny knew, some of them had.

It had taken all the courage she could muster to show up for the advanced yoga class, but Tessa had been right: Penny *was* good enough, even if most people wouldn't think so by looking at her.

As they moved into Natarajasana, Melody wobbled and cursed under her breath. Penny tried not to take too much pleasure in the fact that she was actually stronger and more coordinated than thin, pretty Melody. Realizing she wasn't the worst student in class had been a real boost to her confidence.

She'd originally signed up for yoga because she figured she could use the enforced relaxation in addition to the exercise. Being still and contemplative weren't exactly her strong suits. She preferred to keep busy, and her mind was perpetually racing ahead, making plans for the next activity. But for one hour every week, Penny pushed all those tendencies aside and focused on mindful breathing as Tessa's soothing voice guided her through a series of increasingly challenging poses.

Where it all tended to fall apart for Penny was during corpse pose at the end. It was just so *boring*, lying there on the floor with nothing to do. Today, as she struggled to soften her throat and relax her limbs, her mind fixated on Kenneth and the fact that she'd dated him for two whole months without ever seriously considering whether she actually liked him.

Now that she thought about it, she'd been more in love with the *idea* of Kenneth than the reality of him. He was fine. But he was always working such long hours—at least that's what he'd claimed—they hadn't seen all that much of each other. And she hadn't actually minded. All those times he was supposedly working late or out of town, she hadn't missed his company at all. Even now, when she thought about him with that other woman, she wasn't jealous. She was mostly just mad.

The truth was, she'd never been all that attracted to him. Once the initial excitement of being asked out had worn off, he hadn't made her heart beat faster or her stomach flutter. The sex had been fine, but nothing special. And to be honest, she'd found him a little...boring. He'd talked about his work a lot, but hadn't seemed interested in hearing about hers.

Why had she been with him? His hair was receding, he was short and skinny, and he hadn't shared any of her interests. He only liked dark, gritty movies and dumb reality television shows, and he wasn't a reader—which should have been a deal breaker all by itself.

Her previous boyfriend, Brendon, hadn't been all that great either. She'd thought she loved him at the time, but looking back on it, she couldn't remember why. He'd mocked her fandom friends and her fanfic habit. He'd never wanted to watch her favorite TV shows with her, but she'd spent hours watching football with him, even though it bored it her to tears. Worst of all, he hadn't talked to her before deciding to move to California. He'd just announced he was moving and said she could come with him if she wanted.

Penny had uprooted her entire life for someone who hadn't even cared if she came with him or not. No wonder he'd started cheating on her as soon as he got out here.

What was wrong with her? She shouldn't be settling like that. Sure, she wanted to fall in love and have a family some day, but this wasn't the way to do it. If she didn't love herself enough to expect more, how would she ever find a man who would love her as much as she deserved? She needed to start valuing herself and prioritizing her own needs. Which meant asking for things when she wanted them instead of rolling over at the first hint of resistance.

No, not just asking—demanding.

"All right, good work everyone," Tessa said, shutting off the sleepy music.

Thank God. If Penny practiced much more mindfulness, she was liable to sprain something.

Chapter Five

On Monday morning, Penny went into Antidote and ordered a different drink.

It didn't happen quite as decisively as that, of course. What actually happened was that Penny went to the counter the same as usual, and Caleb rang up her usual order. But when he held out his hand for her credit card, she hesitated.

"Actually, can I..." She trailed off, biting her lip.

She liked her nonfat lattes, but did she really want to settle for the same boring drink every day? Maybe she was missing out on something better. She could stand to be more adventurous. Mix it up a little. She could have a different drink every day of the week if she wanted.

Caleb's eyebrows lifted in surprise. "You want something different?" He was wearing a soft blue henley, and the way it clung to his chest, arms, and shoulders made it difficult to concentrate on coffee.

Penny tore her eyes away from his torso and studied the chalkboard menu on the back wall. "Um. Maybe? I'm not sure." It felt like a big step, even if it was just a coffee order.

"An Americano?" he suggested.

Penny shook her head. A drink comprised of espresso and water seemed even less adventurous than her usual latte.

"Cortado?"

"No..."

She knew exactly what she wanted, but it wasn't on the menu and she was afraid to ask for it. Which was her whole problem. She was so afraid of inconveniencing other people that she never came right out and asked for what she wanted. That was Old Penny thinking, and she needed to let it go.

"What about one of those lavender lattes like you made before? I know they're not on the menu..."

Caleb's eyes sparked as if he were pleased. "Coming right up."

While he made her drink, she went around collecting dirty cups and glasses from the tables and carried them to the dish cart beside the garbage can, because honestly, why couldn't people clean up after themselves when the cart was *right there*?

"You don't have to do that," Caleb shouted to her from the espresso machine. "It's literally my job."

"I like to be helpful," Penny shouted back.

She contemplated the empty tables. Should she sit somewhere else today, just to shake things up even more? Maybe by the window, or on the big orange couch.

She glanced back at her usual spot at the counter, which afforded an unobstructed view of the espresso machine where Caleb was making her latte.

No need to go overboard, she decided, and claimed her old stool.

"Thank you," she said when Caleb brought her drink over a few minutes later. He'd sprinkled dried lavender on top of the foam this time. Penny picked it up and inhaled through her nose, letting the aroma fill her sinuses.

When she glanced up, Caleb was watching her. She blew across the top and took a sip. "Mmmmm. Delicious."

His eyes sparked again, and the corner of his mouth dimpled.

Forget ordering a different drink every day. If his eyes were going to twinkle like that every time, she'd happily order this for the rest of her life. *One lavender latte with a side of gorgeous eye twinkle, please.*

"You should definitely get Reema to put this on the menu," she said.

He ducked his head almost shyly. "Maybe we should start up a secret menu that only the best customers know about."

A silent squeal lodged in her throat at the implication that she was one of his best customers. She'd made it, finally. She was on The List. "Like at In-N-Out."

"Exactly."

The music that had been playing in the background stopped, and it suddenly felt eerily quiet. She hadn't even noticed the music until it stopped, but now its absence was glaring. Caleb threw a glance at Malik, who tossed down the rag he was holding. "On it," Malik said as he disappeared down the hall that led to the office in back.

Caleb turned back to Penny, evidently in no hurry to move along. "It's your turn in the hot seat today."

"For what?"

"I answered all your questions Friday. Now I get to interrogate you."

Penny only barely managed to restrain herself from bouncing on her stool like a manic Bounce Around Tigger. "I'm an open book. Go for it."

"Hmm." His mouth twisted sexily to one side. Having actual conversations with him was amazing, because it gave her an excuse to stare at him unashamed. What a gift. "You work from home, right? That's why you're always in here in the middle of the day."

"Correct."

"And you do something with…chemistry?"

"I'm a patent examiner."

His eyebrows drew together. "What's that involve?"

"Whenever a person or company thinks they've invented something new, they apply for patent protection. I'm one of the people who reviews new applications to determine if their claim makes scientific sense and is legally new and distinct from what's already known."

"Sounds cool."

"It can be, but it can also be dull. Today, for instance, I spent the whole morning reading up on polymers used to make contact lenses."

"Was today one of the cool days or one of the dull ones?" His eyes were finely lashed and shockingly expressive for someone so stolid. The gold depths seemed to flicker as he gazed at her.

Was it warm in here today? Penny squirmed on her stool and looked down at her latte. "Depends how you feel about silicone-based hydrophilic copolymers."

The music started up again, louder than before, and she jumped a little. It was some sort of bass-heavy electronica and hip-hop fusion that sounded out of place for a quiet morning at a low-key coffee shop.

Caleb rolled his eyes at Malik when he emerged from the back. "Come on, man."

"This is good shit. Don't hate." Malik grabbed the tray of dirty dishes Penny had bused and marched them over to the sink.

Caleb shook his head and turned his attention back to Penny. "So how long have you lived in Los Angeles?"

"I moved here from Washington, DC, last year." Her eyes slithered over the curve of his shoulder and down to his biceps. He had his sleeves pushed up, exposing his thick forearms. They were all veiny, with a fine coat of light-colored hair, and his skin was smooth and golden and—

"Is that where you're from originally?"

She cleared her throat and reached for her latte. "Close. I'm from Richmond, Virginia."

Having actual conversations with him was torture, because it gave her an excuse to stare at him unashamed. What a nightmare.

"Family?"

"Mom, Dad, two older sisters—Cassandra and Dana—and my younger brother, Jason. He's a junior at UVA."

Caleb's eyebrows quirked in amusement. "Your siblings are Jason, Cassandra, and Dana? And you're…Penelope?"

Her heart thudded at the sound of her full name on his lips. "My mother's a high school English teacher. Big fan of the classics."

"Clearly." He pinched his lips together, like he was trying not to smile.

Penny wondered what it would take to get him to actually smile. He must be capable of it. His mouth seemed otherwise proficient—supple, dexterous. Perfect, basically. Surely it was able to form a smile. Why was he so reluctant to show it off? Maybe it was so beautiful it turned people to stone. Or made them fall in love with him. That didn't seem too far outside the realm of possibility. Even thinking about Caleb smiling made her feel a little faint.

His eyes fell on her mouth, almost like he could read her mind. *Oh, God, wouldn't that be mortifying?*

Penny licked her lips and looked down at her coffee.

The way he was hanging around and looking at her—if she didn't know better, she might almost think he was flirting with her.

Which was undoubtedly why he didn't usually do it. When a man this gorgeous showed an interest in you, it was easy to get swept away and convince yourself he was being more than just polite. No wonder he avoided chatting with customers other than George.

Penny silently pledged not to give Caleb any reason to think she was misconstruing his attention. He was simply being nice.

Just because her libido was raging out of control didn't mean she should repay his niceness by creeping him out.

The bell rang as a group of new customers came in, and Caleb rapped his knuckles on the counter as he went to serve them.

She blew out a breath as soon as his back was turned, and pressed her fingers to her cheeks. They were burning up. She must be bright red. How embarrassing.

If she and Caleb were going to be friends, she'd need to learn how to talk to him like a normal person, without noticing how gorgeous he was.

Easier said than done.

KNITTING WAS BACK in its regular Monday night slot that week. When Penny arrived—ten minutes late because she'd had to pack up the peanut butter bars she'd made for the group—she cast a nervous glance at the counter.

Malik was still working, but there was no sign of Caleb. Relief warred with disappointment. As much as she liked seeing him, it would be easier to relax and enjoy knitting without him around, distracting her with his good looks and sudden friendliness.

Penny carried her peanut butter bars over to the couch where her friends were waiting for her. While they set upon the baked treats like a flock of ravenous seagulls, she took the smaller container she'd packed and got in line at the counter.

Malik broke into a grin when it was her turn to order. "God, I love Monday nights. It's the only day of the week I don't mind working a double." He tilted his head, trying to see into the container. "What'd you bring this week?"

She slid the contraband toward him. "Peanut butter bars."

"Hey, those are for everyone," Caleb said, coming out of the kitchen with a fresh dispenser of iced coffee. "No hogging them all this time, *Malik*."

Penny's stomach lurched. They should put a bell on him so he couldn't sneak up on people like that. She needed time to gird herself before confronting his handsomeness up close.

"What'll it be?" he asked, taking over at the register as Malik wandered off with the peanut butter bars.

"Mango tea." If she drank coffee this late it would keep her up half the night.

Caleb gave an apologetic grimace. "We ran out. I'm making more, but it'll be another five minutes or so."

"That's okay. I'm in no hurry." She handed him her credit card and added the usual twenty percent tip to the bill.

"Go sit," he said when she pushed the receipt toward him. "I'll bring it out to you when it's ready."

Penny grabbed a handful of napkins and joined her friends in the back corner. They'd already devoured half the peanut butter bars and were chatting excitedly about the previous night's episode of *Game of Thrones*. Everyone in the group watched the show except Penny, who wasn't a fan of all the violence and gore.

From what she could gather, a major character had died last night, which seemed to happen almost every week. Also something involving incest, which—again—seemed to be a frequent occurrence.

"These peanut butter bars are outrageous," Olivia said, changing the subject. "I don't know how you do it."

Penny dug in her bag for the baby hat she'd been knitting on Friday. "It's just chemistry and following instructions. But thank you."

"How are you holding up?" Vilma asked, quirking a motherly eyebrow at her.

"I'm fine!" she replied a little too brightly.

Vilma's eyebrow slanted into skepticism.

"Honestly!" Penny said. "I'm feeling good about the breakup."

"She's feeling so good, she's given up men," Jinny said.

Cynthia lowered her knitting and laid a concerned hand on Penny's knee. "Honey."

"It's a good thing," Penny said, spacing out the mint green stitches on her circular needles. "And it's not forever. I'm just taking some time to enjoy being on my own for a while."

"I think that's very healthy." Cynthia gave an approving nod as she picked up her own needles again. She was knitting a complicated intarsia sweater for her husband's birthday, and her lap was covered with a half dozen different colored yarn bobbins.

Penny didn't mention that she'd been feeling lonely and horny. Not even a week into her no-men resolution, and she was already sick of being single. It was fine though. She just needed to get used to it again. That was what smutty fanfic was for.

Esther leaned forward for another peanut butter bar. "Penny thinks she's too nice, and that's why she keeps getting cheated on."

"Oh, honey, no." Vilma's head tilted in sympathy. "They cheated because they were cheaters. It's their problem, not yours."

Penny shook her head, keeping her eyes on her stitches. "Even if that's true, I bear some responsibility for dating so many of them. I keep choosing cheaters for some reason, and that's on me. I've obviously fallen into a bad pattern and I need to break out of it."

"Do not change yourself for men," Esther said around a mouthful of peanut butter bar. "It's not worth it."

"Okay, but..." Penny hesitated, trying to organize her thoughts. "What if I want to change? What if I'm tired of being the nice girl? What if I want to try being the *fun* girl to see what it's like? Maybe it's better."

"It's not better," Jinny said. "Trust me."

"And you *are* fun." Cynthia nudged Penny with her elbow.

Penny wrinkled her nose. "I have schedules for my schedules. I think I need to practice loosening up a little for my own benefit, if nothing else. Try being more spontaneous. For example—" She glanced at Esther. "How often do you hand-wash your bras?"

Esther blinked. "You're supposed to hand-wash bras?"

Jinny rolled her eyes. "Don't ask her, she's a statistical outlier."

"Okay, how often do you hand-wash *your* bras?" Penny asked Jinny.

"Once a week," Jinny said, looking down at the lacework shawl she was knitting.

Penny narrowed her eyes. "Be honest."

"Okay, every other week," Jinny admitted. "But I own a *lot* of bras."

Penny turned to Olivia. "What about you?"

"Every few weeks, maybe—but I take my work wardrobe to the dry cleaners every week. I think I should get bonus points for that."

"And you?" Penny asked Cynthia.

She shrugged. "Once a month—but I don't wear bras every day."

Penny couldn't imagine walking around without a bra, even in the privacy of her own home. When she'd weighed more, she'd even had to wear a bra to bed at night while she slept.

"Vilma?" Penny glanced at the older woman. "How about you?"

"Never," she said. "I have one of those lingerie bags so I can throw them in the washing machine."

Olivia twisted her mouth to the side. "I don't see what this has to do with you not being fun."

"I hand-wash my bras twice a week, you guys."

"Okay?" Olivia said, still looking confused.

"Twice a week! A fun person does not spend two nights of every week hand-washing delicates."

"But bras are expensive," Jinny said. "You should take care of them."

"Maybe I'm tired of always doing what I should," Penny said with a sigh.

Esther's eyes lit up and she pointed a finger at Penny. "You need one of those boob sling towels!"

"What's that?" Vilma asked, looking up.

"It's like a sling for your boobs that goes around the back of your neck," Esther said. "But it's made of towel material, so it's soft and cozy and absorbs all your underboob sweat. It's for wearing when you get out of the shower or around the house."

"Sounds weird," Cynthia said, wrinkling her nose in distaste.

"It would be nice to walk around my house without a bra," Penny said wistfully. "And without underboob sweat."

Jinny shrugged. "I do it every night."

Esther scowled at her. "You people with your reasonably-sized boobs can't understand what it's like for the rest of us."

"Do you do that thing where you tuck your shirt under your boobs?" Penny asked Esther.

"Yes!" Esther nodded vigorously. "All the time!"

"I think this boob sling sounds like heaven," Vilma murmured as she sipped her wine.

"That's exactly what I'm talking about," Penny said. "That's what I need."

Cynthia's brow furrowed as she reached for her own wine. "A boob sling?"

"Yes!" Penny gave a decisive nod. "I mean, literally yes, I need one of those. But also metaphorically. I need to get out of my rut and try more things that are different and weird."

Jinny looked up, grinning. "Are we talking about sex now?"

"Maybe, but it doesn't have to be." Penny glanced toward the counter and caught Caleb staring at her. She hastily fixed her eyes back on her knitting. "It could be anything, as long as it's different."

"You moved out here," Olivia said. "That was new and different."

Penny shook her head. "But I only did it because Brendon would have broken up with me if I hadn't. It was the safe choice. Or I thought it was, anyway." She'd been more scared of losing him than moving to a new city. That wasn't courage, it was desperation. And then she'd lost him anyway.

Penny might have a name that sounded like a storybook heroine, but she'd never acted like one. She'd never been the type of girl who'd follow the rabbit down the hole to Wonderland, or climb out a window after Peter Pan, or go on an unexpected journey with Gandalf and a band of unruly dwarves. She was the girl who left playtime early to do her homework and straighten her room. She'd never take a risk on an uncertain venture. Not on purpose, anyway. That was the problem with life: even the sure things could pull the rug out from under you. So what was the point of always playing it safe?

"I want to be more spontaneous," Penny said. "Take some risks instead of always sticking to the safer path. I want to hike the steep path and have adventures." She needed to be like Bilbo: stop fussing over the dwarves' dirty dishes and go chase dragons with them instead.

"I prefer the safer paths." Vilma's gaze drifted to Penny. "There are fewer rockslides on the safe paths."

"But the views are better on the steep path," Penny said. "I want better views."

Esther looked confused. "Are we still talking about men?"

Penny sighed. "I don't know, you guys, I just feel like I need to try something different. Instead of rearranging my life to suit someone else, I need to focus on getting what *I* want."

"It sounds like what you want is more sex," Jinny said with a knowing look. "And I applaud that."

"Not just more sex," Penny said emphatically. "*Better* sex."

"Here's your tea," Caleb announced at Penny's elbow

They really need to put a bell on him, she thought as her face heated.

He leaned over to set her mango tea on the table and nodded at her knitting as he straightened. "What are you making?"

"Oh. Um." Penny smoothed it out so he could see. "It's a baby hat."

"Is it for Roxanne?"

"No, I'm making her a blanket. This is for one of my cousins."

He nodded and glanced around the table. "You guys need anything else?"

"I think we're good," Penny said. "Thanks."

His hand brushed her shoulder as he turned to leave, and Penny felt her heart lurch.

"What was that?" Olivia hissed when he was gone, her eyes widening.

"What?" Penny said, keeping her eyes fixed on her knitting.

"Hottie Barista being all friendly with you."

Penny shrugged. "I'm a regular. I get special treatment."

"I'll say." Esther lifted her eyebrows. "He touched your shoulder."

"And smiled," Jinny added. "He never smiles."

"He did not," Penny said. "You're exaggerating."

"He was totally flirting with you," Jinny insisted.

"No, he wasn't. Don't be ridiculous." He was just being friendly. *Platonically* friendly.

Olivia shook her head. "I've never seen him talk to anyone unless he had to."

Cynthia directed a smirk at Penny. "There's your adventure right there."

"I'll bet he smells great." Jinny sighed dreamily. "He looks like he'd smell nice."

"But not *too* nice," Cynthia said, still smirking.

"Yeah, just a little dirty."

"Just the *right* amount of dirty."

Penny shushed them. "Guys, he's right over there. And he's a person, not a piece of meat."

Esther snorted. "I've seen no evidence to support that claim."

"It's definitely weird," Jinny said. "Hottie Barista never talks to anyone."

Penny frowned at her knitting. "His name is Caleb, and he talks to me sometimes."

"I rest my case," Jinny said, arching a smug eyebrow.

"It's only because I'm in here every day."

"I always assumed he was a robot," Olivia said thoughtfully. "A beautiful, lifelike robot."

"He is very attractive," Vilma said.

"You should hit that," Jinny said, nodding at Penny.

Esther shook her head. "Mmm, bad idea."

Jinny turned to look at her as she reached for her wine. "Why? He's gorgeous."

"Reason number one: hot guys are never any good in bed."

"Ouch," Cynthia said. "Damn. What about Jonathan?"

"Yeah." Jinny shot Esther an accusatory look. "Are you saying he's bad in bed, or are you saying he's not hot?"

Esther rolled her eyes. "Neither. He happens to be fantastic in bed and he's hella cute. But he's also smart and sensitive and funny and *those* are the qualities that make him a good lay. Hottie Barista, on the other hand, is an empty vessel. Guys like that don't have anything going for them but their looks. You seriously think there's anything in that pretty head of his other than his own ego? Doubtful."

Penny wanted to defend him, but she knew if she did, they'd just double down on the idea that he was flirting with her.

"What's reason number two?" Vilma asked Esther.

"Don't shit where you eat."

Penny scrunched up her nose. "Gross."

Esther shrugged. "You come here every day, right? He might as well be a coworker. Bad idea."

"Hey!" Jinny protested. "Yemi and I work together."

"No, you don't," Esther said. "You work in the same building, but you don't work together. If you broke up, you'd hardly ever see each other. Not that you're breaking up," she added hastily. "You guys are obviously perfect for each other and you'll be together forever."

"Thank you," Jinny said.

Esther turned back to Penny and hooked a thumb at the counter where Caleb was working. "You bag that prize and then what? You really think he's got long-term boyfriend potential?"

Penny didn't even think he had fleeting encounter potential. The entire hypothetical lacked plausibility.

"Unless there's a happily ever after in your future," Esther went on, "you'll have to deal with an awkward encounter every time you come in here." She shook her head sadly. "Better just to find a new favorite coffee shop."

"I don't want to find a new place to meet," Vilma said. "I like it here."

"They have wine," Cynthia pointed out.

"That's what I'm saying." Esther turned back to Penny. "I mean, sure, he's hot. But is he hot enough to deal with the consequences?"

Jinny gazed across the room at Caleb. "Maybe."

As Penny watched him wipe down the counter, she let her mind wander over the possibility. In detail. Luxuriating in the fantasy. Imagining his mouth and his hands on her. His hard body pressed against hers. His warmth everywhere, filling her up…

Nope. Ridiculous. It could never happen.

"This conversation is absurd." Penny shook her head to clear away the images. "I'm off men, remember?"

"Sure you are," Jinny said. "We'll see how long that lasts."

Chapter Six

*I*t was raining on Wednesday. It never rained in Los Angeles.

It had been overcast when Penny set out for Antidote on foot, but she'd assumed it was just marine layer like always. She changed her tune when the clouds started dumping water on her.

She was two-thirds of the way to Antidote, so she quickened her pace and kept going rather than turn back toward home. It couldn't possibly rain for long; she'd just wait it out at the coffee shop.

By the time she ducked in the door, she was soaked to the skin.

"It's raining!" she announced as she squeegeed water off her face.

"Yikes," Elyse said.

"What are you doing out walking in the rain without an umbrella?" George asked, swiveling on his stool to frown at her. He was the only customer this morning. The rain must have kept everyone else away. Everyone with any sense, that is.

"It wasn't raining when I left the house!" Penny shook out her arms, sending droplets of water flying in every direction. "It never rains in LA!" Her shoes were waterlogged and water dripped off her skirt onto the doormat like the drip line of a tree.

"Stay there," Caleb said and disappeared into the back.

"Now you know better," George said. "It only mostly never rains."

Penny tried to squeeze the water out of her hair. It dripped down her back in a cold stream that made her shiver. "I used to check the weather every single day, you know. But it always said the same thing, so I quit."

"Los Angeles rain likes to sneak up on you. And no one knows how to drive in it. You're lucky you weren't run over."

Caleb came back with a stack of clean dishtowels. "It's all we have," he said apologetically.

"No, this is great. Thank you." Penny grabbed one and toweled off her face and chest.

His gaze came to rest on her décolletage as she patted it dry. Thank goodness her dress had a bright, busy pattern, because the way it was sticking to her could have been very indecent otherwise.

Caleb cleared his throat and bent over to lay a towel out on the floor. "Step out of your shoes onto this."

"I'm not allowed to be barefoot in a restaurant," she protested.

"I promise not to call the health department on you—this time." He put his hand under her elbow to steady her and nodded at the floor. "Come on."

She let herself lean on him, her fingers closing around his large forearm—the very same forearm she'd gazed at longingly so many times—as she slipped out of her shoes. *Too bad he's wearing a sweatshirt,* she thought as she stepped onto the dry towel, scrunching her wet toes in the cotton, *or else I could be touching his bare skin right now.* A shiver raced down her spine at the thought.

He thrust the stack of towels at her, then scooped up her shoes and began drying them off. She reached out to stop him. "Oh, no! You really don't have to—"

He waved her off. "I don't want to have to mop the floor behind you, do I?"

"I can do it! I don't mind."

He shook his head in exasperation. "Just dry yourself off."

She did as instructed while he dried her shoes with the brisk efficiency of a valet out of a historical costume drama. It was both embarrassing and a huge turn-on at the same time. Penny blamed her longstanding crush on Mr. Carson from *Downton Abbey*.

When he was done, Caleb set her shoes on the floor and took Penny's elbow again to help her step back into them. They were still damp and freezing cold, but at least they didn't squelch like wet sponges anymore.

"You good?" he asked.

Penny nodded. She was holding on to his forearm again. His beautiful, thick forearm. She could feel the taut muscles even through his hoodie. She was *great*.

He let go of her and held out his hands for the damp towels. "Lavender latte?"

She nodded, smiling shyly. "Yes, please."

His gaze skimmed over her body briefly before coming to rest on her face and lingering there. Penny stood there paralyzed as the moment stretched out. She'd never looked into his eyes from this close before. Usually there was a counter between them and at least three feet of space.

The corner of Caleb's mouth twitched, and he tilted his head toward the counter. "Go sit down."

She shook off the enchantment enough to give him a curt nod. "Yes, sir."

His mouth twitched again as he turned away to carry the towels into the back.

Penny took her usual stool, shivering as her wet skirt pressed against her legs. She really wished she'd brought a sweater today. Of course, if she had, it would be just as soaked as the rest of her.

"You want the funnies?" George asked, offering a section of his newspaper. Penny shook her head and he went back to reading state and local news.

She crossed her arms and hunched forward as she watched Caleb make her lavender latte. When he brought it to her, she cupped her hands around the bowl-shaped cup gratefully, letting the warmth soak into her cold fingers.

"Your hair's curly," he observed.

Penny reached up to touch her wet hair, which had already started curling up as it dried. So much for all that time she'd spent straightening it this morning. She made a face as she ran her fingers through it, fruitlessly trying to smooth it down. "Yeah, it is."

"It's usually straight."

"I work hard to get it that way." She lifted her latte to her lips, sighing as the hot liquid warmed her from the inside out.

"We missed you yesterday."

She lifted her eyes from her coffee. "We?" She'd had a doctor's appointment, so she'd had to skip her coffee break.

He shrugged. "You know. Me and George."

Penny smiled and took another sip of her latte. "I can't believe you even noticed."

"I always notice you," Caleb said, and Penny's stomach swooped like she was on a roller coaster.

George coughed and rubbed his chest. Caleb looked over at him and frowned. "You okay?"

George waved a hand as he reached into his pocket for a prescription bottle. "Just my angina acting up. Don't mind me."

A chill crept down the back of Penny's neck, and she shivered. Caleb's eyes slid over her arms, noting the goose bumps. "You're freezing."

"I'm fine." She shivered again. *Stupid body. Stop doing that.*

He unzipped his hoodie. "Here. Put this on."

"I couldn't," she protested. Even though she could. And she would.

"I'm not going to let you sit here freezing to death." He shrugged it off his shoulders and passed it over the counter.

Penny accepted the navy blue bundle like she'd just been handed the Golden Fleece. It was soft and heavy, warm with residual body heat. Caleb's body heat, she thought with an exhilarated rush. Putting it on was like being enveloped in a Caleb hug. Or what she imagined being enveloped in a Caleb hug must be like.

"Better?" he asked.

She nodded, clutching the hoodie against her chest like a security blanket. "You're being so nice to me."

The corners of his mouth pulled down. "You sound surprised."

"Well..."

Until two weeks ago, he'd acted like the last thing in the world he wanted to do was talk to her, and now he was making her special drinks and sharing his clothes with her. Was she not supposed to be surprised?

"You didn't think I was nice?"

"Not like this," she said, and he looked down at his feet.

He's shy, Penny realized. That must be why he never talked to anyone or smiled—or part of the reason, anyway.

George coughed again and rustled his newspaper. Caleb's gaze flicked over to him, then back to the floor.

"Honestly, until last week, I thought you didn't like me," she said.

Caleb shook his head. "That's not it."

"Then why were you so distant? Why wouldn't you ever talk to me?"

He shrugged one shoulder. "It's just a habit."

"Being unfriendly?"

"It's easier," he said to the floor.

"Than what?"

He rubbed his palms on his jeans. "Sometimes, if I'm too friendly, women assume I'm flirting with them."

A mortified laugh bubbled out of her throat. "You didn't think *I* was flirting with you, did you? Because I promise you I was not." Caleb looked up with an expression of dismay, and she had the inexplicable feeling she'd landed a punch she hadn't meant to throw.

George coughed again. She looked over at him and saw that he'd broken into a sweat. "George? Are you okay?"

He waved her off and got to his feet, swaying a little.

"George?" Caleb said.

George opened his mouth to speak, teetered, and started to crumple.

"George!" Penny leapt off her stool to grab him. He wasn't a large man, but he was like deadweight in her arms. The best she could do was cushion the fall as they both slid to the floor.

Chapter Seven

"*E*lyse, call 911!" Caleb shouted, rushing to Penny's side and easing George off her.

George's eyes were wide and frightened as they laid him out on the floor, and he was clutching his chest like he was in pain. Penny snatched his jacket off the stool, balled it up, and slid it under his head to try to make him more comfortable.

"George, can you tell me what's wrong?" Caleb asked, kneeling over him.

"My chest," he wheezed. "Hurts." Penny took his hand, feeling useless and frightened.

Caleb pressed his fingers under George's jaw. "You have a heart condition?"

George nodded, grimacing in pain.

"Was that nitroglycerin you just took?"

George nodded again.

Caleb touched Penny's arm. "Do you have any aspirin?"

She shook her head. "Only ibuprofen."

"He needs aspirin."

Penny's mind raced. She could run down the block to Rite Aid, but that might take too long. Or maybe... "Is there a first aid kit here?"

Caleb nodded. "Behind the counter. Under the register."

She pushed herself to her feet and ran around the counter. Elyse was talking into her cell phone, giving the address of the coffee shop to the 911 operator. She stepped back so Penny could reach the red plastic case under the counter. Frantically, Penny dropped to her knees and tore through it, sifting through the Band-Aids and alcohol swabs until she found a small packet of aspirin. "Here!" She stood and tossed it to Caleb.

He caught it and tore it open with his teeth. "George, I need you to chew this up and swallow it, okay? You think you can do that?"

George gave a weak nod, and Caleb lifted his head a little as he slipped the tablet into his mouth. George grimaced as his jaw worked. When he'd swallowed, Caleb gently laid his head back down.

"Ambulance is on its way," Elyse said, the phone still pressed to her ear.

"Tell them it's a probable heart attack," Caleb said.

George's eyes fluttered closed as Penny crouched beside him again and squeezed his hand. "George?"

Caleb reached up to pat George's cheek. "George, wake up. Can you hear me? I need you to keep your eyes open if you can."

George's eyes opened halfway, and Penny let out a relieved breath.

"There you go," Caleb said, sounding impressively calm. "Concentrate on my voice, okay? I need you to stay awake for me."

George's mouth moved like he was trying to talk, but no sound came out. His hand felt cold and clammy in Penny's.

She rubbed it between her palms, trying to warm it up. "Don't worry, George, you're going to be fine. The ambulance is on its way. They're going to take good care of you."

George's hand squeezed hers weakly, then went limp as his eyes rolled back in his head.

"George!" Caleb slapped his cheek lightly, trying to rouse him. "George, open your eyes!"

George's eyes stayed closed this time.

Caleb pressed his ear to George's chest. "Shit," he muttered under his breath.

"What?" Penny asked as Caleb positioned his hands over George's heart and started doing chest compressions. Panic sliced through her gut. Had his heart stopped? Was he breathing? Oh, God—was he dying?

Her Girl Scout troop had taken a CPR class when she was in middle school. It was so long ago, she'd forgotten most of it, but she remembered the instructor telling them to time chest compressions to the beat of "Staying Alive" by the Bee Gees.

It was all she could think about as she watched Caleb bounce up and down, pressing on George's chest at a hundred beats per minute, in perfect time with the song in her head.

One. Two. Three. Four. *Staying alive. Staying alive.*

One. Two. Three. Four…

Oh God, please let him stay alive.

The next few minutes felt like an eternity. Penny and Elyse watched in anguished silence as Caleb performed CPR. A bead of sweat formed on his forehead, and Penny wiped it away with her sleeve before it could fall into his eyes.

How long could he keep this up? How long did George have?

Where is the ambulance?

Finally, she heard a siren in the distance. It gradually grew louder and louder, until it was so loud it hurt her ears. A heavy diesel engine rumbled outside. Flashing red lights shined through the window, and the engine and siren cut out at once, leaving an unsettling silence in their wake.

Penny got to her feet as the paramedics came through the door.

"We've got him now," one of them said, laying a hand on Caleb's back. "I'll take over."

Caleb stood up and stepped back so they could work. "He started having angina about fifteen minutes ago and took one of the nitroglycerin pills in his pocket. A few minutes later he collapsed, and I gave him 325 milligrams of aspirin. I started chest compressions when he lost consciousness."

"How long's he been down?" one of the paramedics asked as he inserted an IV needle into George's arm.

"Three minutes," Penny said when Caleb looked uncertain. "It was three minutes ago." She'd been watching the clock on the wall obsessively, counting the seconds while they waited for the ambulance.

She watched the EMTs transfer George onto the gurney and prepare him for transport.

"You did good." One of the paramedics squeezed Caleb's shoulder as the others wheeled him toward the door. "You might have saved his life."

"Which hospital are you taking him to?" Penny asked.

"Brotman. You know if he's got family?"

"They're in San Jose." His son's name was Mike, she knew that much. If she could remember the name of the company he worked for, she could get in touch with him to let him know what had happened.

Caleb stood beside her, watching through the window in silence as the paramedics loaded George into the back of the ambulance. It had stopped raining at some point and the sun was shining.

"Is he going to be okay?" Penny asked when the ambulance was out of sight.

Caleb nodded, still staring out the window. "Hopefully. They got to him really fast. That's important."

Penny sniffled and swiped at her eyes. Caleb put a hand on her shoulder and turned her toward him.

His brows drew together as his eyes roamed over her face. "Are you okay?"

She nodded again, trying to make it look convincing. She'd never seen anyone have a heart attack before, or even seen anyone taken away in ambulance. What if George died? What if she never saw him again?

Caleb's arms enveloped her, and she sagged against his chest and drew a hitching breath. His hands rubbed comforting circles on her back. "It's going to be okay."

She sniffled, trying not to get snot on his T-shirt. "How do you know?"

"Because he got help right away. The odds are in his favor."

She nodded against his chest. "You were amazing. You knew exactly what to do."

The bell on the door announced the arrival of a customer and Caleb let go of her.

Penny turned her face away and stepped back, putting some distance between them. She dug in her purse for a tissue as Elyse greeted the customer in a hollow voice. She was probably just as shaken up as Penny, poor thing. The woman at the counter ordered a mocha, oblivious to the fact that she'd walked into the middle of a tragedy.

Penny pressed a tissue to the corner of her eyes and made a decision. When she turned back around, Caleb was picking up the trash the paramedics had left behind. "I'm going to the hospital," she said to him. "Do you want to come?"

He straightened, looking conflicted. "I can't. I can't leave Elyse on her own. And I need to call Roxanne and Reema to tell them what happened."

Penny nodded and hiked her purse onto her shoulder. Her eyes fell on George's newspaper lying on the counter. She remembered the look on his face as he'd crumpled to the floor. How fragile he'd seemed.

"Will you call me if you hear anything?" Caleb asked.

"Sure. Of course." She fumbled in her purse for her phone. "What's your number?"

He recited it for her and she added him to her contacts. C-A-L-E-B. She didn't know his last name, so she left it blank.

Which reminded her... "I don't suppose you know the name of the company George's son works for in San Jose? I wanted to call him. I thought he should hear it from someone who knew his dad. I thought it would be better—not that anything can make this better. Easier, maybe. For him." She realized she was babbling and pressed her lips together.

"Bargello," Caleb said. "He works for a software company called Bargello."

"Right." Penny nodded, staring at her phone. She didn't need to write that down. She could remember it. Why was she still staring at her phone?

"Hey." Caleb moved closer. He lifted his hand like he was going to touch her cheek, then stopped and let it drop to his side. "Maybe you should sit down for a few minutes before you try to drive. There's no need to rush off. It'll be a while before they know anything."

Penny shook her head. She didn't want to sit around here, seeing George falling to the floor over and over again. "I've got to walk home first. I'll be fine."

Caleb nodded, but he didn't look happy about it.

Why would he? There was nothing to be happy about today.

Chapter Eight

*P*enny still had Caleb's hoodie. She didn't realize it until she was sitting in the waiting room of the cardiac care unit.

The volunteer at the desk was a kind elderly woman wearing a red bib and a name tag that said "Joan." She wasn't allowed to tell Penny anything about George's condition because she wasn't family, although she'd been very apologetic about the need to protect patient privacy.

George's son Mike was on his way though. Penny had gotten in touch with him at his office and explained what had happened. He'd called the hospital himself, then found a seat on a flight leaving in an hour, but he wouldn't be here until three thirty. Penny had a long wait ahead of her.

She looked around the waiting room, which was half full of worried-looking friends and family. There was a water cooler and a coffee pod machine off to one side. A selection of herbal teas and granola bars. A small bowl of wrapped peppermints. A television was tuned to CNN, but the volume was turned down low, so it was just a dull murmur in the background instead of an insistent squawk. Penny had chosen a seat facing away from it. She didn't need the news making her even more anxious. There was a fish tank across from where she sat. Angelfish and tetras swam in slow, peaceful circles.

The volunteer at the desk was reading a mystery novel. Every once in a while someone would come out of the doors leading to the cardiac care unit and speak to her in hushed tones. She'd point them to one of the waiting families. Sometimes they'd be led into the back, or sometimes the doctor or nurse would speak to them for a moment and then disappear again, leaving them to continue their vigil.

Penny wished she had her knitting with her so she'd have something to do that didn't require concentration. She'd been trying to read *Star Wars* fanfic on her phone. Finn and Poe were handcuffed together and locked in a meat freezer, forced to huddle for life-saving warmth. It was one of her favorite tropes, but she kept reading the same paragraph over and over without digesting a word.

She swiped to her contacts and stared at Caleb's name. She wanted to text him, but she didn't have any news yet. He'd probably be worried though. He might appreciate an update, even if it was just to say there weren't any updates yet.

She typed out a message. *George's son is on his way. They won't tell me anything until he gets here.*

Caleb's reply came within seconds. *Thanks for letting me know.*

I've still got your hoodie, Penny typed. *I'm sorry.*

I'm glad you've got it. Hospitals are cold.

Penny was glad too. It made her feel less alone.

She'd been too upset to properly appreciate the hug Caleb had given her while it was happening. But she could still remember how it felt to have his arms around her. If she closed her eyes, she could almost feel them again. The thick firmness of his muscles. The reassuring warmth of his body. The way he smelled: like coffee and something subtly spicy.

The same way his hoodie smelled. She pulled it up over her nose and inhaled. It was almost like having him with her.

Whenever the doors to the cardiac care unit opened, everyone in the waiting room would go silent for a moment, their heads all swiveling to see whose turn it was to be spoken to. Someone had just come out—a handsome Indian doctor wearing scrubs and tennis shoes. He consulted with the volunteer, and then came over to where Penny was sitting. "Are you here for George Simkin?"

Penny swallowed. "Yes." The doctor was tall and lanky like a basketball player, and he towered over her.

He held out a hand. "I'm Doctor Ramesh."

"Penny Popplestone." He had soft hands, but a firm handshake. "I was at the coffee shop when George collapsed. We're friends."

Doctor Ramesh sat down in the chair beside her. "I understand his family lives out of town."

She nodded. "I called his son. He's flying down from San Jose, but he won't be here for a few hours. Is George okay?"

The doctor gave her a reassuring smile. "He's awake and stable. We're about to take him into surgery."

"Oh. Okay." That felt like good news. At least it wasn't bad news.

"The procedure should take about three hours, but sometimes it can take longer, so there's no need to worry if it does. As soon as we're done, I'll come out with an update on his condition." He spoke kindly, but with brisk efficiency, like he'd given this speech a thousand times before. "After surgery, he'll go to recovery for a couple hours. Once he's awake, he can have a family member come back and see him. Hopefully his son will be here by then."

Penny nodded, feeling overwhelmed. Doctor Ramesh gave her an encouraging smile and got to his feet.

She watched him disappear through the double doors before she got out her phone and called George's son. It went straight to voicemail, which hopefully meant he was on the plane already. She left a message repeating what the doctor had said.

When she was done she typed out a text to Caleb with the same information.

She stared at the screen as she waited for him to reply. And waited. And waited.

She was on the verge of giving up when the phone buzzed in her hand with an incoming call. From Caleb.

She went out into the hall to answer it. "Hi," she said, trying to keep her voice steady.

"Hey." His voice sounded deeper on the phone. Huskier. "That's good news."

"It is, right? I thought so, but—"

"No, if he's awake it's definitely good."

Penny let out a long breath and squeezed her eyes shut. Hearing Caleb's voice made her feel a lot better.

"Are you okay?"

"Yes," she said, rubbing her eyes. "Just worried. And I hate hospitals."

"Me too." She heard the sound of the milk frother in the background.

"You're at work still?"

"Yeah. Roxanne came in and sent Elyse home. She was pretty freaked out."

"Poor Elyse." Poor all of them.

"I better get back to work," Caleb said. "You sure you're okay? Is there anything we can do?"

"No, I'm fine. There's nothing to do right now but wait."

"Okay," he said. "I'll see you later."

Penny went back into the waiting room and settled in for the long wait.

Two hours later, George's son showed up. He was short and wiry, just like his dad, only with a little more hair. He gave Penny a hug when she introduced herself. "My dad's told me all about you."

"Really?"

Mike nodded and rubbed his palms on his business casual khakis. "He talks about everyone at that coffee shop like they're family."

Penny swallowed around the lump in her throat. "He's like family to us too."

The volunteer brought over a clipboard of forms for Mike to fill out. While he was working on them, Penny offered to get him something to eat, and he accepted her offer gratefully.

She came back ten minutes later with a granola bar and a banana for herself and a hamburger and french fries for Mike.

"Thank you so much," he said. "For everything. It's nice to have someone here so I don't have to wait alone."

While he ate his hamburger, Penny recounted the episode at the coffee shop that morning, telling him how quick-thinking Caleb had been to recognize what was happening, administer aspirin, and start CPR. She also told him what the paramedic had said about it maybe saving George's life.

They killed the next hour making hushed small talk in the waiting room while they waited for George to get out of surgery. Mike's wife was staying in San Jose for another two days with their son, but they were coming down Friday afternoon as soon as she picked him up from school. Hopefully George would be well enough to see his grandson by then.

After a while, they ran out of things to say and fell into an edgy silence. Penny glanced at the clock on the wall for approximately the one thousandth time. Any minute now, the doctor might come out with an update—or it might be another hour or two.

She took out her phone and deliberated texting Caleb again but decided against it. If he was waiting anxiously for an update, it would be mean to keep getting his hopes up by texting him when there wasn't any news.

She'd just put her phone away again when she saw Caleb standing out in the hall.

He was watching her with his hands in his pockets like he was trying to make up his mind whether to come in. When she smiled at him, he nodded in acknowledgement and started toward her.

"Caleb!" She was so happy to see him she almost jumped up and hugged him again, but something about his body language stopped her. "I didn't know you were coming!"

"I just got off work and thought I'd wait with you." His eyes flicked over to Mike, who'd stood up when he approached.

"Mike, this is Caleb," Penny explained. "From the coffee shop."

Mike stepped forward and hugged Caleb. "Thank you. Penny told me you saved my dad's life."

"I didn't do that much," Caleb muttered as Mike clung to him. "It wasn't a big deal."

Mike let go of him and reached up to rest a hand on his shoulder. He was at least five inches shorter than Caleb. "I'm so glad you were there. I can't even imagine what might have happened if Dad had been at home alone."

"Don't think about that," Penny said, shuddering at the thought of George lying on the floor of his house alone, possibly for hours.

Caleb shifted his weight, looking uncomfortable. "Is there any word yet?"

"Still in surgery." Penny sat down again. After a moment's hesitation, Caleb took the chair next to hers.

"You know, Dad talks about you all the time," Mike said, sitting on Penny's other side and leaning forward to talk to Caleb across her. "I feel like I know you. Both of you."

"We see George practically every day," Penny said. She darted a glance at Caleb, who was staring at the floor, and nudged him with her elbow. "Don't we?"

He looked up and nodded. "Yeah. He comes in every day for

his bottomless drip coffee." He was doing that monotone thing he used to do to her before he'd started being friendly.

She couldn't tell if he was upset or just shy, but obviously she was going to have to carry the conversational baton alone.

While Mike and Penny chatted, Caleb sank into silence beside her. It felt weird to have him sitting right next to her. She was pretty sure they'd never been this close for an extended period of time before. At the coffee shop he was always standing, usually with a counter between them. Now he was only inches away. Sharing an armrest. Their knees side by side.

His fingers drummed a nervous beat on his thigh. He must be worried about George. Penny wanted to reach over and take his hand in hers, as much for her own comfort as his, but she wasn't sure he'd like it. Instead, she stood up and asked if anyone wanted any coffee.

Mike requested cream, no sugar, and when she looked at Caleb he mumbled a half-hearted, "Black, thanks."

She went to the coffee pod machine and made two styrofoam cups of coffee.

"Thanks," Mike said when she brought his coffee to him.

She held out the other cup to Caleb. "This is a switch, isn't it? Me bringing you coffee instead of the other way around." His fingers brushed hers when he took it from her, and their eyes met and held.

"Penny's been great," Mike said. "Keeping me company and bringing me food."

"She's good people," Caleb agreed, and Penny felt herself blush.

At five thirty, Dr. Ramesh came through the double doors. He was wearing one of those patterned surgical caps like they wore on *Grey's Anatomy*. His had dolphins on it.

Penny introduced him to Mike, and Dr. Ramesh told them that George had come through surgery like a champ. He described in detail the procedure they'd done, and said George had a long recovery ahead of him, but he should be just fine. Mike hugged the doctor and then hugged Penny. He was a hugger.

Dr. Ramesh said the nurse would come get Mike in a little while and take him to see his dad. He shook Mike's hand, and disappeared into the back again.

"I'm going to call my wife," Mike said, pulling out his phone.

Penny turned to ask Caleb if they should go and realized he'd already left.

She caught sight of him heading for the stairs at the end of the hall and hurried after him. "Caleb," she called out as she followed him into the stairwell. *"Wait."*

He stopped on the landing below her and turned around.

"Where are you going?" she asked when she drew even with him.

He shifted his feet but didn't say anything. His chest rose and fell like he was breathing hard.

She edged closer, peering into his face. "Were you just going to leave without saying goodbye?"

He pressed his lips together and looked down at his feet.

"I don't understand you. How can you be so sweet one minute and so remote the next?"

When he looked at her, his eyes were dark and intense.

Penny froze, every nerve in her body on high alert. "What is it? What's wrong?" His expression shifted like he was deliberating something. "You can talk to me."

He let out a deep breath and moved closer, lifting a hesitant hand to her face. She opened her mouth in surprise as his fingertips caressed her cheek. His eyes drilled into hers. Hypnotizing flecks of gold danced in the depths of his irises. His eyelashes lowered as his fingers slid into her hair. He tilted her head back.

"Penelope."

The sound of her name on his lips sent an electric ripple through her body. She felt faint. Oxygen was a distant memory.

He let out a rough breath and pressed his mouth against hers.

Penny's brain short-circuited. Hottie Barista was kissing her. Kissing! Her!

Fortunately, she didn't need her brain for this. As his lips moved over hers, her body reacted instinctively. Her fingers curled into his arms and her mouth opened, angling against his. Lapping him up.

What had started out slow and careful quickly intensified into something much deeper. Hungrier. Teeth grazed her lips and she shuddered a sigh.

Caleb pulled back, his eyes searching her face like he was asking for forgiveness—or permission.

She answered by pulling his mouth to hers again with a hand curled around the back of his neck. His body pressed against hers, warming her from tip to toe. They were both panting and breathless. Gulping for air as their mouths melted together. She was dimly aware that he'd backed her up against the wall. That they were in the stairwell of a hospital that smelled like antiseptic. That someone could walk in on them any second.

She didn't care. All she cared about was the feeling of his lips on hers. The hardness of his body. The heat building inside her.

Her fingernails scraped over his scalp and he made a huffing sound into her mouth. She kissed him harder, rising up on her toes. His hands clutched her hips, his fingers digging into her flesh.

A door slammed overhead and they jolted apart. They stared at each other, frozen, as footsteps echoed down toward them. There was a creak of a door being pulled open. Another slam. Silence.

Caleb's face was flushed, his expression grave. Penny reached up to touch his cheek.

His long eyelashes fluttered closed. He caught her hand. Moved it off his face. "I should go."

He started down the stairs without a backward glance. She wanted to go after him, but her legs were so wobbly she wasn't convinced she could manage stairs. She was shaking. In shock.

Her mouth opened but all that came out was a ragged gasp. She couldn't even make herself call out after him.

Her chest heaved as she listened to his footsteps pounding away from her. All the way down, three flights of stairs to the ground floor. He must be sprinting. A door finally slammed at the bottom, and Penny was alone in the stairwell.

What just happened?

The cold cinderblock wall behind her started to seep into her bones, jerking her back to reality like a splash of ice water. Shivering inside Caleb's hoodie, she pushed herself upright and ran a hand through her bedraggled hair, smoothing it back down where his fingers had been only moments ago.

His nearness had intensified his scent on the hoodie. She felt like she was drowning in it.

She wanted to drown in it even more.

Why did he kiss me?

More importantly: *How can I get him to do it again?*

Chapter Nine

*P*enny went back to the waiting room in a daze and made both her and Caleb's goodbyes to Mike. As she rode downstairs in the elevator, her mind replayed the kiss with Caleb on an infinity loop.

That was...wow. Caleb had kissed her.

And it had been hot. Super hot.

Except then he'd just...left? Which sucked.

Was he repulsed? Embarrassed? Ashamed?

Penny felt herself getting a little mad. *He* was the one who'd kissed *her*. It wasn't like she'd been throwing herself at him. In fact, she'd been doing pretty much the exact opposite of that. If he hadn't wanted to kiss her, *why had he?*

Had the kiss been that bad? Penny didn't think so. She was a habitual overachiever, which meant she'd worked hard to perfect her kissing technique and had received a lot of compliments in the past. She felt pretty confident she was a good kisser. Caleb had sure seemed to be enjoying himself in the moment.

Could he have a girlfriend?

It was possible, she realized as a sinking feeling formed in her gut. He'd never mentioned one, but he'd never mentioned a lot of things. It was only recently he'd started opening up about himself at all. Maybe he'd been hiding a girlfriend all this time. Penny felt sick at the thought. And even angrier.

By the time she got home, it was seven o'clock and she'd missed a half day's work. She should probably try to make up some of the hours now. Those technical specifications weren't going to read themselves.

Instead, she called Olivia.

"What's up?" her friend said when she answered.

"So many things." Penny sank back into the cushions of her couch. "I don't even know where to start."

"Chronological or ascending order of importance. Pick one." Olivia had a direct and ordered approach to everything, which was exactly what Penny needed right now.

"Chronological." Penny couldn't even begin to rate the day's events according to importance, so she started with George's heart attack and the ensuing hours waiting around the hospital for him to get out of surgery.

"Oh, wow, Pen."

"That's not even all of it," Penny said, squeezing her eyes shut.

"What else?"

"Hottie Barista kissed me."

"Whoa," Olivia said. "Back the fuck up. When did he do that?"

"At the hospital." Penny realized she was starving and went into the kitchen. "When Mike went to call his wife, Caleb tried to sneak off and leave."

"He pulled an Irish goodbye," Olivia said knowingly.

"Exactly!" Penny grabbed a container of leftover beef stew out of the fridge and put it in the microwave. "So I went after him and followed him into the stairwell."

"And?"

"And he kissed me," Penny said, feeling warm again at the memory.

"Just like that? Without saying anything?"

"Practically. It was definitely out of nowhere. One second he was trying to sneak away and the next he was staring at me really intensely and then...he pushed me up against the wall and kissed me."

It must have been a moment of temporary insanity. That was the only explanation Penny could think of. A stressful day, emotions running high. The two of them alone together in an unfamiliar environment. Maybe he'd forgotten who she was for a second and mistaken her for someone he was attracted to.

"Huh," Olivia said. "What'd he say after?"

"Nothing! He just ran off." Her stomach twisted. That part of it had been sort of humiliating.

"He kissed you out of nowhere and then ran away without a word?"

"Pretty much. All he said was, 'I have to go.' And then he literally sprinted down the stairs to get away from me. It's weird, right?"

"*Yeah*, it's weird. How was the kiss?"

Penny touched her lips, smiling. "Outstanding."

"Nice. Congrats, I guess."

"But what do I do now?"

"What do you want to do?"

Penny thought about Caleb's fingers sliding into her hair. The gentle scrape of his teeth on her bottom lip and the taste of his tongue. "I want to kiss him again."

"I thought you swore off dating?"

"That was before a super-hot guy kissed me in a hospital stairwell."

"Fair point."

The microwave dinged and Penny reached for a potholder. "I'm going to see him tomorrow and I don't know how to act." She carried the steaming container over to the table. "Do I pretend it never happened? Do I follow his lead and see how he acts?"

"No, fuck all that," Olivia said. "He kissed you and you deserve an explanation. You're not a character on a badly written TV show. Don't be too gutless to have an adult conversation. Be direct. Ask him outright what the fuck the deal is."

Penny's stomach clenched in apprehension. "Just like that? Just walk right up to him and say, 'Hey, Caleb, why did you kiss me and run off?'"

"Why not? It's not like *not* talking about it is going to erase the fact that it happened or make it any less weird. So you might as well deal with it and move on. One way or the other."

Penny stirred her soup and tried to imagine herself having a dialogue like that with Caleb. She could barely manage benign, easy conversations with him. How were they going to talk about something like this? "I don't know," she said. "I don't think I can do it."

"It's either that or never go back there again. Ghosting's the only other option."

Penny sighed. "This is exactly what Esther warned me about."

"Yep."

"I don't want to ghost," Penny decided. "I like Antidote. I'm not giving it up because of him."

"Then you should make him talk to you."

Sure. Make Caleb talk. Easier said than done.

AT ELEVEN THE NEXT MORNING, Penny set out for Antidote. Her legs felt like jelly, even though it wasn't a spin class day.

She still had a lot of work to catch up on from yesterday, and if she was going to visit George in the hospital this afternoon, it would cut into her work time even more. Probably she should skip her coffee break today, but that would mean not seeing Caleb, which wasn't an option. The anticipation might actually kill her if she put it off for a whole other day. Plus, she didn't want him thinking he'd scared her off.

She still hadn't decided what she was going to say to him.

Her stomach hurt every time she thought about it. But it also went all fluttery at the prospect of seeing him again. A happy kind of flutter, like you get when you have a crush. Her stomach was hurting and fluttering simultaneously, and it was making her nauseous.

Her trepidation increased with every step that carried her closer to Antidote, and to Caleb. To her impending death by mortification.

No, you know what? He's the one who should be embarrassed.

She'd done nothing wrong. He was the one who'd kissed her and run away. *He'd* acted weird, not her. Olivia was right—he owed her an explanation. It wasn't like Penny was expecting him to marry her or anything. She just wanted to know what was going on in his head. And also, if he had a girlfriend. That wasn't too much to ask of someone who'd kissed you.

Her pulse pounded in her ears as she approached Antidote. She clutched the door handle in a white-knuckled grip, took a deep breath to steel herself, and pulled it open.

Malik was working the register today and Caleb was at the espresso machine with his back to the door. The sight of his muscled upper back pulling his T-shirt tight across the top of his shoulders sent a shiver of lust-slash-dread down Penny's spine.

"Penny!" Malik called out as she got in line behind a woman in workout clothes.

Penny saw Caleb's hands still at the sound of her name, but he didn't turn around. So that was how he was going to play this.

"I heard you were here when George keeled over yesterday," Malik said when he'd finished ringing up the woman ahead of her.

"Yeah." Penny glanced at Caleb again. He was still turned away from her, pretending not to hear, even though he was only a few feet away and it was quiet in the shop except for the muted sound of electro jazz playing on the sound system. Malik must have picked the music today.

It felt like an invisible wall stood between her and Caleb. Like she didn't exist to him anymore. He'd hit the reset button on their relationship and gone back to ignoring her.

Malik shook his head. "Must have been scary."

Penny nodded, trying not to remember it. "It was."

"George is doing okay though, right?"

"Yeah. I talked to his son this morning. He says they're moving him out of the CCU and into a regular room today."

Caleb did turn around at that. His eyes found Penny's and held them for a moment before skating away again. He set the coffee he'd made on the counter, called out the customer's name, and went to make the next drink.

"You want the usual?" Malik asked Penny, already keying it into the register.

"Yep." She really wanted a lavender latte, but she was too chicken to ask for it. Malik probably wouldn't know what it was anyway.

She paid for her plain nonfat latte and went to take her usual seat at the counter. As she sat down, her gaze lingered on George's empty stool, two over from hers, and her chest squeezed.

He was going to be fine. No need to get all teary again.

When she tore her gaze away, she caught Caleb watching her with a frown on his face. As soon as their eyes met, he turned away again.

What? The heck?

This was getting stupid. She needed to talk to him. But how? Not in front of Malik. She'd have to wait until he went into the back. Or maybe Caleb would go into the back and she could follow him.

She tried to think of ways to get him alone while she watched him work the espresso machine, but she kept getting distracted by how attractive he was. She couldn't believe she'd actually kissed him yesterday. Those hands had been on her body. Those hips had pressed against her hips. That mouth had been on her mouth.

Focus. She needed to figure out how she was going to get him alone, and more importantly, what she was going to say to him once she did. She was torn between wanting to yell at him and wanting to ask him out on a date, neither of which seemed like the best course of action.

He was wearing a soft gray T-shirt, and tantalizing glimpses of his tattoo kept peeking out from under the sleeve. She'd had her hand on that biceps yesterday. She could have pulled his sleeve up and explored that tattoo up close, if only she'd thought to do it. Would she get another chance?

Her longing grew as she watched him, making it impossible to think of anything else. Lust scrambled her brain. She didn't know what she was going to do, but she knew what she *wanted* to do. She wanted to do Caleb.

She was still daydreaming when he finally brought her drink over and set it in front of her. "Hey," he said without meeting her eye.

At least he'd said something. He hadn't tried to skulk away. Yet.

"Hello." Penny stared at his mouth. She couldn't help herself. Her mind flashed back to kissing him. To the sweet softness of his lips. The prickle of his stubble on her skin. His tongue exploring her mouth.

Nope. Stop. She pushed the image away and opened her mouth to speak—

The shop bell rang as a trio of businessmen came in, talking loudly. Caleb gave her an apologetic look and moved away to help them.

Sighing in defeat, Penny looked down at her latte. It had three hearts in the foam and lavender sprinkled on top. She lifted the mug to her lips and sipped. He'd made her a lavender latte without being asked.

What did that mean? Was it a sign he still wanted to be friends? A peace offering? Or an apology?

She didn't want him to apologize. She wanted him to want to kiss her again. That wasn't too much to ask, was it?

She drank her latte while Caleb made the businessmen's drinks. Two Americanos and a flat white. They carried them to a table by the window where they began arguing about the Dodgers' pitching staff. Malik was leaning against the counter staring at his phone, and Caleb was slicing lemons with his back to her.

Penny got up and went to the register. Malik glanced up at her and she shook her head. "Caleb," she said, trying not to let her voice shake.

He set the knife down and turned around. His expression was as blank as stone.

"Can we talk?" Penny tilted her head toward the back. "Privately." Was it her imagination, or did his eyes widen momentarily in fear?

He wiped his hands on a dishtowel and nodded. "Sure."

She trailed after him down the back hallway, past the restrooms. He halted in front of the office door and turned around to face her. It was quieter back here. The voices of the businessmen had faded to a dull murmur, blending with the white noise hum of the refrigerator case at the end of the hall.

Neither of them spoke. They were standing close enough that she could see the gold in his eyes. As they stared at one another, the memory of the kiss floated in the air between them. Their fevered breaths. The way he'd moaned into her mouth. Penny licked her lips.

"I owe you an apology," Caleb said.

The words punctured her thin bubble of hope. "I see."

"I shouldn't have kissed you like that."

"Why not?" she heard herself say a little too loudly.

He flinched at the challenge in her tone. "What?"

"Why shouldn't you have kissed me?"

The bell on the front door jangled, and there was a murmur of voices as more customers came in. Malik was out front. He could handle them.

Caleb shuffled his feet like he was itching to escape. "Um…"

"Do you have a girlfriend?" Penny asked.

He shook his head at the floor. "No, nothing like that."

She rested her hands on her hips. "Did you not mean to do it? Am I supposed to believe it was some sort of accident? That you tripped and fell onto my face?"

"No, of course not, I—"

"Because I'm trying to understand why you'd do something like that and then run off and leave me standing there. And why you're apologizing now for kissing me instead of for running off."

"I'm sorry for that part too," he said quietly.

"It wasn't very nice."

"You're right, it wasn't. I'm sorry." God, he was beautiful when he was being contrite. It made it impossible to think straight.

Penny stared at his collarbone, which was also stupidly attractive, but not quite as distracting as his face. "So why did you do it?"

"Run off? Or kiss you?"

"Both. Either. Why are you being so weird about all of it?"

"Um." He shifted his weight, lowering his eyes to the floor. If she hadn't been standing between him and escape, he might have actually bolted like a horse.

She crossed her arms. "Did you not *want* to kiss me?"

"No, I…" He trailed off, rubbing his palms on his thighs.

Penny waited. She was prepared to wait all day if that was what it took.

He looked up. "I've wanted to kiss you for a long time."

That stopped her in her tracks. "W—what?"

His eyes looked into hers. "You heard me."

Something burned in her chest, constricting her voice to a whisper. "But you don't even like me."

"That's not true." He looked pained.

How long was a long time? Since last summer when he'd started working here? Did that mean—could she have been dating *Caleb* instead of Kenneth? She tried to picture it. Caleb asking her on a date, taking her out to dinner. Smiling across the table as he tried to charm her, hoping for a goodnight kiss at the end of the evening. She couldn't even picture the smiling part, much less the rest of it.

She tried to clear her throat and made a choking sound instead. "You *acted* like you didn't like me."

"I was trying to keep my distance." His expression turned reproachful. "You had a boyfriend."

"Who was a cheating jerk. Which you could have told me at any time." If Caleb had ever given her even the slightest hint he was actually interested in her, she would have dropped Kenneth like the flaming bag of dog poop he'd turned out to be.

"I was afraid you'd hate me if I was the one to tell you."

Unbelievable. Literally, it was impossible to believe this man who'd barely acknowledged her existence had actually been attracted to her all this time. It was inconceivable, and not in the *Princess Bride* sense of the word.

And yet...he *had* kissed her. It hadn't been a half-hearted kiss either. That was a serious kiss he'd given her. Deadly serious.

Penny swallowed. "I don't have a boyfriend anymore."

Caleb gazed at her for what felt like a long time. "I'm moving to Mississippi in a month."

"What?" It was the second time he'd knocked the wind out of her in this conversation.

"I'm starting med school at the University of Mississippi in the fall and my dad got me a summer job at a clinic there."

"Med school? Wow. That's—wow."

"That's why I'm sorry." He looked genuinely sad. "Because I'm leaving soon."

"I see." Her whole body had gone numb. Pins and needles prickled in her fingers, and she balled them into fists.

The shop bell jangled again and Caleb's mouth twisted into a regretful grimace. "I have to get back to work."

"Sure," Penny mumbled as all her fantasies came crashing down. She felt like she'd been run over by a truck and left by the side of the road. "Good talk."

"I'm sorry," he said again as he moved past her and away.

Not as sorry as she was.

Chapter Ten

*P*enny stood in the hallway alone, trying to get her bearings back.

Caleb had liked her. *Did* like her. But he was leaving. Moving away. In a few weeks, they'd never see each other again.

It wasn't fair. They'd missed their chance before she'd realized they even had a chance.

She went into the restroom and washed her hands, just so she'd have something to do. So she wouldn't have to go back out and face Caleb yet.

As she stood at the sink staring in the mirror, her gaze went to the reflection of the stall behind her. Her mind flashed back to the night she'd come in here to cry, when Caleb had come to check on her.

He'd actually cared. She still couldn't quite believe it. Her mind was reeling. It was too much to process at once. She needed to go off and think. Somewhere that wasn't here. Someplace where Caleb wasn't.

She pushed her way out of the bathroom. The back door they used for deliveries beckoned to her left. The urge to slip out without having to see Caleb was strong, but she'd stupidly left her purse on the counter—unattended. What had she been thinking?

She hadn't, obviously.

Penny hurried out of the hall, breathing a sigh of relief at the sight of her purse still sitting where she'd left it, next to the remains of the lavender latte Caleb had made. He glanced her way, his hands stilling as he fastened a to-go lid on the iced coffee in his hand.

Penny made a beeline for her purse, avoiding his eyes as she snatched it off the counter. Amazingly, she managed to keep her composure until she was out the door.

As she hurried down the sidewalk, she sucked in a ragged breath, panting like a cross-country runner. Her heart was pounding in her chest, but it eased a little with every step that carried her farther away from Antidote and Caleb.

She tried to use the walk back to her apartment to clear her head, but she couldn't stop fixating on the cruel unfairness of it all. The heart-stoppingly gorgeous guy she'd been crushing on for months had been crushing on her right back. How often did that even happen? Never. Not to her, anyway.

But it didn't matter, because he was moving away. They'd missed their window. If only she'd known. If he'd given some indication—*any* indication—of how he'd felt. They could have shared so many kisses by now. They could have shared so much more than kisses. She could have seen him naked. Run her fingers over the washboard abs she just knew were hiding under his clothes.

Darn it.

By the time she got home, Penny wasn't just frustrated, she was angry. Caleb had wasted so much time by making her think he wasn't interested. If only he'd said something sooner...

She couldn't dwell on it anymore. She had too much work to do to catch up from yesterday. And she'd promised to visit George today.

She sat down at her computer, opened up the application she

was working on, and tried to push Caleb and the abs she'd never get to touch out of her mind.

PENNY HESITATED outside the door of George's hospital room, clutching a bouquet of balloons in her fist. Maybe she should have brought flowers instead? She'd thought balloons might be more cheerful, but now she worried they were too juvenile.

When she peeked her head in, she saw that the curtain was drawn alongside the bed, but Mike was sitting in a chair by the window working on a laptop. He looked up and waved her into the room.

"Dad? Someone's here to see you."

Penny stepped around the curtain to the foot of the bed. George looked small and shriveled under the pale blue blanket, with all kinds of tubes hooked up to him. A machine beside the bed regulated his IV drip and displayed his blood pressure and heart rate.

His mouth stretched into a thin smile and he wiggled his fingers in greeting, too weak even to lift his hand. "Hey, kid." His voice was as weak as the rest of him.

Penny handed Mike the balloons she'd brought and went to take George's hand. It was cold and fragile in hers. Like blown glass. "How are you feeling?" she asked.

George grunted. "Like someone opened up my chest and moved everything around. I guess I'll live though. That's what they tell me anyways." At least he still sounded like his old grumbly self.

"You'll be back on your feet in no time," Penny said. "You're too stubborn to let a silly thing like a heart attack slow you down."

"Sure," he said. "That's me."

Talking clearly took a lot out of him, so Penny only stayed a few minutes and did most of the talking herself.

"I'll come back when you're feeling stronger," she promised, leaning over to kiss his cheek.

He squeezed her hand. "Sorry I gave you and everyone else a scare."

"You can make it up to us by getting better."

He nodded, his eyes already fluttering closed as Mike walked her to the door.

Penny took the elevator downstairs and got into her car, feeling shaken. Sure, George was old, but not *that* old. He'd always seemed so healthy and energetic. One minute he'd been full of life, and the next he'd nearly died.

It was easy to forget just how tenuous and unpredictable life was. You never knew when something would be taken away from you.

As she sat in her car thinking about George and life and missed opportunities, Penny made a decision. A scary decision.

She wasn't giving up on Caleb without a fight. She refused to spend the rest of her life wondering what could have been. So he was leaving in a month. So what? That still left them thirty days together, give or take. They could do a lot in thirty days.

So much.

Just because there was an expiration date hanging over their heads didn't mean they couldn't enjoy each other's company in the meantime. She was new Fun Penny! She didn't need commitment. She didn't even want it.

This was exactly what she'd been looking for: adventure, spontaneity, risk. Living in the moment with no strings or expectations. This was her chance.

Penelope Popplestone was taking the steep path—rockslides be darned.

PENNY'S NERVES were a jangling mess when she walked into Antidote the next morning. It was one thing to decide to go after

Caleb, and quite another to actually do it. She wasn't used to doing the pursuing. This was new territory for her.

But that was good. That was what she wanted. Unexplored vistas. Why should she always sit back and wait for a man to make the first move? Hadn't she just been thinking that she needed to get better at asking for what she wanted?

Okay, maybe a man as gorgeous as Caleb wasn't the safest choice for her inaugural attempt. But at least she had hard data that he was interested in her. That was a pretty good starting place.

"Morning," Caleb said when Penny stepped up to the register. He wore the wary expression of a dog afraid of being kicked, but at least he wasn't ignoring her completely.

Penny gave him her warmest smile, trying to set him at ease. "Good morning."

"Lavender latte?" he asked, relaxing a minute amount.

"Yes, please."

He rang her up without another word and went to make it while Elyse took over at the register. Penny watched him, trying to work up the courage to make her move. It was Friday, and he didn't usually work on the weekends unless they were short-handed. If she didn't do it today, she might not have another chance until Monday. She didn't think she could wait that long— not when the clock was already counting down toward his departure.

"I still have your hoodie," Penny said when Caleb brought her latte over. "I meant to bring it back to you, but I keep forgetting." This was a lie. It was sitting on the arm of her couch. She'd looked right at it as she was walking out the door today and decided not to bring it. Truthfully, she wasn't ready to give it up yet. It was the only piece of him she had.

"It's okay," he said, already starting to edge away. "Don't worry about it."

He wasn't going to make this easy for her, was he?

"I went to see George yesterday at the hospital," she said.

That stopped him. He turned back to her. "How's he doing?"

"Pretty well, I think, considering." She sipped her latte, waiting to see if he'd say anything else. When he didn't, she said, "You should go see him."

He nodded, looking less than thrilled at the prospect.

"I know he'd appreciate it. He adores you."

"I'll try." The way he said it sounded more like *no way in hell*.

Whatever, she wasn't his mother. It wasn't her job to nag him about social niceties. New Improved Penny didn't do that kind of thing for men anymore.

"So med school, huh?" She tried to keep her voice light, like she was just making friendly conversation.

A muscle tightened in his jaw. "Yeah."

"I had no idea. How old are you?"

"Twenty-three. I took a gap year after college to save money." He grimaced. "And to work on my MCAT scores."

Penny was twenty-five, which meant she was chasing after a younger man. Somehow that made it even more enticing.

He shifted his feet and stared at the floor, clearly desperate to get out of the conversation. Any second now he'd make his escape. If she left it up to him, they'd go back to the way things were before, when he'd barely acknowledged her existence. And then in a month he'd be gone. She'd never see him again.

Unless she did something.

Here goes nothing.

"I've been thinking about what you said yesterday."

He lifted his eyes from the floor. "Oh."

"Yeah." Penny looked around. It was quiet in the shop. Now was as good a time as any. "Can we...?" She tilted her head toward the back where they'd had their *tête-à-tête* yesterday.

"Hey, Elyse," Caleb said without taking his eyes off Penny. "I'm taking a break. You'll be okay on your own for a few, right?"

"Uh huh." She waved him off without looking up from her phone.

Penny slid off her stool and followed Caleb into the back. This time, she was clearheaded enough to bring her purse with her. Her knees felt a little wobbly though, and she put a hand on the cinderblock wall to steady herself.

You can do this. You've got nothing to lose.

Except my pride.

He stopped in front of the office door again and turned to face her. "What's up? Is everything okay?"

She nodded. "I've been thinking about what you said yesterday and..." She took a breath. "I don't accept it."

His brow crinkled. "You don't accept what?"

"I don't care that you're leaving."

His brow crinkled even more. "Thanks?"

"I didn't mean it like that. I care that you're leaving, obviously."

"What are you trying to say?"

"I'm saying, I'm not looking for long-term commitment. Maybe I just want to have some fun with no strings."

He stared at her. "Are you serious?"

"Completely. One hundred percent."

Footsteps plodded toward them as a customer headed into the men's restroom.

She couldn't do this in a hallway with people going in and out of the bathroom. Penny grabbed Caleb by the arm and dragged him into the office, pulling the door shut behind them.

She'd never been in there before. It was the size of a large closet, and the smell of coffee was overpowering but also deliciously comforting. Metal shelves covered two walls, packed with bulk supplies: napkins, cups, bags of coffee beans, dish soap. Next to a metal filing cabinet, a cheap particleboard desk held a laptop and a stack of invoices. Every available surface was cluttered, and

Penny's fingers itched with the urge to tidy and organize everything.

"What are we doing in here?" Caleb asked.

"Talking." Her heart pounded in her chest. If she was wrong about this, she'd never recover from the humiliation. But she saw something in his eyes that gave her courage: longing. "Maybe more than talking."

His gaze traveled down her body and he swallowed hard. She watched with a sense of triumph as his throat constricted. The way he was looking at her—she wasn't wrong. He wanted her as much as she wanted him.

Okay, then.

She stepped into his personal space and felt a thrill when he didn't step back. Another triumph. "Tell me you don't want to kiss me again."

He sucked in a sharp breath, but didn't speak.

She smiled, gaining confidence. "Tell me you don't want to kiss me, right now, and I'll leave you alone forever."

Still nothing.

She laid a hand on his chest. His pec was like granite. She slid her hand down his torso, to the abs she'd fantasized about. His breath hitched as her fingers traced the hard ridges. Talk about granite...

"Penelope." He sounded tortured. Poor thing.

She looked up at him with her hand spread out on his stomach. A mere inch above the waistband of his jeans. "What? Tell me to stop if you want. Say it."

He grabbed her and crushed his mouth against hers. Penny's purse slid off her shoulder and hit the floor with a *thunk*.

Their last kiss had started out sweet and tentative, but there was nothing tentative about this one. It was rough and desperate and messy. His tongue explored her mouth with wanton determination as he pushed her up against the shelving unit. Some sort of paper product fell on them, glancing off her shoulder, but neither of them paid any attention. All their attention was consumed by each other.

Her hands gripped his shoulders, fingernails digging into the muscle for better purchase. One of his palms moved over her breast while the other cupped her ass. As their hips ground together something hard and heavy pressed into her stomach. Penny moaned, arching against him.

Caleb let go as abruptly as he'd grabbed her and took a step back. "This is a bad idea." He ran a hand through his hair.

"Why?" Her voice rose in disappointment. It wasn't a bad idea, it was a fantastic idea.

"Because I've tried long-distance relationships and they never work out."

"I agree." Penny watched his chest rise and fall. "Long-distance relationships are the worst."

"So..." His tongue ran over his lower lip and she knew he was tasting her there.

She stepped toward him again. "So what?"

He shoved his hands in his back pockets, like he needed to physically restrain himself from reaching for her. "So it's a bad idea to start something now when there's no future in it."

Penny put her hand on his chest. "I'm not saying we should have a relationship. I'm saying we should have sex."

He blinked. "Oh." The sound warmed the air between them.

"That's all you have to say? Oh?" Her fingers smoothed over his T-shirt.

"I don't—"

"Want to?" she challenged.

He shook his head. "I don't think we should." So he *did* want to. He was just being a chicken.

"Why?"

His expression softened into regret. "Because I don't want you to get hurt. I can't do that to you."

Penny made a sound of frustration. "I'm a big girl. I promise not to get attached."

His eyes bored into hers, challenging. "You sure about that?"

Not really. But she wanted to find out. Consequences be damned.

Her fingertips curled into his shirt. "I don't want to wonder what it could have been like."

"You don't think we'll regret this?" Lust pinked his cheeks as he glanced down at her hand on his chest.

Was it her or was the room getting smaller? "I think we'll regret it even more if we don't. At least once, to get it out of our system."

"Once?" He blinked, and she could swear he looked almost—disconcerted. "You think that'll be enough?"

Penny smiled. "Let's find out."

Indecision twisted in his expression. His eyes flicked to her mouth, and she knew he was thinking about kissing her again. His control was slipping. She almost had him. She rose up on her toes, straining toward him—

"I can't," he said flatly.

She dropped back on her heels and took her hand off his chest. She wouldn't force herself on him. If he said no, he said no. "That's too bad." She struggled to keep the disappointment out of her voice.

His eyes dropped to the floor, shoulders slumping.

Projecting an attitude of cool nonchalance, she picked up her purse, took her phone out, and typed a quick text. She smirked in satisfaction at the way he jumped when his phone vibrated.

"That's for you," she said, her pulse pounding at her own boldness.

"What is it?" He fumbled his phone out of his pocket and frowned at the screen.

"My address. Just in case you change your mind."

Without waiting for him to respond, she yanked the door open and walked out. He didn't follow her.

No one looked up as she emerged from the back. They were all in the same positions they'd been in a few minutes ago, like flies trapped in amber or an exhibit at the natural history museum. Twenty-first century humans at a coffee shop.

It felt like Penny had stepped out of a time machine back into the present day. Like the last five minutes hadn't happened to anyone but her. She called out a goodbye to Elyse and hurried out the door without looking back.

Penny had made her offer. It was up to Caleb now to accept it. Or not.

Chapter Eleven

*S*he couldn't believe she'd done it.

Just...*thrown herself* at Caleb like that.

Even more amazing was that he hadn't seemed to mind. In fact, he'd seemed to enjoy it quite a lot for a minute there. Until he'd changed his mind.

At least she'd tried. She could feel proud of herself for that much. She'd made a pass at a super-hot guy without completely making a fool of herself. How about that for New Improved Penny's first foray into uncharted territory?

She spent the rest of the day trying to catch up on work while visions of Caleb tried to superimpose themselves over the prior art for the thermoplastic polyurethane cell phone case on her computer screen.

At five o'clock, she logged out and drove to the hospital to visit George. He was looking better tonight. Sitting up in bed, talking a little easier. She stayed a half hour this time, and George even did some of the talking, complaining about the food and the noise and the nurses who woke him up at all hours of the night.

When she got home, she was lucky enough to squeeze her small Kia Soul into a cramped space on the street two blocks from her building. Her apartment didn't have an assigned space, and this time of day the street parking situation resembled a scene from *Mad Max*. In the year since she'd moved to Los Angeles, she'd become an expert parallel parker.

As she walked up the sidewalk, Penny noticed a man standing in front of her building, staring up at it. Fear prickled at the back of her neck until the stranger's silhouette resolved into a familiar build with a slouch she knew well, and a dizzying shot of adrenaline surged through her veins.

It was Caleb.

She said his name and he turned to her in surprise, his face contorting into the guilty expression of a kid caught with his hand in the cookie jar—or standing outside the cookie jar creepily staring at it, in this case.

Penny stopped in front of him. He smelled like coffee, even standing outside with two feet of space between them, and it immediately triggered a sense memory of their kiss in the storeroom. Her mouth watered in response.

"What are you doing here?" she asked, trying to sound calm.

It had been disorienting enough to see him at the hospital, outside of Antidote. But that was nothing compared to seeing him here, where she lived. On *her* turf. It was like a character from a television show had stepped off the screen and materialized at her front door.

He looked sheepish. "Definitely not stalking you outside your apartment."

"It's not stalking if you've been invited." She could barely hear herself speak over the racing of her pulse. The Indy 500 was thrumming inside her ribcage.

He plunged his hands into his pockets. Was she really such a temptress that he felt the need to handcuff himself around her all the time?

"Where's your boom box?" she asked. "Aren't you going to

hold it over your head and play Peter Gabriel at me? I assume that's why you're here."

The corner of his mouth twitched. "I guess I must have forgotten it." She adored that mouth twitch. She wanted to devour it.

"That's too bad. I love Peter Gabriel." She stared into his eyes, caught in their mesmerizing spell. Outdoors, the gold in them seemed to glow even brighter, taking on glints of copper and bronze.

"I've been trying to talk myself out of knocking on your door."

A little spike of hope kicked her in the back of the knees. "For how long?" she asked, fighting off the urge to do a little victory dance right there on the sidewalk.

"About ten minutes."

"How's it going?"

He shrugged, hands still deep in his pockets. "So-so."

She was starting to feel faint. "Caleb?"

His eyes dropped to her mouth. "Hmmm?"

"Do you want to come up?"

He shook his head. "Yes."

A laugh burst out of her like a champagne cork. And then a miracle happened.

Caleb smiled.

An unrestrained, genuine smile curved his lips, lighting up his whole face as it shone out of his eyes. It was even more beautiful than she'd imagined. It was like the rain clouds had parted and a beam of sunlight appeared from the heavens to create a double rainbow.

Penny grinned in response. "I didn't know you could smile. You should do it more often."

His smile dimmed a little, but didn't completely disappear. It was still a single rainbow. "I smile."

"Not like that. Not like you mean it."

"I'm just selective about who I smile at."

"I feel honored to have finally passed the test."

Regret flashed in his eyes. He looked down at the sidewalk and shook his head. "I don't know why I'm here."

"Yes you do." Every muscle in her body was quivering with need. She wanted to leap at him and lavish him with kisses, but she held herself back. He was still skittish, like a lost dog. If she moved too quickly she might frighten him away.

A car with a faulty muffler cruised by like a shark, in search of a parking space. She waited until it had passed. "Okay, well, this has been fun, but I'm going upstairs. Are you coming with me?"

A muscle twitched in Caleb's jaw. He had a great jaw. Perfectly angled, leading to a strong chin. Just the right amount of stubble for maximum sexiness. "I shouldn't."

"So you say." She held her hand out to him and waited.

He stared at it with a mixture of wariness and longing, as if she'd offered him drugs. Her self-esteem swelled two sizes like the Grinch's heart. Caleb wanted her. It felt good to be wanted.

When he finally slid his hand into hers, she could swear she saw stars. Was that sound the local high school's marching band practicing in the distance or a chorus of Whoville Whos raising their voices in song?

Goose bumps shimmied down her arm as his calluses scraped against her palm. They locked eyes again. For a moment they just stood there on the sidewalk holding hands. Getting used to the feel of it. Bracing themselves for what came next.

It's happening.

Struggling to contain her elation, Penny tugged him up the walk to her building. Her apartment was on the second floor, and they continued holding hands as they climbed the cement steps. When they got to her door with its welcoming wreath of dried flowers, Penny regretfully released his hand to fish her keys out of her purse.

Caleb stepped up behind her when she slid her key into the lock. Heat radiated off him as his front pressed against her back.

His fingers moved through her hair, brushing it aside, then his lips grazed her neck.

Abandoning the keys in the lock, she spun to face him. They were so close her breasts grazed his chest. He put one hand flat against the door beside her head; the other reached up to trace her cheekbone. She shivered as his rough fingertips trailed over her skin. He bent his head, and their noses brushed. His breath whispered across her cheekbone, then he pressed a soft kiss to her temple.

A sigh escaped her lips as her hands fisted in his T-shirt, tugging him closer. His hand trailed down her neck to her shoulder, his thumb settling in the cradle of her collarbone. He pressed his forehead against hers. "I should go."

Her stomach sank like a lead weight. "No, you shouldn't." She gave his shirt a hopeful little tug. "You should definitely come inside."

He pulled back and shook his head. "I can't."

Annoyance flared within her. He couldn't just keep teasing her and then disappearing. "Relax. I'm not going to jump you." The corner of her mouth pulled into a smirk. "Unless you want me to."

His eyes darkened. "You have no idea."

Another tug. "Then come inside." She was never letting go of this T-shirt. He'd have to pry it out of her rigor-mortised fingers.

"Penelope." Her name came out as a growl. She'd never heard anything sexier in her life.

"Caleb. Come inside." She shoved the door open and he let her pull him over the threshold. She didn't let go until she had the door closed behind them.

His eyes traveled around her apartment, taking it in as she slipped out of her shoes and set her purse on the dining table. There wasn't a ton to see. The space was dominated by a dinette with four chairs and a big cozy couch with a hand-knit throw draped across the back. On one wall stood a bookcase overflowing with Blu-rays and old schoolbooks, and in the middle of the room sat a leather ottoman with a wooden tray that served as a coffee table. There wasn't even space for a second armchair—something she considered extremely fortunate at the present moment.

She gestured to the wicker mat beside the door where she'd put her flats. "Take off your shoes."

He obeyed, bending over to untie his scuffed work boots before lining them up carefully next to hers.

"Do you want something to drink? I was going to make some tea, but I've also got beer and wine. Or I could make you coffee!" she added. "Wouldn't that be a treat?"

He straightened and shoved his hands in his back pockets, looking amused. "Tea's fine."

"Make yourself comfortable." She went into the kitchen to put on the kettle. "Spicy chai or orange zinger?"

"Chai."

She got out two mugs and put a teabag in each. Spicy chai for him and orange zinger for her. "Do you take anything in your tea?"

"Black, please."

She went to the bathroom while the tea was steeping to do a quick hair and makeup check and apply a fresh coat of deodorant. Just in case.

He was staring at the contents of her bookcase when she came out. "You watch a lot of TV shows," he said as she dumped the tea bags into the trash.

She carried his mug of chai to him and gazed at the bookcase fondly. "These are my most favorite shows. The ones I like to watch over and over."

"Why buy it when everything's on Netflix?"

She blew across the top of her tea to cool it off. "Everything's *not* on Netflix. Sometimes they drop a show, and then you can't watch it when you want to. I like knowing that I can always watch my favorite shows in an emergency."

His brows drew together in amused incomprehension. "A TV emergency?"

"Yes! When I've had a bad day, I like to zone out on the couch and watch something that will make me feel better."

"Does that happen a lot?"

"All the time."

She took her tea to the couch and sat down. After a moment's hesitation he followed, leaving plenty of space between them. She turned toward him and he did the same, mirroring her position. They regarded one another silently as they cradled their tea.

The chai in his mug scented the air with spices. It smelled the way his skin had smelled. The memory of it made her feel warm all over. The heat started low, and spread up through her chest and into her face.

"What?" he said warily.

She sipped her orange zinger. "Nothing."

"You're staring at me."

"You're staring at *me*."

He shook his head. "This is weird, isn't it? Tell me it's weird for you too."

"A little."

She'd used up all her bold plays getting him here, and she didn't have a next move. It was one thing to screw up her courage to kiss someone who'd already kissed her once. But now that he was in her apartment, she had no idea what to do next. Was she supposed to seduce him? She wasn't used to being that girl. She *wanted* to be that girl, but she didn't know how.

She'd always relied on men to make the first move. They set the pace and she followed it. But if she let Caleb set the pace, he'd be in Mississippi before they'd made any real progress. Every instinct she had was urging her not to let him get away—not without a taste test, at least.

This was her chance to be the girl who had fun instead of good little Penny. To have a meaningless fling with a hot guy who was about to disappear from her life forever. She wanted this. Not only because he was so, *so* hot, but because she wanted to prove to herself that she could have hot sex simply for the sake of hot sex. No commitment, no attachment, no feelings.

She set her mug down and laid her hand on the couch between them, palm up. "You don't have to be scared of me. I don't bite."

The corner of his mouth twitched. "That's disappointing."

She grinned at him. "Maybe if you ask nice."

He graced her with another of those dazzling smiles as he placed his hand in hers. She'd always thought the term "panty-melting" was dumb when she read it in stories, but seeing that smile, it felt keenly apropos.

"I don't even know your last name," she said, tangling their fingers together.

His thumb stroked over her knuckle. "Mayhew."

"Caleb Mayhew." She rolled it around on her tongue like a sip of expensive wine. "I like it."

"It's not as good as Popplestone."

"Few things are." She turned his hand over and cradled it in both of hers like a palm reader. "Your hands are so rough."

His fingers flexed. "Sorry."

"No, I like it." She ran her fingertips over the calluses, imagining how they'd feel on her body. She never knew calluses could be so sexy.

"It's from lifting weights."

"I knew you worked out. A body like yours doesn't happen by accident."

He started to pull his hand away but she held on fast, locking her eyes with his. "Why does that make you uncomfortable?"

He held her gaze for a moment before lowering his eyes with a light shrug. "It gets old, only being appreciated for my looks."

She traced the veins in his wrist with her fingertips. "I appreciate lots of things about you."

He took a drink of his tea. "Yeah, right."

"I appreciate the way you make coffee."

He snorted.

"You make the best latte art of anyone."

"Great."

"I always liked that you were nice to George. I'm a little jealous, to be honest."

He lifted his eyes. "Of George?"

"That you talked to him when you wouldn't talk to me. You know, it's not my fault you haven't let me get to know you. It's not like I haven't tried."

Caleb's eyes flicked away. "I was intimidated by you."

It was Penny's turn to snort. "Yeah, right."

"I was. You're so smart and beautiful and confident. You seem like you have your whole life together."

"Come on."

"It's true."

"You're going to medical school, so obviously you're smart and you've got your life together too."

He scowled into his mug. "It's all an illusion."

"I just wanted to be your friend. Why wouldn't you let me?"

He leaned forward to set his tea on the coffee table before answering. "I didn't see the point of making friends when I knew I was going to be leaving soon."

She imagined him as a little boy, saying the same thing as he moved from one new school to another, and it broke her heart. She curled her fingers into his palm. "There doesn't need to be a point to having friends."

"I'll bet you have a lot of friends."

"And I'll bet you don't have very many."

When he didn't say anything, Penny turned his hand over and laced their fingers together. Her whole body ached for him. Being this close to him was suffocating. But she made herself wait. She needed to be patient. She didn't want to scare him away.

He swiveled his head toward her. "Do you still just want to be my friend?"

"No," she said quietly. "Not just. Not since you kissed me."

He looked down at their clasped hands. "Were you surprised when I did that?"

She took a chance and scooted toward him on the couch. "Yes. But it was a good surprise. The best."

His fingers squeezed hers. "I didn't mean to do it. It just happened."

She scooted a little more and the couch cushion helpfully tipped her toward him. "Do you regret it?"

"No." He lifted his other hand to her face and pushed a strand of hair behind her ear.

"Do you want to kiss me again?" she asked as his fingertips explored the curve of her jaw. Desire was surging like an electric current inside her. She'd never felt this helpless and this powerful at the same time.

He took his time answering. "Yes."

"Why don't you?"

"Because I'm afraid if I start, I won't be able to stop."

"Then don't stop. I'm not made of glass. You're not going to break me."

Something stirred in the depths of his eyes. "Maybe you're going to break me."

She almost laughed. "Somehow I doubt it."

His smile washed over her. "Did you know you're the best part of most of my days?"

She blinked at him. "Me?"

"You. You're amazing, Penelope."

"If I'm so amazing, why aren't you kissing me?" She'd meant it to sound light and teasing, but it didn't come out that way. Because that was the question, wasn't it? What was wrong with her that he kept holding himself back?

His frown deepened and she looked away.

"Hey." He tilted her chin toward him. His eyes roamed over her face, so soft and deep, she could sink right into them.

She wanted him to kiss her so badly, every nerve ending in her body was craving it. But she'd been the forward one last time. She wasn't doing it again. There was signaling your interest in someone and then there was relentlessly throwing yourself at them. If he wanted to kiss her again, he had to decide to do it.

"Penelope." He looked sad. Regretful.

He was about to tell her he hadn't meant it. She could already hear the excuses. That she was a great girl, just not his type. How he liked her a lot, but not in *that* way. He'd just gotten carried away in the moment when he kissed her before. This wasn't what he wanted. *She* wasn't what he wanted.

His lips parted, and she braced herself to hear that she'd been an experiment. A mistake.

Instead, he pressed his mouth to hers.

Her whole body sagged in relief, tipping her toward him on the couch even more. His arm slipped around her as he softly—so softly—kissed her mouth open. When their tongues touched the taste of his spicy chai mingled with her orange zinger. It tasted like Christmas morning. Like coming downstairs and getting that first glimpse of all the presents under the tree. Promise and possibility and wonder.

He sighed against her lips, and that was how she knew. He *wanted* her. He wanted this. At least as much as she did. His hand cupped her jaw, his fingertips stroking her skin as his mouth moved over hers slowly. Intently. Savoring her like a new and wonderful flavor of ice cream.

Feeling emboldened, she twisted her body toward him and swung her legs up onto the couch, tucking them beneath her. The arm around her tightened, pulling her even closer. Encouraging her. She slid a knee over his thigh and he let out a low groan as it settled between his legs.

He kissed her harder and she ground her hips against his

thigh. She couldn't help herself. She was lost in the softness of his lips and taste of his tongue. The prickly scrape of his stubble. Her knee slid up higher between his legs and he groaned again, head lolling back and eyes closing. She smiled smugly, reveling in the newfound feeling of power over him.

His hand glided up her spine as he gazed at her with hunger in his eyes. Experimentally, she moved her knee again and laughed as he groaned a third time. The hand on her spine slid into her hair. His fingers grasped the nape of her neck, pulling her mouth to his as his other hand grabbed her leg and moved it so she was straddling both his legs.

She nipped playfully at his lower lip and shifted her weight until she was comfortably settled in his lap. "Is that okay?" she asked, afraid she might be too heavy for him.

His hands cupped her ass. "Better than okay." Gifting her with another of his rare smiles, he gave her cheeks a squeeze.

So many smiles. She felt blessed. No wonder he was so careful about showing them to anyone. The women who came into the coffee shop would throw their underwear across the counter if they saw Caleb smile like this.

Penny gazed down at their legs, marveling at the size and strength of his thighs. They were even bigger than hers. But where hers were soft and pliant, his had been chiseled out of marble like a Michelangelo.

She caught sight of the tattoo on his biceps and reached for it. Pushing up his sleeve to expose the full length of it, she ran her fingers over his skin, tracing the words as she read them: *Transit umbra, lux permanet.*

"What does it mean?"

He played with a strand of her hair. "Shadow passes, light remains."

"I like that." She smoothed her hand down his arm, unable to believe this was really happening. She'd never been this close to anyone half as good-looking as Caleb. Looks had never mattered to her as much as personality—or at least that was what she'd always told herself. In truth, an opportunity like this had never presented itself before. And now here she was sitting in this gorgeous man's *lap*, for crying out loud. What was even her life right now?

She placed her hand on Caleb's chest and felt his heart thud against her palm, quick as a rabbit's. His chest rose and fell, his breathing heavy, and it shocked her to realize it was because of her. She'd made his heart speed up and his lungs heave just by touching him.

She slid her hands down his torso, enjoying the heady feeling as his rib cage expanded under her hands with every breath. He watched her with dark, heavy-lidded eyes as she ran her fingertips over his abs. Following the ridges like a topographical map, she settled her hands on his waist. There wasn't an ounce of give to it. Not a single pocket of excess fat to be found. She could only imagine what he must look like under that T-shirt. Images from the cover of *Men's Health* danced before her eyes. There was definitely a six-pack under there, and she longed to see it. Did she dare lift his shirt up?

No, not quite. Not yet anyway.

She stroked his stomach with her thumbs, smiling as his muscles contracted at her touch. "So I'm the best part of your day, huh?"

"You have no idea." He lifted both his hands to her face, cupping it gently as he drew her in for a kiss. Their mouths met in a slow, luxurious slide. One of his hands curled into her hair while the other traveled to her shoulder, then over and down to graze the side of her breast as his fingers spread over her ribs.

She let out an embarrassing little whimper and felt him smile against her mouth.

"All this time I had no idea you even liked me," he murmured.

She pulled back to stare at him. "Are you kidding? I was always nice to you."

He pressed a kiss to the corner of her jaw. "Yeah, but you're nice to everyone."

"Well, that's true." She ran her fingers through his hair as his lips moved down her throat.

"How was I supposed to know you weren't just being polite?" His breath heated her skin as he pressed a series of open-mouthed kisses over her throat.

"I *was* being polite, but you could have given me some encouragement. Then I would have been more than just polite." Teeth nipped at her skin and she shivered.

"I was afraid to. I knew I was leaving."

"Not for months." Her fingers tightened in his hair as her chest clenched. "We could have had so much time."

She felt him hesitate. "I was sort of seeing someone last year."

"Sort of?"

"We were...let's say engaged to be engaged."

Swallowing an irrational flare of jealousy, she lifted his head to look in his eyes. The pain she saw in them made her throat burn. "What happened?"

"She didn't like where I got into med school. She'd been hoping for somewhere a little more exciting than Jackson, Mississippi."

"I'm sorry."

He shrugged like it was all water under the bridge. *Que será, será.* "In retrospect, I dodged a bullet there." His mouth dropped to Penny's shoulder and she let her eyes fall closed as he kissed his way to her cleavage with intense concentration. "I thought about doing this, you know. Every day you came into the shop I thought about it. You have no idea." His index finger trailed down her chest and settled in the crevice between her breasts. "But then you started flirting with that guy Kenneth."

"Only because he flirted with me first. It could have been you." She lifted a hand to Caleb's face. "I would have preferred you."

He leaned back and gazed at her with eyes that had turned to dark, inky pools. His pupils were so wide she could barely see the gold in his irises anymore. "And now it's too late."

"It's not," she said, trying to keep the desperation out of her voice.

"I'm trying to warn you off me, and you're not making it easy."

She clenched her thighs around his. "I like being on you."

His eyes closed and he let out a low groan. "You know what I mean."

She bent her head toward him, her lips just barely brushing against his. "You like it too."

His eyes opened and locked with hers. "I do." His hand dropped to her hip. *Yes*, she thought as it slid down the outside of her thigh. *More of that.* His fingers ceased their journey and tightened on her thigh. "That's why I should go."

Just like that, her happy bubble burst. Again. "No, you shouldn't."

"I have to." His hands clenched around her waist and he moved her off him like she weighed nothing.

"Why?"

His eyes avoided hers. "I have somewhere I have to be tonight. I'm sorry. I can't stay." It sounded like a lie. He stood up, wincing as he adjusted his pants.

Serves you right, she thought vindictively. She hoped he ran into her elderly downstairs neighbor, Mrs. Jourgensen, on his way out.

"I'm sorry," he said again as he put on his shoes.

Penny nodded and stared at the floor. The words *please don't go* hovered on her tongue, but pride prevented her from saying them aloud.

When he had his shoes on, he came back to the couch and stood in front of her. "Penny."

"What?" she said without looking up.

"Penelope." He caught her hand and pulled her into his arms.

She lacked the fortitude to resist him. Her arms wrapped around his waist as she pressed her face into his chest, breathing him in. *Change your mind,* she thought fiercely. *You don't want to leave. Stay with me. Kiss me. Make love to me.*

He held her tightly. Then he kissed the top of her head and gently extracted himself from her grasp. "I'll see you Monday," he said, and let himself out of her apartment.

Well, crud. She'd gotten close this time, but still no cigar.

And, man, did she want his cigar. She wanted it bad. She was starting to feel like Charlie Brown. Lying in the grass after Lucy had yanked the football away yet again, wondering why this kept happening.

Something was holding him back. But was it really just his fear of hurting her? Or something else?

She felt like she was wearing him down though. He'd wanted her. That much she was sure of. Maybe if she'd been a little more aggressive. Maybe if she'd come right out and *asked* him to stay...

Next time.

Next time she'd have more courage.

She just had to make sure there was a next time.

Chapter Twelve

"*H*ow do you seduce a man?" Penny asked when she went for coffee with some of the women from her yoga class the next morning.

Melody shrugged. "I honestly haven't the faintest idea."

Tessa reached for her coffee, shaking her head. "Definitely not my area."

They both turned to look at Tessa's girlfriend Lacey, who had the body of a female wrestler and a face that could be on the cover of *Vogue*.

"Why is everyone staring at me?" Lacey asked. "Just because I'm bi you assume I'm some kind of loose woman? That's a vicious stereotype."

Tessa's eyebrows lifted in amusement. "A 'loose woman'? Did we time travel back to the Jazz Age?"

"Come on," Melody said, poking Lacey in the arm. "I know you've dated more men than me."

Lacey shook her head. "I've *slept* with more men than you. Sex isn't the same thing as dating."

"But that's exactly what I want," Penny said. "I don't want to date him. I just want to sleep with him."

"Wow," Lacey said, looking surprised.

"What?" Penny could be a loose woman if she wanted to. There was nothing wrong with being a loose woman. It was called being in charge of your own sexual desire.

"I thought you were off men," Melody said.

Penny shrugged and sipped her latte. "I'm off relationships. Meaningless sex is still on the table."

"Who are you trying to have meaningless sex with?" Tessa asked, resting her chin in her hands.

"It doesn't matter," Penny said. "It's just this guy."

"I'm going to need more details if you want my advice," Lacey said, letting her long, black hair out of its ponytail. "Spill."

Penny stared at her coffee. "He kissed me the other day, so I know he's attracted to me, but I'm having trouble getting him off first base."

"Maybe he's trying to be a gentleman," Melody said.

"But that's the whole problem. I don't want him to be a gentleman, I want him to bang me like a screen door."

Tessa's eyes widened. "Penny!"

"What? What's wrong with that?"

Lacey grinned. "Nothing's wrong with that. High five, girl." Penny reached across the table to slap her palm.

Melody frowned. "But maybe he's taking it slow because he wants more than just meaningless sex."

"Not an option," Penny said. "He's moving away in a few weeks."

Lacey nodded. "You want a goodbye bang. One for the road."

"Yes!" Penny leaned forward excitedly. "That's exactly what I want! How do I get him to do that?"

Everyone looked at Lacey again. "Seriously?" she said.

Tessa smirked at her. "Everyone at this table who's successfully seduced a man into your bed, raise your hand."

Lacey lifted her chin in Melody's direction. "You. Raise your hand."

"Nope." Melody shook her head. "My seduction technique amounts to following a man around like a lovesick idiot for months hoping he'll notice me eventually. I don't recommend it."

Penny looked hopefully at Lacey. "Come on. You've got to have some wisdom you can give me."

Lacey rolled her eyes. "Okay, fine. Here it is: men are dogs. They don't need to be seduced."

"How does that help me?" Penny asked, confused.

Lacey knocked back the last of her coffee and pushed the cup away. "You're overthinking this. Men's brains are in their dicks. If you try to be coy or subtle about it, they won't catch on. You want this guy to sleep with you, just be direct. Come right out and ask him to."

"You mean like one of those survey memes? 'Do you want to sleep with me? Yes or no.'"

"Exactly like that. Men are always looking to get off. If he's even the least bit interested in you, he'll say yes. He won't be able to help himself."

Penny felt like Caleb had been pretty good at helping himself so far, but maybe Lacey had a point. Maybe she'd been holding back too much. Waiting for *him* to take it to the next level instead of grabbing the reins herself.

Maybe instead of trying to flirt with him, she should just proposition him. Point blank.

After coffee, Penny went home and took a shower. As she stood under the hot spray, she contemplated the best way to implement Lacey's advice. Waiting until Monday was out of the question. Not only would she likely combust with unrequited desire long before then, it was too difficult to talk to him when he was at work. Too many distractions and avenues of escape presented themselves at the coffee shop. It needed to happen someplace private where they could speak alone. Preferably somewhere they could immediately act on their urges, should he accept her offer.

What Penny really needed was a do-over of yesterday's encounter. She needed to get him back in her apartment, where she just happened to have plenty of privacy, a bed, and a generous supply of condoms.

That was a booty call, right? When you issued an invitation for the express purpose of having no-strings sex. That was what she wanted.

Penny tried to imagine herself calling Caleb on the phone and saying the words aloud. Her stomach quaked in fear at the mere thought. She knew herself well enough to know she'd never be able to blurt it out. Once she had him on the line she'd almost certainly chicken out.

But she could send a text. That way, there'd be no getting tongue-tied or weaseling out. She could take her time composing it, considering her words carefully, and send them into the ether without having to hear his voice or look him in the eye. Perfect.

But what to say? Penny had never composed a booty call text before—she'd never even *had* a booty call.

As soon as she finished drying her hair, she did what she always did in a situation like this: she got on the internet and did a search for "best booty call texts."

The results were…eye-opening. And not entirely helpful. No way in heck was she typing anything as openly filthy as a lot of what was in the listicles she found online.

But it helped her familiarize herself with the etiquette, at least. The general pattern seemed to consist of an innocuous opening salvo inquiring as to your intended partner's present availability. If that was answered in a promising manner, an invitation followed. Whether that invitation included sexually explicit specifics or a transparent offer to participate in a sex-adjacent activity like pizza and Netflix seemed to be a matter of personal preference. Either way, the goal of meeting up at a time and place conducive to sexual activity was achieved.

Penny considered her opening salvo. She and Caleb hadn't

done any casual chatting via text, which meant they didn't have an established rapport in the medium. She was charting new territory.

First things first: establish his current availability.

Are you working today? she typed and hit send.

That seemed innocuous enough. If the answer was no, she could implement phase two.

The three little dots appeared that meant he was typing a reply, and Penny's heart leapt into her throat as she waited for them to materialize into an answer.

No. I'm off until Monday.

Whew. That was the first hurdle cleared.

Now came the hard part: the actual proposition.

She held Lacey's advice firmly in her mind. *Be direct.* If she equivocated by inviting him over for pizza and Netflix, he might come up with an excuse to decline. But if she came right out and invited him over for sex, he wouldn't be able to say no. Theoretically. According to Lacey's hypothesis, if he wanted to sleep with her even a little bit, he wouldn't be able to help himself in the face of such a bold invitation.

Penny trusted Lacey. She was beautiful and confident and refreshingly frank. And from what Penny had gathered, before Lacey had settled down with Tessa, she'd had a busy and fulfilling social life. Which was exactly what Penny wanted. Especially the fulfilling part.

She took a deep breath and typed her next text.

Do you want to have sex? Yes or no?

She hit send before she could change her mind.

Her heart settled in her throat as she watched the message status change from "delivered" to "read." What if he said no?

If he did, then at least she'd tried. She wouldn't have to live with any regrets.

Just crushing humiliation.

But that was fine. She would only have to face him for a

limited time. In a month, he'd be gone, and she could forget this ever happened.

The three magical little dots appeared again. Penny waited. And waited.

The dots disappeared.

Her heart sank into the pit of her stomach. What was she thinking? She should have known better than to get her hopes up.

The dots reappeared again. Penny was getting seasick from all the emotional highs and lows.

She watched the dots flicker on her screen, trying not to let herself be too hopeful. He was probably thinking of a nice way to say no. That was why it was taking so long. He was composing some long excuse to let her down easy.

A single word appeared on the screen.

Yes.

Penny nearly dropped the phone in shock. It had worked. She couldn't believe it.

Her fingers trembled with excitement as she typed her next text.

How fast can you get to my apartment?

His reply was almost immediate.

Give me half an hour.

Chapter Thirteen

She might not have known much about booty calls, but Penny knew enough not to dress up for one. Instead, she put on her most flattering pair of lounge pants—the soft heather gray ones that hugged her butt cheeks just so—and a thin white T-shirt with a deep V-neck that showed off her cleavage and a hint of the hot pink bra she was wearing underneath. She applied some makeup, but not too much. Just enough to bring out the green in her eyes and lend her a little more confidence.

She couldn't believe she was really doing this! Never in her life had she slept with someone she wasn't in a committed relationship with. She'd always adhered to the three date rule—at a minimum—because that was what "nice" girls were supposed to do.

Being not nice was a lot more fun.

While she waited for Caleb to arrive, Penny bustled around tidying her already immaculate apartment, because she needed to be doing something or else she'd explode. Cleaning helped keep the nervous panic at a manageable level.

She washed and put away the water glass she'd been drinking out of. Straightened everything on the coffee table so it was at perfect right angles. Fluffed the pillows on the couch and on her bed. Brushed her teeth and wiped down the bathroom sink and counter. Finally, after she'd run out of other things to do, she resorted to pacing aimlessly from room to room.

Exactly twenty-four minutes after Caleb's last text, he knocked on Penny's door.

She adjusted her bra and cast one last look around her apartment to make sure everything was perfect. Then she checked her makeup one last time in the mirror beside the door before she pulled it open.

Her heart lurched in her chest at the sight of him standing there in all his beautiful glory. She hadn't seen him all day, and the sheer force of his attractiveness hit her anew. But it was more than just his physical appearance that affected her. It was his presence —some ineffable quality that seemed to change the atmosphere around him. She didn't understand it. They barely knew each other. And yet, something intangible clicked into place at the sight of him. A feeling of relief. Of completion.

His hair was ruffled and damp, and he smelled strongly of the spicy soap he used. He must have jumped into the shower before coming over.

Penny froze, suddenly unable to recall whether she'd remembered to apply deodorant after her shower. The urge to lift her arm and do a sniff check seized her, and she clenched her hands into fists to keep them pinned at her sides.

Caleb shuffled his feet on her doorstep, his eyes darting uncertainly to the apartment behind her, and she pulled herself together enough to offer him a smile. "You're here."

The tension in his shoulders relaxed a microfraction. "I'm here."

"Come in." She stepped back to admit him, but as he moved past her into the apartment, she leaned toward him to steal a shameless sniff. She couldn't help it. He smelled so good. She had to find out what that soap was so she could bathe herself in it every day.

Despite his recent shower, the subtle scent of coffee still clung to him. It must have settled into the hoodie he was wearing. This one was a dark charcoal gray, and it hugged his shoulders and biceps in a way that should be illegal in public. Penny couldn't wait to peel it off him.

While he took his shoes off, she shut the door and twisted the deadbolt, which slid home with an ominous *thunk*. They were locked in now. No escape. Like Finn and Poe in the meat freezer, minus the imminent threat of hypothermia.

Penny wasn't sure what to do next. Her internet search had failed to cover this part, and she was unfamiliar with the standard etiquette. Should they spend a few minutes making small talk, or get right down to business?

She elected to fall back on good manners, which had always served her well. "Do you want a beer or something?" she asked Caleb, who was now standing uneasily in the middle of her living room. Maybe this would be less awkward with a little social lubricant to smooth the gears.

He shook his head. "No thanks."

So much for social lubricant. Now what? Straight to the personal lubricant stashed in her bedside table? Her mind shrank away from the possibility of an escalation that abrupt.

"Are you as nervous as I am?" she asked, hoping honesty would help break the ice.

His brow creased. "Maybe we shouldn't—"

"I swear to God," she interrupted before he could get any further, "if you try to leave again I will *murder* you."

The corner of his mouth quirked in amusement. "Okay, then."

"Just because I'm nervous doesn't mean I don't want to do this."

"Are you sure?"

"Yes. Okay? Do you believe me now, or do I need to say it a dozen more times?"

"I believe you."

"Are *you* sure?" she asked him, suddenly afraid that in her quest to be assertive, she might have accidentally pressured him into something he wasn't a hundred percent on board with.

He took long enough to answer that she'd almost convinced herself he was going to say no. "I'm sure if you are."

"Okay." She let out the breath she'd been holding. "Good. That's settled, then."

They regarded one another warily. Neither of them inclined to make the first move, apparently.

Penny broke the impasse by starting for the kitchen, because it was her safe place. As long as she was playing hostess she knew what to do with herself. "I'm getting a beer. Are you sure you don't want—"

Caleb grabbed her elbow as she passed and spun her toward him. His arms banded around her as his mouth crushed hers. It was so sudden and so forceful it stole her breath, and she gasped against him.

He started to pull back, but before he could get away she wound her hands around his neck to stop him. She pressed his mouth open as their lips came together again, and he breathed out a sigh of relief.

Rather than the slow, precise, exploring kisses of the day before, this was more like an open-mouthed slide. Urgent, fumbling, and rough. Heat shuddered through her as his hands moved over her face, her hair, her shoulders, like he couldn't get enough of touching her.

She scrabbled at his chest and pushed his hoodie off his shoulders and down his arms. Once again, only a single thin layer of T-shirt stood between her and what she was certain was a magnificent torso. As they kissed, she pressed her fingertips to his chest, groping him shamelessly, feeling her way down like she was reading a page of braille. Their tongues tangled as she traced the dense flesh of his pectorals, the individual bones of his rib cage, the rock-hard ridges of his abs.

When she got to his waist, she dipped her fingers under the hem of his shirt in search of bare skin, and he generously pulled his T-shirt over his head, tossing it onto the floor behind him.

Penny's gaze consumed him, enraptured. Devouring every perfectly defined bulge and taut valley. "Wow."

Caleb watched her watching him, his expression heated but also a little leery. "What?"

"You're just..." She gestured at him. "You're just so *wow*."

His hands squeezed her hips. "You're pretty wow yourself."

She wanted to protest, to point out they weren't even playing in the same league, much less the same division, but before she could, his tongue was in her mouth again and she forgot what she was going to say. His hands cupped her ass as he pulled her against him, his hardness grinding into her until she felt like she was going to pass out.

She needed him to be naked as soon as possible. She needed both of them to be naked. *Right. Now.*

Caleb must have shared her impatience, because he started moving them toward the couch.

"Not here," she murmured between gasping kisses. "Bedroom."

He spun her around and started pushing her in the other direction. They tripped and shuffled and kissed their way to her bedroom, bumping into doorjambs and bouncing off walls and pieces of furniture before making it to the Promised Land.

Penny's calves hit the edge of the bed, and the intensity of their kissing increased with their proximity to the site of their imminent coupling. Caleb's bare arms wrapped around her, holding her tight against his chest as her hands roamed over the broad, smooth planes of his back. One of his hands cupped her breast, and as his thumb traced delicious circles around her nipple through the fabric, she clung to him for dear life, blind with lust.

His fingers found their way to the drawstring of her lounge pants. He fumbled with it for what felt like an eternity before letting out a grunt of frustration, and she pushed his hands away to help him out. As soon as she had the knot undone, he took over again, hooking his fingers into her waistband and sliding her pants down her hips. As they fell to the floor at her feet, Caleb grasped the hem of her T-shirt and greedily lifted it over her head.

Penny tensed, ever self-conscious about her belly fat. Not that he couldn't have guessed what she looked like under her clothes, but exposing herself to a man for the first time always magnified her fear of being judged.

Caleb didn't appear to be judging her though—at least not negatively. His eyes widened, taking on a look of awe as they zeroed in on her breasts.

They were supported by her prettiest, most flattering bra. It wasn't easy finding comfortable bras in her size that didn't resemble a skydiving harness. Penny had paid an outrageous price for this one—a lacy pink demi cup that lifted her boobs like a Ren Faire beer wench—but the way his eyes had just glazed over made it worth every penny.

"Wow," Caleb said, licking his lips.

She felt herself blush, her chest and cheeks prickling with heat, and tried to step into him to escape his unabashed appraisal, but his hands grasped her shoulders, holding her at arm's length.

"Not so fast. Let me savor this for a second." He slid a hand over the top of her cleavage, so entranced you'd almost think he'd never seen breasts before. Goose bumps broke out on her arms as his calluses dragged across her skin. He pressed his fingertips into the flesh experimentally, watching it give. Then he slid a single finger under the strap of her bra and slipped it off her shoulder.

He brushed her hair back and bent down to press a kiss to her shoulder. Penny leaned into him, wanting to feel his arms around her again. Wanting to feel wrapped up and safe.

His hands smoothed over her back, then with one adept flick of his fingers he unclasped her bra. He peeled it off and let it fall to the floor as he gazed at her naked breasts in open admiration.

It took everything she had to resist the urge to cover herself. She wasn't used to being stared at so brazenly—or with such reverence. His palms smoothed over her breasts, squeezing gently, and he lowered his mouth to them. Penny heard herself let out a low moan as his lips caressed her. His hot breath seared her skin, making her knees feel weak again as his tongue traced a sensuous trail.

She curled her fingers into his hair and gave it a tug. "Get up here." She needed to kiss him some more, and then she needed him to take his pants off, because she wanted to feel him inside her as soon as humanly possible.

As their mouths came together again, she fumbled with the button on his jeans. He reached down to help her out and together they pushed his jeans down, both of them clumsy in their impatience.

She watched him step out of his pants, her vision tunneling as it sank in that Caleb was standing in front of her completely naked except for a pair of black boxer briefs. His body was even more beautiful than she'd imagined in her fantasies. Her gaze tracked up his calves and over the striations in his quads, until it froze on the bulge in his underwear. *Sweet Jiminy Christmas.*

His hands captured hers. "Are you okay?"

She looked up into soft brown eyes, creased with concern, and smiled. "So okay. You have no idea." How could a man this attractive possibly be this sweet? It defied the laws of nature.

Penny rose up on her toes and kissed him. His hands grasped her hips and yanked her toward him, his hardness pressing against her stomach as his hands explored and caressed her. He guided her back onto the bed, laying her down with such gentle care she felt like a queen, and kissed his way down her body, removing her lacy thong before settling himself between her thighs.

She shuddered with pleasure as his stroking fingers and tender mouth lavished her with attention. She'd never felt anything like it. Never felt so desired—so *desirable*. It wasn't the first time a man had gone down on her, but it was the first time she'd actually enjoyed it. The first time it hadn't seemed like a burden, performed grudgingly out of a sense of obligation. And it was definitely her first time with a man who knew what he was doing. Caleb seemed to sense instinctively what she needed, responding to her every moan and quiver until he had her gasping out his name and breaking into a million pieces beneath him.

"You're so beautiful," he murmured, kissing her thigh as she lay there panting and trying to remember how to talk. He kissed her stomach, and a spot between her breasts, then his lips brushed against hers. She opened her eyes and found him gazing at her with a self-satisfied smirk. "So I guess that was okay?"

"More than okay." She reached for him, curling her fingers into his hair, because she wasn't even close to being done with him yet. All of her insecurities had been washed away by that glorious orgasm, and for once in her life she felt uninhibited and in control.

As his lips caressed hers, she reached between them and slipped her hand inside his underwear. He groaned and kissed her more roughly. She loved the heavy hardness of his body on hers, the weight of him pressing down on her. And she loved the way he shuddered and jerked against her, helpless in her grasp.

"I want you," he panted. "Please? Will you let me fuck you?"

A heady rush flooded her pleasure centers. This beautiful man was not just in her bed, he was actually begging for her. She was in charge, and Caleb was putty in her hands. It turned her on even more, something she wouldn't have thought possible in her heightened state, but apparently she had reserves yet to be tapped.

"Condoms are in the bedside table," she said, releasing him.

He wrenched himself away and jerked the drawer open. Once he'd found his prize, he yanked down his underwear and climbed back onto the bed.

Penny tried not to stare at the magnificence that more than lived up to her imaginings. Instead, she snatched the foil packet away from him with a vehemence bordering on the violent and tore it open with her teeth as she reached for him again. He went to his knees before her on the mattress, his muscles trembling as she rolled the condom on.

When she was done, she pulled him down onto her, basking in the heaviness of his body weighing down on her and the head-to-toe heat of his bare skin touching hers. Their eyes locked as he pressed into her, and the solemnity of his gaze made her heart stutter. She arched her hips against his, biting her lip at the exquisite pressure as she felt herself stretching to accommodate him.

His breath caught and he jerked against her, the sweet shock drawing a loud gasp out of her.

"Okay?" he asked, frowning slightly as he struggled to hold himself still.

She smiled and reached up to stroke her thumb tenderly across his cheekbone. "Better than okay."

The intensity of Caleb's eyes ignited an unexpected flare of emotion in Penny's chest. The concentrated earnestness. The restrained passion. The hint of uncertainty. It was too much.

She pulled him into a kiss as she surged against him, craving more of him. He held her tightly and rocked her with careful control, setting a torturous rhythm that drove her mad with desire. She shuddered beneath him as his hardness moved against her softness. His mouth crushed hers, his breath fevered and uneven, and she dragged her fingernails down his back, urging him on, feeling alive and utterly lost at the same time, swept away by the ebb and flow as he carried her to the edge of ecstasy.

Penny heard herself cry out as the dam inside her burst, and she clung to him as she rode the swell of pleasure. She was still half gone when she felt Caleb's muscles tense, and his fingers tightened where they clasped the back of her neck. His head dropped to the pillow beside hers, his beard dragging across her cheek as he moaned into her hair.

She held him as he slumped against her, and they lay together spent and satisfied, chests heaving and sweaty limbs entwined.

Chapter Fourteen

*C*aleb lifted his head and smiled at her. "Wow."

She grinned at him, feeling a bubble of pride as she smoothed his hair off his forehead. "Ditto."

"Hang on." He shifted off her, leaving behind a splash of cold air when he got up to dispose of the condom. A few seconds later, he crawled back into the bed and wrapped her up in his arms.

Penny sighed happily and snuggled her back against his front, still not quite believing she had Caleb in her bed in all his naked glory. Any moment now, surely, she would wake up and realize it had all been a dream. A wonderful, extraordinary, marvelous dream.

His hand smoothed down her arm. "Comfortable?"

"Mmmm." She couldn't remember ever feeling this secure. The practical part of her brain whispered that she should get up and go to the bathroom so she didn't get a UTI, but she couldn't bear to leave his arms just yet. If she got up, he might decide to leave. What if this was their one and only time together, and she never had another chance to lie here with him like this? She wasn't ready for it to be over yet.

Just a little longer, she told herself. Then she'd get up.

"No regrets?" Caleb said, nuzzling into her hair.

"Not a one." She rolled over in his arms so she could look at his gorgeous face. "I do have a confession to make: I've never done that before."

His eyebrows lifted. "Could have fooled me."

"Not *that*." She laughed. "I've done that. I meant invite a guy over just for sex."

"Ah." He rolled onto his back, lifting his arm to make a space for her. She nestled against him and laid her head on his chest as his arm resettled around her shoulders.

"I wish I could have more," she said, running her fingertips over his magnificent abs.

"What? That wasn't enough for you?"

"I don't think I'll ever be able to get enough of you."

He laid a hand on her hair. "Penny—"

"I know." She waved his concerns off with a flick of her hand. "You're leaving. I'm not getting attached. I'm just saying. You're not gone yet. A month is a long time."

He tangled their fingers together on his stomach. "Not that long."

"We could have a lot of outstanding sex in a month."

"Is that so?" His thumb stroked the inside of her palm, sending a shiver of goose bumps over her skin.

"Sure, why not?"

He was quiet for a moment. "You don't think it'll make it worse?"

She lifted her head and rested her chin on his chest. "What could possibly be worse about getting to have lots more sex?"

His fingers combed through her hair. "I don't know."

"You don't have anywhere else to be tonight, do you?"

"No."

"How about tomorrow?"

"Not until work on Monday."

"Sounds to me like we've got plenty of time." She smiled coyly. "Unless you're too tired?"

He let out an amused breath. "Give me five minutes."

"Perfect!" She brushed a kiss across his lips as she pushed herself upright. "I'm going to pee. Don't go anywhere."

"HUNGRY?" Caleb asked when Penny's stomach let out an ear-splitting growl an hour later.

They were still recovering from their second go-round, and he was lying with his head on her belly, so the untimely squawk had occurred right into his ear.

"I guess so." She was starving, now that she thought about it. She hadn't eaten since lunch six hours ago, and two rounds of sex burned a lot of calories. According to her fitness tracker app it was actually only seventy-two calories for every fifteen minutes, but it felt like she and Caleb had burned a lot more. Her app also claimed an average load of male ejaculate had five calories, which she would definitely be leaving off today's food log.

Penny nearly offered to get up and cook dinner for both of them, until she remembered that was what the old Penny would have done. She'd vowed not to mother the men in her life anymore—not that Caleb was *in* her life, exactly. He was just passing through. But still. Now was as good a time as any to start building better habits.

"Do you have eggs?" he asked, propping himself up on one elbow. "I can make us omelets."

Her mouth fell open in shock. "You can cook?"

"I can cook omelets," he said with a shrug. "Why do you look so surprised?"

"I don't think I've ever known a man who could cook before."

"How do they feed themselves?"

"When I'm not around? I honestly don't know. Pizza and frozen dinners I think."

"Well, I can't afford that." He dropped a kiss on her stomach before rolling out of bed and reaching for his underwear. "It was either learn to cook for myself or starve, and starving seemed like even less fun than cooking." He pulled his underwear up and bent to kiss her on the lips. "I'll find something to make us," he said, and padded out of the room.

Penny went to the bathroom and put on her bathrobe before following him into the kitchen. She found him bent over, digging through the contents of her fridge, and she leaned against the counter to watch, wishing she could take a picture to preserve the moment for eternity. Would that be wrong? Her phone was just in the living room—

"What is this?" He pulled out a plastic container and shook it at her.

"Shredded chicken." She tiptoed to the coffee table and grabbed her phone.

"Can I use it?"

"Sure." Back in the kitchen, she made sure her volume was off and opened the camera app.

"Do you have any green onions?"

She focused on his ass and snapped a shot. "Bottom drawer." She took a few more pictures, just in case the first one was blurry.

"Wow, look at all this produce. You must eat really well."

"I try." She took a step to the side and switched to live picture mode so she could make a GIF of his abs rippling.

He straightened and shut the fridge, his arms full of ingredients. "What are you doing?"

"Taking a picture of you."

"What for?"

She put her phone down and went to kiss him. "What do you think it's for?"

He shook his head, smiling as he carried his spoils to the counter. "I don't want to know."

"What sorts of things can you cook?" she asked as he laid the ingredients for his omelets on the counter. Besides chicken and eggs, there was cream cheese, spinach, olives, and green onions. This was going to be some omelet.

He pulled a knife out of the block and started chopping onions. "Nothing fancy. I eat a lot of chicken and a lot of beans and rice. Different combinations of vegetables, depending on what's on sale."

"And omelets."

He looked over at her and smiled. "And omelets, almost every morning."

No wonder he looked so good. He ate like a bodybuilder. Of course, so did Penny, pretty much, and she looked like a teddy bear with boobs. It helped to be genetically gifted. Which Caleb definitely was. *So* gifted.

She sat at the breakfast bar to watch him cook. She'd never had a man cook in her kitchen before, much less one as attractive as Caleb. It was a bit like seeing Bigfoot casually strolling through the housewares department at Walmart.

"Do you have an omelet pan?"

"Cabinet to your left."

He set the pan on the stove to heat while he broke two eggs into a bowl and added a splash of water. When the pan was hot, he added a thin sliver of butter, stirred the eggs, and poured them into the pan. Penny watched him nudge the eggs around with practiced ease. He really did know what he was doing. She felt like she'd found Willy Wonka's Golden Ticket, only instead of a Golden Ticket it was something even more rare: a man who was good in the kitchen.

When he'd layered the other ingredients and the eggs were perfectly cooked on the bottom, he folded them over and slid a picture-perfect omelet onto a plate. Penny couldn't have done better herself.

"Go ahead and eat," he said, handing it to her. "Don't let it get cold while I make mine."

She got out two forks and two paper napkins and carried them to the small dining table, choosing the seat with a view of the kitchen—and Caleb's perfect ass.

The omelet was so pretty it almost seemed a shame to cut into it. Not enough of a shame to stop her though. Not when it smelled this heavenly and she was so hungry she was practically drooling. She lifted a bite to her lips and closed her eyes in ecstasy. It tasted every bit as good as it looked—fluffy and flavorful and fantastic.

"Does it taste okay?" Caleb asked without turning around.

"Are you kidding? This is incredible. You should consider a career as an omelet chef."

"And give up barista-ing? Never."

He slid his omelet onto a plate, turned off the stove, and took the seat across from her at the table. "I guess you must have liked it okay," he said, nodding at her half-empty plate.

She grinned at him. "It's the second best thing I've had in my mouth today."

He choked on the bite of omelet he'd just taken, and she got up and patted him on the back on her way to the kitchen. "Let me get you some water for that cough."

"You're full of surprises."

She set out two glasses and opened the fridge. "Why? Because I made a dirty joke?"

"Yeah. I mean, you always seemed so..."

"Innocent?" she suggested as she filled both glasses from her Brita jug. That was what everyone thought about her. Sweet, good little Penny. The "little" in her case being figurative, of course. Because of her size, men tended to assume she was inexperienced. Naive. Desperate.

"Wholesome."

She wrinkled her nose. "Thanks."

"I don't think I've ever heard you swear."

She shrugged as she carried the water to the table. "My parents discouraged it—strenuously—so I never got into the habit. But that doesn't mean I disapprove when other people do it. I'm not a prude."

"So you didn't mind when I did it?"

"You mean earlier, when…" When he'd been naked in her bed, begging to fuck her. Her cheeks heated at the memory. "No, that was hot."

"I was a little worried I might have offended you."

"Definitely not. Feel free to talk as dirty as you want." She propped her chin in her hand as she watched him eat his omelet. "Can I ask you something?"

"Sure."

"Did you really have somewhere to be yesterday when you left?"

He glanced up. "Did you think I was lying?"

Yes. She shrugged. "I don't know. Maybe."

"I really had somewhere I had to go."

"Have you got another girl on the side?" she teased. "More than one, maybe?"

"No." He shook his head and stabbed at his omelet. "I went to see George in the hospital."

"Oh." Penny sat back in her chair, ashamed for being so suspicious. "That's nice. I'll bet he was happy to see you."

"He was. I almost didn't go though." He flicked a glance at her. "I wanted to stay with you."

A warm tingle traveled down her spine. "I'm glad you went. I think he's missed you."

"They're transferring him to a rehab facility next week."

"Yeah. Mike told me."

"Did he also tell you he wants to move his father up to San Jose?"

Penny frowned. "George won't allow that."

Caleb shook his head. "I'm not sure he'll have a choice."

"First you're moving away and now maybe George too?" He

looked pained, so she tried to put an optimistic spin on it. "Maybe George will be happy to be closer to his family. Just like I'm sure you'll be happy in med school."

Caleb pushed his chair back and stood up. He scooped up both their plates and carried them to the sink.

Penny followed him. "I can do the dishes."

He shook his head and turned on the water. "My mess, my dishes."

"You cooked for me. It's the least I can do." As she said it, she thought about all the meals she'd made for past boyfriends, and how she'd always wound up doing the dishes too. She could count on one hand the number of times one of them had helped clean up. What a bunch of selfish jerks.

Although...it was possible they'd offered at first and she'd turned down their assistance. She had a particular way she liked things done, and it was easier to just do it herself than supervise someone else and make sure they did it right. Maybe it had been her fault. Maybe she'd trained them not to help by insisting on doing it all herself.

Caleb handed her a dishtowel. "We'll do them together."

"Deal," Penny said, accepting it with a smile.

He washed and she dried. It turned out he didn't need any supervision. He knew how to wash dishes just fine.

"I should probably go," he said when she'd put the last dish away, and Penny felt her stomach drop.

She closed the cabinet and turned toward him. "Why?"

"It's getting late."

"It's seven thirty. That's late to you?"

"I wake up at four a.m. most weekdays."

She moved closer and slipped her arms around his waist. "You don't work tomorrow. You told me you don't have anywhere to be until Monday."

His hands slid up her arms and over her shoulder blades. "I didn't say I had to leave. I said I should."

"Why?"

Her bathrobe was gapping in the front, and he licked his lips as he stared at her breasts. "I don't want to overstay my welcome."

"Unpossible." She tightened her arms around him. "Stay."

He looked torn. "You sure?"

"Do you want to stay?"

His eyes fell on her breasts again. "Yes."

"Stay."

Chapter Fifteen

"How have you never seen this show before?" Penny asked, leaning back against Caleb's chest. "It's so funny."

They were curled up on her couch together, watching *Brooklyn Nine-Nine*. At least, she was watching it. He mostly seemed to be playing with her hair. Which was perfectly fine with her.

"I don't have a TV," he said, twisting a strand around his finger. He'd put his T-shirt back on, tragically, but he was still in his underwear. Penny still wore her pink chenille bathrobe.

"You can watch it online." That was what everyone did these days. Penny knew plenty of people who didn't have TVs.

"I don't have internet at my house."

She swiveled in his arms to gape at him, wincing as her hair caught around his finger. "You don't have internet? How do you live like that?"

Caleb gently unwound her hair and kissed her head where it had pulled. "It's too expensive. I've got it on my phone, but I have to be careful about my data."

"But...what do you do? How do you pass the time?"

The corner of his mouth quirked. "What do you think people did before the internet?"

"I have no idea." She'd asked her mother about it once, when she was a teenager. Her mother said people had talked to each other more. Caleb didn't seem like he spent his free time talking to people though.

"I go to work. I work out. I cook dinner. That takes up most of my time. After that I usually read books until I fall asleep."

Penny seized on this small glimpse into his life outside Antidote. "Like actual hard-copy books?" she asked, reaching for the remote to pause the episode, since neither of them were watching it.

"Yeah, there's this place called the library where they let you check them out for free."

"Wild. I'm not sure I've cracked a book made of paper since college. I do all my reading on my phone."

He reached for her hand, turning it over in his to trace the lines of her palm. "I do that sometimes too, but I like browsing the shelves at the library and the feel of holding a real book in my hands."

"Do you live alone?" She didn't know anything about where he lived, other than it was less than half an hour away.

"I have two roommates. We live in a three-bedroom rental house." He found a freckle on her wrist and drew a circle around it with his fingertip.

"Do you like them?" she asked, suppressing a shiver.

"They're fine. We all work a lot, so we don't see that much of each other." His gaze lifted to her chest and settled there.

"Do you have any friends?"

He tugged at the collar of her robe to give himself a better view of her cleavage. "There's a few guys from college who are still around. We get together every once in while, when we can make our schedules work. Not often."

It sounded like a lonely life. Penny supposed it was only

temporary for him. He was just biding his time until he moved on to the next phase. She couldn't imagine living like that for a whole year though.

He stroked a hand down the side of her neck, pulling her closer as his mouth dipped to her ear. Her eyes fell shut when his lips grazed her earlobe, his warm breath sending a scatter of goose bumps down her arms.

"Your hair smells nice," he murmured, nuzzling against her temple.

"I washed it just for you."

"I'm honored."

She turned her head to capture his lips, and they breathed out matching sighs, enjoying the slow tussle of tongues and lips and teeth. Caleb's fingers curled into her hair while his other hand dropped to her leg. It slid up under the bottom of her robe, seeking higher ground. She let out a shuddering gasp when he found it. "You really want to have sex again?"

"Yes." His breathy growl lit her up like a marquee.

"You're insatiable," she said, smiling as he untied her robe. How much testosterone did he have? He was like the Energizer Bunny. He just kept going and going.

He kissed his way down to her neck. "Like you said, we might as well make the most of the time we have."

"I said that, didn't I?"

He stopped kissing her. "Unless you don't want to?"

"No, I want to. I definitely—" Her breath caught as his mouth found her breast. "*Definitely* want to." She started to get up so she could pull him off the couch, but his hand clamped on her wrist, dragging her back down. "Come on," she said, giving him a fruitless tug. "Let's go to the bed."

He didn't budge. "Or we could stay here."

"No." She pulled out of his grasp. "Not here."

He peered up at her. "Why won't you let me have sex with you on your couch?"

"Because this is where company sits!"

"So?"

"So upholstery is harder to clean than sheets."

He gave her one of his rare smiles—which weren't so rare after all, she was discovering. "I love it when you talk dirty."

"How's this for dirty? The condoms are all in the bedroom."

"Good point." He scooped her up and carried her into the bedroom.

WHAT A WAY TO WAKE UP, Penny thought when she opened her eyes Sunday morning. She was warm and naked, with Caleb's hand cupping one of her breasts and his stomach warm against her back.

Imagine having this every day. She pushed the thought away. Going down that road would only lead to disappointment. She couldn't have this every day. Only for the next four weeks.

She reached for her phone on the nightstand and Caleb stirred behind her, nuzzling into her hair. "What time is it?"

"Ten o'clock." She couldn't remember the last time she'd slept this late.

He shifted on the bed and rolled her onto her back.

How dare he look so good in the morning? she thought as his face came into view. His hair was rumpled, but in a way that made him look even sexier. Meanwhile, after all that sex yesterday, she must look like Medusa. He didn't seem to mind, however.

He curled his hand around her neck and kissed her, morning breath and all. His stubble was longer and tickled more than it had yesterday, but it was also softer and she liked it a lot.

"Do you have to be anywhere today?" he asked as she scraped her fingernails through his beard.

On Sundays she usually went to the nursing home. But they could do without her for one day. "Nope, nowhere at all."

He gifted her with a heart-exploding smile. "In that case, shall I make us breakfast?"

"Another omelet?" she asked hopefully.

"They are my specialty," he said, dropping another kiss on her lips before he rolled out of bed.

How did I get this lucky? Penny thought as she watched his backside walk away.

"CAN I USE YOUR SHOWER?" Caleb asked when they'd cleaned up the breakfast dishes. "I'm getting a little ripe."

Penny fastened herself to his side. "I hadn't noticed."

He turned his head to kiss her forehead. "You could join me if you want."

"Are you trying to say I'm stinky?"

"No, I'm trying to get you naked in the shower with me."

"Oh. In that case, I accept."

When he stepped into the shower, she was so hypnotized by the sight of water sliding over his perfect golden skin that she could only stand and gawk. "Get in here," he said, reaching for her wrist to give her a tug. She stepped into the spray, oblivious to the water soaking her hair as she watched the droplets pool and channel in rivulets down his body, caressing every perfect muscle and vein.

"Is this the shampoo you use?" He lifted one of the half dozen bottles to his nose.

Penny shook her head to clear it. "I think it's the conditioner you like the smell of. The one next to it."

He set the shampoo back in the shower rack and turned to face her. His eyes skated down her body, appreciating every inch of it with the same intoxicated stare she'd been giving him.

Just when the self-consciousness of being scrutinized threatened to overwhelm her, he stepped toward her and lowered his mouth to hers. His arms wrapped around her as the hot water poured over them, slicking their skin and washing away her insecurities.

He reached for a bottle of body wash and began to lather up her chest, his hands smoothing over her breasts, down her ribs, across her hips. Then he turned her in his arms and did the same to her back, buttocks, and thighs. When he traded the soap for shampoo and began to wash her hair, it was by far the most sensual thing that had ever happened to her.

Penny let her eyes fall closed, transported to a place outside ordinary time and reality as Caleb's fingers massaged lather into her scalp. He rinsed it with the care of a professional beautician, then repeated the process with the conditioner, taking his time as the mango scent steamed around them.

By the time he finished rinsing the conditioner out, she was so relaxed she was nearly comatose. She stumbled a little when he turned her toward him again, but his strong hands held her fast.

"I can't believe how beautiful you are," he murmured as his lips skimmed over her jaw.

Her hands roamed over his slick, hot muscles. "*You* can't believe it? I can't believe you're even real."

His mouth captured hers, and then his hand tightened on her hips and he pushed her up against the cold, hard tile. She squeaked in shock, but he held her firmly, mischief sparking in his eyes as he gazed at her. She wriggled in his grasp, opening her mouth to protest, and he kissed her again, hard enough that she forgot to mind the cold tile on her back.

When he dropped to his knees before her, she had to brace her hands on the wall to keep herself upright.

I take it back, she thought as his hands gently spread her thighs, *this is the most sensual thing that has ever happened to me.*

"CAN we watch some more of that show we started last night?" Caleb asked when they got out of the shower.

"Sure." She hadn't thought he'd been watching it. "Did you like it?"

"Yeah, it was funny."

He certainly wouldn't have to twist her arm to get her to watch one of her favorite TV shows. Usually it was the other way around.

When she reached for the hair dryer, Caleb's hand closed over hers. "Will you let it dry curly so I can see it?"

Her eyes met his in the mirror. "Really?"

"Really." He reached up to wind a damp ringlet around his finger. "I love your hair curly."

Okay, then.

They spent most of the day on the couch watching *Brooklyn Nine-Nine*, with Caleb's laughter reverberating against Penny's back. It was pretty much the best day ever.

When they took a break for lunch, he made the rest of the shredded chicken into chicken salad with Greek yogurt and walnuts and grapes, served on a bed of leafy green lettuce, and they ate on the couch in front of the TV. They were still watching hours later when dinnertime rolled around, and they ordered Chinese food, which Penny insisted on paying for because Caleb had made three meals in a row.

"But you provided all the food," he protested.

"That's the easy part," she said, knowing he was on a budget. "You're my guest. I'm paying for dinner."

They ate dumplings and beef with broccoli, and made it all the way to season two before eleven o'clock rolled around and Caleb sat up on the edge of the couch and said, "I really need to go."

"You have to be at work early," Penny said sadly.

"Really early."

"I guess you can go home now. I've held you hostage long enough."

He stood up, and Penny caught his hand in hers. "I had a great weekend with you," he said, squeezing her hand.

"Me too. I don't want it to be over yet."

"Me neither, but—"

"I know. Work. Early." She pushed herself off the couch and walked him to the door.

"I'll see you tomorrow?" he said when he'd put his shoes back on.

"Of course. Same as always." Except it wouldn't be the same as always, because now they'd seen each other naked. Everything was different.

He kissed her long and slow, sliding his fingers in her hair, and she let her head fall back against his hand as she melted into him. "Goodnight," he said, far too soon. He stroked his thumb across her cheek, brushed another kiss against her forehead, and let himself out.

Chapter Sixteen

*P*enny was pretty sure she was walking funny on Monday.

Eight orgasms in twenty-four hours was definitely a record for her. Her prior record was two, and that had been an unusual achievement. Clearly, she'd been doing herself a disservice by dating unexceptional men.

It made spin class something of an unpleasant adventure. Hopefully no one noticed her wincing through the cooldown. But after spin class she had work, and after just a few hours of work she'd get to see Caleb again.

It was hard to concentrate on the application for a golf ball mold she was working on, because she kept checking the clock every five minutes to see how much time had passed. Never in the entire history of the universe had a morning crept by so slowly.

Finally, eleven o'clock came and she logged out of her computer and set out for Antidote. She was wearing her favorite floral-print dress today, the one with bright pink and orange peonies on it, with glossy pink lipstick to match.

She wasn't exactly sure what would happen when she saw

Caleb again, and she started to get a case of nervous butterflies on the walk over. They hadn't talked about where they stood now or what was next. Whether what happened this weekend was a one-time thing or something they might do again.

No strings, she'd said. That meant he wasn't obligated to see her again. Maybe he wouldn't want to, now that he'd gotten what he wanted.

We both got what we wanted, she reminded herself. She was the one who'd propositioned him. Impermanence was built into the package. They were just killing time, a couple of grown adults having some fun. They didn't even qualify as friends with benefits —at most they were acquaintances with benefits.

Maybe it would be better if they didn't do it again. He might be right: the more they saw of each other, the harder it would be when he left. They should probably forget it ever happened and go back to the way things were before. Barista and customer, nothing more. Acquaintances *without* benefits.

But when Penny caught her first glimpse of Caleb through the glass door, it stole her breath away. Had he somehow gotten more gorgeous overnight? She felt like he should have lost some of his mystique now that they'd been intimate. But no. Her newfound knowledge of exactly what lay under his clothes only dialed up the volume on her attraction. Exponentially.

Control yourself, she thought as her knuckles whitened on the door handle. It wouldn't do to fawn all over him like a lovestruck ninny. That wasn't what they were to each other. *No getting swept up.*

She waited for her breathing to normalize before she pulled open the door. Caleb was taking an order from a trio of women fresh out of a yoga class, and he glanced up at the sound of the shop bell. A jolt of heat shot through her as their eyes met and his glance turned into a stare. He didn't smile, but his mouth quirked in that way Penny had come to recognize as the next best thing, and she relaxed a little.

"Did you get that?" the blue spandex-clad woman said, sounding annoyed.

Caleb tore his gaze away from Penny. "Skinny soy half-caf macchiato," he recited, typing it into the register. "What else?"

"I can't make up my mind," the woman in purple spandex said, stepping forward and leaning on the counter so her cleavage was displayed to maximum effect. "I'm feeling adventurous today. What do you think I should get?"

The woman in red spandex giggled as blue spandex rolled her eyes, and Penny felt an involuntary surge of jealousy. The thought of Caleb making a lavender latte for another woman roused her little green monster. That was *her* special drink; it wasn't for any random woman who thrust her breasts at him.

"Our iced coffee is our most popular drink," Caleb said in a disinterested monotone, his eyes fixed on the register screen instead of the purple spandex breasts heaving in front of him, and Penny let out a relieved breath.

Purple spandex waffled over her order a while longer while Elyse started making blue spandex's macchiato. When it became clear Caleb wasn't going to flirt back, purple spandex gave up and ordered an iced coffee. Blue spandex paid for all their drinks, and they went to find a table, tittering and whispering to each other like a trio of brightly colored birds.

And then Penny was standing alone in front of Caleb. When their eyes met again, she felt herself flush as she flashed back to their weekend escapades.

Act natural, she chided herself. *Play it cool.*

"Penelope," he said in the same low voice he'd used when they were in bed, and another jolt of heat shot through her. So much for being cool. At this rate she'd die of the convection effects before she'd even placed her order.

"Good morning," she replied, struggling not to smile too wide. *No simpering.*

"Your hair's curly."

She nodded and touched her hair. She'd decided not to bother straightening it this morning. At some point in her life she'd internalized the idea that fat girls shouldn't have big hair—as if skinny hair could fool people into thinking she was a skinny person. It was ridiculous, now that she thought about it. She wasn't skinny and she never would be, no matter what her hair looked like. Curly hair was pretty too, so why not save herself a lot of time and trouble and embrace her natural hair instead of trying to make it something it wasn't?

Caleb's mouth twitched. "I like it."

"Thank you."

"Do you want the usual?" He'd switched to the same impersonal tone he used on every other customer, but he was staring at her mouth now.

She licked her lips and was pleased to see a muscle tighten in his jaw. "Yes, please," she said and held out her card.

His fingers brushed hers as he accepted it, lingering for an extra-long moment before pulling away.

"How was your weekend?" she asked as he swiped her card. "You look tired."

The corner of his mouth curled faintly. "Someone kept me up late two nights in a row." He pushed her card and the receipt toward her. "And you look beautiful."

Penny felt her cheeks heat again and glanced around to see if anyone had heard. Fortunately, Elyse was too busy struggling with the espresso machine to pay them any attention. Penny scribbled a signature on the receipt and pushed it back toward Caleb.

He covered her hand with his, his fingertips stroking the back of her wrist. "Your drink will be ready in a minute." He gave her hand an extra squeeze before he let go and turned away.

Alrighty, then. So much for him not wanting to see her.

Penny slid onto her usual seat at the counter and watched as Caleb warmed a stainless steel pitcher of milk and added a handful of dried lavender. Elyse was still struggling to make the spandex trio's orders, and he helped her out while the lavender steeped for Penny's latte.

After a few minutes, he strained the lavender out, then took a large mug from the warmer and pulled a shot of espresso while he steamed the infused milk. When it was done, he brought it over and set it in front of her. He'd made a single heart in the foam.

It doesn't mean anything, Penny reminded herself. *He makes hearts all the time.* Still, her pulse raced as she lifted the cup to her lips and blew across the top.

He rested his hands on the edge of the counter, leaning his weight on them as he watched her take a cautious sip. "How is it?" he asked, staring at her mouth again.

She licked the foam from her lips and saw his eyes darken. "Delicious as always."

"I get off at two," he said, leaning toward her a little more.

"I have to work until five." She stared at his lips, wondering how bad it would be if she launched herself across the counter at him.

"I thought you worked from home."

"I do, but I have to actually work when I'm supposed to be working."

He leaned closer still. "Can I come over when you're done?"

"Yes," she said, before she remembered it was Monday. "No. Sorry, I can't tonight. I've got knitting." Which meant she needed to bake something beforehand, and she hadn't gone to the store this weekend because she'd been too busy having sex.

"Right," Caleb said, straightening. "Of course."

Penny considered bailing on knitting, but it seemed like a bad idea. She'd already skipped the nursing home yesterday for him. She couldn't put her whole life on hold for a month to have sex. Tempting as it might be, it would be unhealthy to give up all her routines for him. Those routines existed for a reason; she needed them more than she needed him. Even if, at the present moment, she *wanted* him more.

No strings went both ways, she reminded herself. She wasn't required to reschedule her life for him. That was the old Penny, who gave up things that were important to her. No more. If Caleb wanted to spend time with her, he could fit himself into her schedule.

"You could come over after?" she suggested, trying to sound casual. Like it didn't matter one way or another if he did. Although she really hoped he would.

"It'll probably be too late. I need to get to sleep early tonight."

"Right," she said, swallowing her disappointment. "Because you start work at the crack of dawn." That was a perfectly legitimate reason. It didn't mean he didn't want to see her. He was just being practical. *Casual.* Just like she was.

He nodded, his expression gone flat. "Yeah." The bell rang as a new customer came in, and he gave her an apologetic look as he moved to the register.

There was an annoyingly steady stream of customers after that, which prevented Caleb from coming back over to talk to her. When he wasn't taking an order or making a drink, he was clearing tables or fetching supplies out of the back. She had to content herself with staring at him while he worked, but after a while it started to feel creepy so she pulled out her phone and opened the fanfic she'd been reading last week. But every few paragraphs she'd find herself glancing up at Caleb again. Occasionally their eyes would meet and her heart would leap into her throat, but he never came back over to talk to her.

After thirty minutes had passed, she got up to bus her dishes. "I've got it," Caleb said, coming up behind her and taking the cup out of her hands. "I'll see you tomorrow?" He posed it like a question. Like she didn't come in every single weekday.

She gave him a smile. "Of course."

He didn't smile back, but then he never smiled at work.

"Have a good day," she said on her way out the door, like he was just her barista and not someone who'd given her eight orgasms over the weekend.

WHEN PENNY WALKED into Antidote on Tuesday, Caleb was nowhere in sight. Her heart gave a little lurch of panic.

"I'll be right with you," Malik called over his shoulder from the espresso machine.

"Take your time," Penny said. She stared up at the menu, pretending to deliberate over her order. They hadn't added her lavender latte to the board, and she wondered if Caleb had ever talked to Reema about it. It wasn't exactly a drink that could be made quickly; perhaps it wasn't practical. Which meant she'd have to give them up when he left.

"Hi, Penny!" Charlotte called out from the couch, where she was surrounded by philosophy books and stacks of papers again today.

Penny turned and waved. "Hello!" Charlotte was wearing a bright purple dress with a Peter Pan collar, and the streak in her hair was now a coordinating shade of lilac. "I love that dress!"

"Thank you. I love yours too."

Penny smiled and struck a pose, flipping her hair off her shoulder in her best impression of Gloria Grahame in *It's a Wonderful Life*. "This old thing? I only wear it when I don't care how I look."

Caleb came out of the back with a tray of clean dishes and stopped short at the sight of her.

Penny felt her chest prickle with heat and cast her face down to hide her blush.

"Americano for Drew," Malik called out, setting a drink on the counter. He turned to Penny. "You want the usual, beautiful?"

"I got her," Caleb said, putting down the dish tray and moving to the register. Malik shrugged and went to put away the clean dishes, leaving him to it. "You want the old usual or the new usual?" Caleb asked without meeting her eye.

"The new usual if it's not too much trouble."

Penny assumed he didn't want to advertise that they'd slept together, which was fine with her. The only person she'd told so far was Olivia. Penny had been texting her updates on the latest developments in the Caleb saga, but she'd made her promise not to say anything to anyone at knitting last night. She didn't want to put her choices up for debate by the group, or listen to any Negative Nancies who might try to rain on her fun parade with their common sense and reason.

The fewer people who knew, the better. In a few weeks Caleb would be gone, and she didn't want everyone treating her like a brokenhearted war widow.

"I don't have knitting tonight," Penny said quietly as she handed him her card.

"Yeah?" he replied as he swiped it through the card reader.

"Yeah." She screwed up her courage for the next part: "Do you want to come over?"

He tore off the receipt and slid it across the counter toward her. "What time?"

"Five-ish? I'll text you when I'm done with work."

He nodded. "Okay."

"Okay," she said. "It's a date." His expression changed, and she realized what she'd said. "Not a date," she amended. "Not like a *date* date. We're not dating, so we don't have dates. I just meant figuratively."

"I know what you meant."

"Okay," she said again. "Whew."

AT FOUR FORTY-FIVE, Penny shut down her computer and texted Caleb: *I'm done.*

It took him almost three full minutes to respond. *Just finished working out. Be over as soon as I shower.*

Penny thought about him all sweaty and glistening and pumped up.

Don't shower, she texted back. *Don't even change your clothes. Come over now.*

Seriously? he replied.

Seriously.

"OH MY HECK," Penny said when she answered the door. "You look so hot right now."

Caleb looked down at his sweaty tank top and then back up at her. "Really?"

She grabbed the front of his shirt and dragged him inside her apartment. "Get in here, quick, so I can tear those sweaty clothes off you."

He put his bare arms around her and kicked the door closed as they spun around. His damp clothes stuck to her skin as he pulled her close. His body was like a furnace, putting off so much heat it singed the hair on her arms. He pinned her up against the door, pressing his full weight into her for maximum sweaty contact. "Isn't this gross?" he asked, his mouth twitching in amusement.

She ran her hands up his biceps and over his shoulders. "There are a lot of words I could use to describe you right now, but gross is nowhere on the list."

His lips curved. "What kind of words?"

She pressed her face into the crook of his neck. He smelled beachy, like salt and fresh air. "Hot." She pressed her lips to his collarbone. "Kissable." His skin tasted like seawater. She wanted to lick him all over. "Delectable."

His fingers curled into her hair and dragged her head back. Then his lips were on hers as his tongue plunged into her mouth hungrily. He cupped her ass and jerked his hips against hers. She moaned into his mouth as he ground against her, and his hands tightened, lifting her up.

I am amazing at this no-strings thing, she thought as he carried her toward the bedroom. *Why didn't I try this ages ago?*

"Why did you want to be a doctor? Was it because of your dad?"

They were lying on their sides, face-to-face in her bed. Still naked, and far too comfortable to move out of their cocoon of warm blankets.

Tiny furrows sprouted across Caleb's forehead. "I guess you could say that."

"Did you want to be like him?" she asked, reaching out to smooth his furrows away with her finger.

"No, not at all."

She dropped her hand to his arm, skimming her palm over the smooth curve of muscles. "What's he like?"

Caleb's face settled into a scowl. "Rigid."

"I'm sensing you aren't really close."

"Keen perception, Mr. Holmes."

"But you still wanted to be a doctor just like him?"

"It was the only way he'd pay for my college. Also, it seemed like the least I could do."

"Why?"

He rolled onto his back and stared up at the ceiling. "Because I didn't go into the army like I was expected to."

"So?"

"I was trying to make up for disappointing him."

Penny propped herself up on her elbow so she could see his face. "He was disappointed you didn't go into the army?"

"More like livid."

"But it's your life."

"The Colonel doesn't see it that way. He invested his time and money bringing me up. In exchange, it's my duty to be the kind of son he wants me to be. A carbon copy of my old man."

"You call your dad The Colonel?"

His mouth twisted into a smirk as he turned his face to hers. "Not to his face."

"Now I'm picturing Colonel Sanders." She reached out to ruffle his hair. His attractiveness magnified exponentially when it was tousled. So unfair.

His eyes closed as she ran her fingernails over his scalp, and he sighed with pleasure. "He is definitely nothing like Colonel Sanders. More like Colonel Kurtz from *Apocalypse Now*."

"I've never seen it."

He rolled toward her, pulling her closer as he buried his face in her chest. "Don't. You're too nice for that movie."

"I'm not that nice," she said, feeling defensive.

He looked up from her cleavage. "What's wrong with being nice?"

"Nice people get treated like doormats."

His mouth moved up to her neck, leaving a trail of lazy kisses. "Only by dicks. You can stand up for yourself and still be nice."

"Like you stood up to your dad?"

He let go of her and rolled onto his back again. "My dad's a dick. He treats everyone like a doormat, whether they're nice or not."

"I'm sorry you had to grow up that way."

His expression turned stony as he stared at the ceiling. "Let's talk about something else."

It hurt to see him all twisted up in knots because of his father. She wanted to make it better. To know him, so she could help him. "Where does your mom stand on all this?"

"She doesn't. She does whatever my dad expects her to do." He was starting to sound annoyed, so she tried another tack.

"Was there something different you would have wanted to do? If your dad hadn't pressured you to become a doctor."

"I never thought about it."

"You must have. Come on." She reached out to pinch his nonexistent love handles. "What did little Caleb want to be when he grew up?"

"I don't want to talk about this," he snapped, loud enough to make her jerk her hand back.

"Sorry." George had warned her it was a sore subject; she should have believed him.

Caleb rolled toward her and gathered her up in his arms. "No, I'm the one who's sorry." He kissed her forehead, cradling her against his chest. "I shouldn't have yelled at you."

She blinked away tears. "I didn't mean to pry."

"I just don't like talking about my dad."

"I'm sorry." She'd just thought if she could get him to talk about it, he might feel better. Clearly, that was a mistake.

"Stop apologizing when I'm the one who acted like a jerk."

"You're allowed to not want to talk about things. It's not like we're in a relationship. We don't have to share everything with each other."

She felt him go rigid. "Right," he said, letting go of her.

"Did I say something wrong again?" He'd gone back to staring at the ceiling.

"No. You're right. We're not in a relationship."

"We can talk if you want to. I'm happy to listen if—"

"I said I don't want to talk. Can we just drop it?"

"Okay."

He sat up and reached for his clothes. "I should probably go. It's getting late."

It was only seven o'clock.

"Are you mad?" she asked, watching him get dressed.

"No."

"You seem mad. Although it's a little hard to tell, because you're about as expressive as a wooden post. I can never figure out what's going on inside your head."

"You don't want inside my head."

"I'm just trying to get to know you."

The look he threw her way made her heart squeeze in her chest. "Why? We've got an expiration date, remember? You said you were only looking for a good time. Fun and easy. No strings."

"I know." Only she wasn't having fun anymore—and clearly neither was he.

"I'm just giving you what you wanted." He leaned down and kissed her cheek. "I'll see you." The way he said it sounded like maybe it wouldn't be a such a tragedy if he didn't see her again.

Penny gathered the sheets around her, wondering what had happened as the door slammed behind him.

Maybe she wasn't so amazing at the no-strings thing, after all.

At half past eleven the next day, Penny pulled open the door of Antidote, unsure what kind of reception she'd get from Caleb. Assuming he was even working today. He might not be—

Caleb's head swiveled at the sound of the bell, and he froze as his eyes met hers. His expression wasn't exactly warm, but she wouldn't call it cold either. More like guarded.

He was in the middle of filling one of the large grinders on the counter, and as they gazed at one another, a few errant coffee beans made a break for it and went skittering away. He swore under his breath and turned his attention back to his task.

Penny walked across the linoleum to the register, clenching her purse strap as she waited for him to finish. Elyse was leaning against the counter staring at her phone, and she glanced up at Caleb and then over at Penny, eyebrows lifted in silent inquiry. Caleb shook his head at her as he swept the stray coffee beans off the counter, and Elyse went back to whatever she was reading on her phone while he stowed the bag of beans under the counter and made his way to the register.

"Hi," Penny said, lifting her eyes to his face. He looked even more chiseled and intimidatingly handsome than usual this morning, which did nothing to bolster her courage.

"Hi." He rubbed his palms on his jeans and his mouth twisted into a grimace. "I'm sorry if I was a jerk last night."

"You weren't," she told him, even though he sort of had been. She was still smarting from the unexpected flash of anger. "I'm sorry if I put my foot in my mouth."

"You didn't."

He was lying just as surely as she was lying, the apology he'd offered no more sincere than hers. They stared at one another across the counter. Neither of them having any fun.

"So everything's okay?" she asked, feeling like it was anything but.

"Sure," he replied in his old monotone. "Everything's great."

"In that case, can I have a lavender latte?" She hated how small her voice sounded, like a scolded child asking for a special favor.

"Of course." He rang her up and went to go make it. When it was ready, he dropped it off without a word and retreated out of conversational range. A plain fern leaf adorned the foam. He hadn't even bothered to sprinkle dried lavender over the top.

Their no-strings fling seemed to have crashed and burned.

Penny sat at the counter, watching Caleb take orders and make drinks as she sipped her latte. In between customers, he tried to teach Elyse how to make foam designs. They pulled shot after shot of espresso and Caleb stood over Elyse's shoulder giving directions as she poured the steamed milk. He didn't so much as glance Penny's way, much less come over to talk. No more flirting for her. He'd put up his walls again.

Maybe it was for the best. They'd spent an awful lot of time together the last few days. If she wasn't careful, she might start wanting more than the easy fun she'd promised him. And she wasn't allowed to have more. He'd be gone soon, and the closer she let herself get to him, the harder it would be to give him up.

Might as well let go of him now.

She finished her latte and went home.

Chapter Seventeen

*S*ince Caleb obviously wasn't coming over that night, Penny decided to go visit George in the hospital. On the way, she stopped off at Antidote to get him a cherry Danish. Even though she knew Caleb probably wouldn't be working this late, she still felt a stab of disappointment when he wasn't there.

This was definitely getting out of hand. No strings meant she should be able to let him go at any time. Without pining.

"When did you start eating pastries?" Roxanne asked when Penny ordered George's Danish and a nonfat latte for herself to go.

"It's for George," Penny told her. "I'm on my way to visit him at the hospital."

"Awww, tell him we miss him."

Penny took her Danish and latte and drove to the hospital. When she got to his room, George was alone and sitting up in bed, pushing a square of lime Jell-o around on his dinner tray. He wore a burgundy velour robe over his hospital gown, and seemed to have gotten a lot of his strength back.

"What'd you bring me?" he asked, eying the paper bag in her hand with interest.

She set it on the rolling table beside his dinner tray. "A cherry Danish."

He perked up as he peeked into the bag. "From Antidote?"

"Of course."

The balloons Penny had brought were holding up well. They sat on the ledge along the window beside a couple bouquets of flowers and a stack of DVDs.

"You know the way to an old man's heart." He took the Danish out of the bag and broke off a piece as he shot a longing look at the coffee in her hand. "No coffee for me?"

"I didn't think you were allowed."

"I'm not." He waved her over. "Let me at least sniff it. All they've got is decaf in this joint. Tastes like bilge water."

Penny took the lid off her coffee and held it under his nose. He'd shaved and combed his hair, and if it weren't for the hospital setting and the wires still attached to his arm and chest, he'd almost look back to his old self. "Smells like heaven. Did Caleb make it?"

"No, he's not working tonight." Penny moved a stack of newspapers so she could sit in the chair beside the bed. "Roxanne made it and she said to tell you she misses you."

"She's a good kid. I'm sad I won't get to meet her rugrat."

"Of course you will. Aren't you getting out of here soon? You'll be back at Antidote before you know it."

George shook his head. "They're moving me up to San Jose. Mike and Jennifer don't want me living down here alone anymore, and I guess they've got a point."

"Oh," Penny said, feeling bereft. George really was leaving too.

"They're moving me into some kind of special apartment complex for 'active seniors.'" He emphasized the last two words by making disdainful air quotes with his fingers. "It's a fifty-five and up community. Wall-to-wall geezers like me."

"That doesn't sound so bad," Penny said, thinking of the

nursing home where she volunteered, which was essentially a hospital with a dreary rec room in the middle of it.

He scowled. "I hate old people. All they do is complain."

Penny smiled into her coffee cup. "They're not so bad. You get used to the complaining."

"I like being around young people. Keeps me from feeling old and decrepit."

"You'd prefer a youth hostel, then? Or one of those Silicon Valley rental houses full of brogrammers mainlining Red Bull and Cap'n Crunch all hours of the night?"

He took another bite of Danish and chewed thoughtfully. "Maybe. At least they won't die on me left and right."

"I wouldn't bet on it. Guzzling all that 24-Hour Energy can't be good for them."

He sighed and shook his head. "I don't like change."

"I don't either," Penny said, feeling a sharp stab of sympathy. "Won't it be nice to be closer to your family though? You'll get to see your grandson more often."

"That part's terrific. It's everything else that's the pits. Los Angeles has always been my home."

"You'll make new friends in San Jose, just like I did when I moved here from DC. Maybe even a few who aren't geezers."

"Sure." He nodded, looking unconvinced. "Mike's already talked to a real estate agent. We're signing the papers to put my house on the market tomorrow."

Her heart gave a little squeeze. "That's fast." She'd thought it would take longer to get everything arranged. That she'd have more time before he left.

He picked at the crust of his Danish. "I lived in that house for forty years. Barbara and I bought it when she got pregnant. It's where we raised our family."

"I'm sorry." Penny swallowed the lump stuck in her throat. "That must be hard."

They never covered that part of happily ever after in the fairy tales. How even if you found your perfect soul mate, one of you was likely to be left alone at the end. Maybe it would be better not to pair up in the first place. At least that way you'd be used to living alone.

George waved his hand like it didn't matter. "It doesn't do any good to hold on to things. Sometimes you just gotta let go and move on." He wadded up the paper bag his Danish had come in and tossed it into the trash can. "Enough about me," he said, narrowing his gaze at Penny. "What's wrong with you?"

"Nothing's wrong with me," she said, shaking her head as she lifted her coffee to her lips.

"Bullpucky. You seemed down even before I started telling you my sob story. What gives?"

"I'm fine." She tried to sound like she meant it but fell pathetically short of the mark.

George's eyes sharpened. "How's Caleb?" he asked, far too perceptive.

"Caleb's fine." She hesitated. "Did you know he's going away to med school?"

"Yeah, he mentioned something about that." Caleb seemed to tell George everything. She wondered how much he'd told George about her. "He's leaving pretty soon, right?"

"On the twenty-fifth." His new job started the day after Memorial Day, and he had to drive down there and get settled in first. Only twenty-two days left before he was gone.

George nodded, watching her closely. "How do you feel about that?"

"I'm happy for him, of course." She remembered the way he'd taken charge when George had his heart attack. How calm and capable he'd been under pressure—and how caring. "He'll make a great doctor." That was what mattered, not the minor inconvenience it posed to her life.

"You're not going to miss him?"

She already missed him, and he wasn't even gone yet. But like

George had said, there was no use holding on to things you couldn't have. Better to make your peace with reality and move on.

"I'm going to miss *both* of you," she said.

George grunted. "Gimme another whiff of that coffee."

She leaned forward and passed it to him.

"Mmmm," he sighed, inhaling deeply. "You think they have coffee this good in San Jose?"

"I'm sure they do."

WHEN PENNY GOT home from the hospital, she paced around her apartment, feeling restless and glum as she thought about George and his wife of forty years and the house full of treasured memories he was giving up.

And here she was feeling sorry for herself over Caleb, a man she barely knew. She needed to get a grip. This was supposed to be a casual fling, which meant she shouldn't be having all these *feelings* about him. The whole point was to walk away before things got real.

She pulled open the refrigerator and glared at the stacked containers of leftovers inside, arranged by date and waiting to be eaten. None of them held any appeal. She shut the fridge again and leaned her back against it, surveying her empty apartment with dissatisfaction.

It hurt to admit it, but maybe Caleb had been right. They never should have started anything in the first place. She didn't seem to be cut out for casual flinging.

The smart, logical thing to do was keep her distance from him.

She didn't want to be smart or logical though. She wanted to call him. Just the thought of hearing his voice made her heart flutter. She wanted to see him again so much it was a physical ache, like hunger pangs. She wanted to feel his arms around her. His skin under the pads of her fingers. His breath warm on her neck as his hands roamed over her body, rough and gentle by turns.

She pulled out her phone and stared at his picture in her contacts. It was one of the ones she'd taken of his backside when he was going through her fridge. Her thumb hovered over the call button as she tried to remind herself what George had said about moving on.

While she was debating with herself, she got a notification for a new text message—from Caleb.

Hey.

Before she'd pulled herself together enough to type a response, he added: *Can I come over?*

This was obviously a sign. Her fingers trembled as she typed out the word *Yes.* There was no possibility of saying no.

But was he coming over because he wanted to see her? Or to let her down gently? Had he had the same realization as her? That their fling was in danger of becoming something more, and needed to be put out of its misery?

As she headed to the bathroom to brush her teeth—just in case he wasn't coming over to dump her—there was a knock on her door. She detoured into the living room and peered through the peephole.

Caleb's familiar bulk shifted uneasily on the other side.

She threw open the door and his eyes lifted to hers. A chemical reaction occurred as they gazed at one another, but it wasn't just about heat. This felt more like synthesis than combustion. Two simple compounds combining into something more complex.

Before she had time to consider the implications, he moved toward her, cradling the back of her head in his palm as he pressed warm lips to her forehead. "I missed you." His nose bumped against hers as they leaned into one another, their breaths syncing and slowing in relief.

Whatever was happening between them had already grown out of her control. It was too late to protect herself now. The horses had stampeded through the open barn door and were hurtling toward inevitable heartbreak.

She might as well enjoy the ride in the meantime.

Penny curled her fingers in the front of Caleb's shirt as she lifted her face to his. His hand slid through her hair to cup her cheek. He kissed her forehead again, and then her lips.

This is it, she thought, closing her eyes as she felt her body relax. *Equilibrium.*

PENNY LAY with her head pillowed on Caleb's arm as she meditated on the perfection of his torso. His eyes were closed, and his chest rose and fell in slow, relaxed expirations under her hand. She watched her fingertips explore the smooth trough of his breastbone, test the firm muscle of his pecs, and trace the ridges of his ribs.

They hadn't talked about what they were doing, or what was happening between them, although it seemed obvious something had changed. Penny was scared to bring it up, afraid that shining a light on it would cause it to disappear, like ice crystals melting in the sun.

If Caleb knew how strong her feelings had become, he'd surely insist on ending things immediately. She couldn't let that happen. She'd made her bed, and she intended to lie in it as much as possible while she still could. Consequences be damned.

"I went to see George tonight," she said, when the silence started to feel too weighty.

Caleb's eyes cracked open, and he turned his face toward her. "How's he doing?"

"Mike's moving him up to San Jose."

He nodded somberly. "That's probably for the best."

"He has to give up his house. The one he and his wife lived in for forty years. I can't even imagine."

"I've never lived anywhere longer than four years, so neither can I." His eyes looked almost black in the dim light.

She felt a chill and pulled the sheet up over her chest, scooting closer to absorb more of his warmth. "My grandparents have lived in their house since they got married. They raised all their kids there. I think it would kill them to have to sell it and move somewhere else. Poor George. It makes me so sad to think about it. All those memories."

Caleb's hand touched her hair. "You can't live in the past. He'll be better off closer to his family."

"I know." She sighed. "It still makes me sad."

His arm tightened around her, and his lips brushed the top of her head. "One thing I learned from moving around so much as a kid: home's not a place. It's the people you're with."

She pressed her face into his neck, breathing him in. The scent of coffee had become an aphrodisiac. She'd never be able to smell it again without getting turned on. A warm hand slid down her back, and she pulled his face to hers, enjoying the slow drift of pleasure as their mouths met in a leisurely kiss. She would happily stay in this moment forever, if only she could find a way to stop time.

"It's getting late," Caleb said.

Penny looked at the clock and saw that it was almost eleven. It really was late this time.

"I should go." He sat up and threw the covers back.

She reached for him. "Don't."

"I have work in the morning." He sounded apologetic. Like he wanted to stay.

"Don't go," she said, squeezing his forearm. "Sleep here."

His brow furrowed in indecision. "Are you sure?"

"I'm sure. Stay the night."

He did.

PENNY'S KNEES went to jelly as soon as she saw Caleb standing behind the counter at Antidote the next morning. Like a silly, lovestruck schoolgirl. You'd think she'd be past that sort of reaction to him by now, but apparently not. Maybe she'd never get past it.

He wasn't even his usual flawless self today. His shirt was rumpled, his hair faintly lopsided, and his designer stubble looked rough around the edges. He was still transcendently beautiful, and last night she'd slept with those tree trunk arms wrapped around her. A very small, very petty part of her wanted to climb up on the counter and shout the news to the world.

His alarm had woken him before dawn, and he'd dressed in the dark before slipping out of her apartment with a soft kiss and whispered goodbye. She'd managed to mumble something vaguely resembling "Have a good day" before rolling over and falling right back to sleep in the warm spot he'd left behind. When her own alarm had gone off a couple hours later, she'd spent a few disoriented seconds believing the whole thing had been a dream.

There were no other customers in line, so as soon as she was certain her legs would support her, Penny walked straight up to the register.

"Morning," Caleb said in his monotone customer service voice, but his eyes were soft as they gazed at her. "You want the usual?"

"Yes, please," she replied, staring back at him. Roxanne was rearranging the pastry case just a couple of feet away, so Penny refrained from saying anything else.

Caleb held her eyes for a moment before he rang her up and went to make her latte. When it was ready, he brought it over and set it in front of her. He'd made a pair of hearts in the milk.

"You need anything else?" His eyes were mischievous, as if he were daring her to say something lascivious.

"Nope," she said, refusing to take the bait. "I'm good."

He didn't hang around to chat, instead occupying himself with busywork: collecting dirty dishes, rinsing them at the sink, wiping down the condiment bar and refilling the containers of sugar and creamer. But he kept directing furtive looks her way. Every once in a while their eyes would meet, and his mouth would twitch, and then he'd turn away and pretend to be busy.

No wonder it had taken her so long to realize he liked her, if this was his post-coital flirting. Thank God he'd lost his head and kissed her at the hospital, or she would have forever remained cheerfully oblivious to the fact that he was interested in her.

She took her phone out and pretended to read, but she was hyperconscious of every movement Caleb made. She kept following him out of the corner of her eye, until finally she just gave up and blatantly stared at him. He was making a cappuccino and she watched him top it off with foam, his mouth settling into a cute little frown of concentration as he poured the milk. His tattoo was peeking out of his T-shirt, and it gave her an intoxicating thrill to remember how she'd traced it with her fingertips.

He carried the cappuccino to the counter and called out the customer's name. His eyes fell on Penny and she smiled, but he still didn't come over. Instead, he pulled out his phone. She watched him type something into it, wondering who he was texting.

Her phone buzzed in her hand, and she jumped—he'd texted her.

You're staring, the message said. She looked up at him and shrugged. He shook his head, amusement twinkling in his eyes, but stayed where he was.

You're nice to look at, she typed back. *Are you afraid to come talk to me?*

Yes.

She smiled at the screen. *Little old me? I don't bite.*

I have evidence to the contrary.

She stifled a laugh and glanced up to find him smiling at her. He shook his head and turned his back on her.

You liked it, she typed back.

She could see his triceps twitch as he typed another text, and she tapped her finger against the side of her phone while she waited for it to come through.

That's why I'm staying over here. I might not be able to resist temptation.

To do what? she wrote back.

She'd never considered herself a temptation to anyone before. It was exhilarating to wield that kind of power.

Jump over the counter and besmirch your reputation.

She crossed her legs, suddenly very aware of her clothes touching her bare skin.

Come over and besmirch me tonight instead?

The three little dots flickered as he typed his answer. *What time?*

I've got my weight training class at six, but I should be done by 7:30.

Don't shower after, he texted back. *Don't even change your clothes.*

Chapter Eighteen

"*Y*ou don't have to push me," Caleb protested as Penny herded him out of her apartment on Sunday morning. "I'm going."

They'd spent the last four nights together at her place. In fact, they'd spent almost every free minute they had together.

It was a dangerous game Penny was playing, but she'd moved beyond caring into the sweet embrace of nihilism. She'd be crushed when Caleb left no matter what, so she might as well soak up every second she could until then.

Her one concession to rationality and common sense was maintaining all her usual activities, even when it meant kicking Caleb out of her apartment so she could go to yoga or her weight training class. Or, like today, to volunteer at the nursing home for two hours.

"I'm going to be late if we don't hurry. You have your phone, right?" As she dug in her purse for her keys, the plate of short-bread cookies she was juggling started to tip precariously, and she let out a squeal of alarm.

Caleb deftly relieved her of the capsizing baked goods, which he'd helped her make this morning. He was surprisingly handy with a rolling pin and cookie cutter for someone who looked like he should be modeling underwear for Calvin Klein. "Yes I have my phone," he said with an indulgent grunt, "and ten dollars in my pocket that says you've never been late for anything in your life."

Penny fished her keys out of her purse and opened her mouth to protest, but he cut her off.

"And arriving on time doesn't count as being late, Amy Santiago."

She twisted her head to beam at him as she locked the door. "Did you just make a *Brooklyn Nine-Nine* reference? I'm so proud of you, I'm going to let that dig about my punctuality go without comment."

They'd made it through another season over the last few days and only had three more to go. Caleb didn't know it yet, but she already had plans to make him watch *The Good Place* next. They should just have time to get through it before he left.

Penny felt a pang of unease at the thought of the drop-dead date looming over them, but pushed it to the back of her mind as she started for the stairs with Caleb following behind with her cookies like a dutiful footman.

"But I'll have you know my punctuality is admirable," she added.

"Is this you letting it go?" he asked in sardonic amusement.

"It's good manners," she said. "For the record."

"I'll have the court reporter make a note." They reached the bottom of the stairs and turned in the direction of her car. "What time will you be back from entertaining the elderly?" he asked, drawing abreast of her on the sidewalk.

"Two-thirty."

"Perfect. That'll give me time to do a load of laundry while you're gone."

He didn't even have to ask anymore. It was just assumed he'd come back to her place later.

They'd conveniently avoided the subject of how much time

they were spending together. Penny lived in constant fear that Caleb would suddenly feel the need to back off again in some sort of misguided attempt at gallantry. As if anything could protect her from what was coming.

"You know, I've never seen where you live," she said as they approached her car.

"It's not much to see."

She opened the rear hatch of her little white Kia. "I don't care. I want to see it."

He leaned into the car to set the plate of cookies in the cargo area. "No, you don't."

"Why?" She arranged her yoga bag up against the cookies to keep them from sliding around and turned to face him.

"Because it's a dump."

"It's where you live."

He shook his head. "You're going to be disappointed."

"Invite me over."

He reached up and closed the tailgate. "My roommates might be there."

"So? I want to meet them."

"Why?"

"They're your roommates."

"I barely know them."

"Invite me over."

"You're relentless," he said, but his eyes were glinting with affection.

"And you're stubborn. I'm starting to think you're hiding a secret wife or a harem or something and that's why you don't want me to see where you live."

"That's ridiculous. How could I afford to support a harem on a barista's salary?"

She prodded him in the chest with her index finger. "If you want to have sex tonight, you have to invite me over."

"Penny," he said on an exasperated sigh.

"What?"

"Do you want to come over to my place later today?"

She rose up on her toes and kissed his cheek. "I thought you'd never ask."

CALEB WASN'T LYING. His place was a dump.

He lived near LAX, in a cobalt blue stucco house with a ghastly white ironwork railing stretched across the front. A stunted, half-dead banana tree squatted in the middle of a patchy lawn next to a driveway so cracked it looked like a window someone had thrown a rock through. The doorbell had a piece of duct tape over it, so Penny pulled open the rusty burglar bars and knocked on the white paneled door.

Caleb answered it wearing a gray tank top and baggy athletic shorts. A sheen of sweat glistened on his face and arms. "You've been working out!" she exclaimed in delight.

The corner of his mouth lifted. "Just for you."

She threw herself into his arms and he kissed her, spinning her around so he could shut the door.

The inside of his house was no better than the outside, she discovered as soon as she'd finished kissing him. The walls and trim and fixtures were all painted a dingy, yellowed white that made her think of rotten eggs, and the floor was covered with patterned orange ceramic tile that must have dated from the nineteen fifties.

"Don't take off your shoes," Caleb warned, following her gaze to the floor.

Footprints muddied the tile and drifts of dust bunnies crowded in the corners. It didn't appear to have been swept or mopped since the house was built.

"My roommates don't believe in cleaning, and I got tired of being their maid. We're currently engaged in a war of attrition. These floors are the hill I'm going to die on."

"Are you winning?" Penny lifted her foot and her shoe tried to stick to the floor, reluctantly letting go with a sticky sound.

Caleb let out a dispirited sigh. "I'm pretty sure they haven't even noticed."

Her fingers itched for a broom. And a mop. And possibly some napalm to burn the whole place to the ground. "You know, I could—"

"Don't you dare. This is why I didn't want to invite you over. I knew you'd want to clean, and you're not allowed."

She took in the rest of the living room. There was a couch covered in mustard yellow corduroy, two ancient vinyl La-Z-Boys that had been patched so much they were at least thirty percent duct tape, and a cheap veneer coffee table covered in beer bottles, coffee mugs, old pizza boxes, and dirty paper plates.

"It's nice," she said, trying to be polite.

"No, it's not." He kissed the tip of her nose. "You shouldn't lie. You're terrible at it."

She struggled for something positive to say. "It's got good bones. And the tile isn't the worst I've ever seen." Although it was definitely in the top ten. Top five, even.

"The rent's cheap." Caleb looked around in distaste. "That's the best thing I can say about it. But it's only temporary."

Right. Temporary. Just like *she* was only temporary. Was he slumming it with her like he was with this dump he lived in?

He put his hand on the small of her back and guided her through the living room. "Come on, I'll give you the tour."

"Yay." She edged toward the mess, drawn to it like ferrous metal caught in a magnetic field. "Maybe I could just—"

"Nope," Caleb said, pulling her back. "It's their mess and it'll stay until they clean it up."

The sight of it was physically painful to her. If she had a garbage bag, it would only take a minute to tidy up the worst of it. "Yes, but—"

"Don't look at it." Caleb took her by the arm and led her into the kitchen.

"Now I know why you always want to come to my place."

"The fact that you're there also has something to do with it too," he said, and she couldn't help smiling in response.

The kitchen was slightly less revolting. The floor, which was covered in more of the orange tile, was horrifically filthy, but only half the sink was full of dirty dishes. And the Formica counters actually looked as if they had been cleaned sometime in the current millennium.

"I have to cook in here," he explained. "So I try to keep it relatively sanitary. I refuse to do their dishes though."

Penny turned her back on the dirty dishes so she wouldn't be overwhelmed by the compulsion to wash them.

"You want something to drink?" Caleb asked.

She eyed the vintage avocado Frigidaire rumbling in the corner, imagining what horrors must lie inside. "No, thank you."

"Probably smart. You don't want to have to use the bathroom. Trust me."

Penny turned her eyes to the patio door at the far end of the breakfast nook and the weight bench that lay beyond. "Is that where you work out?"

"Yeah."

"Can I see?" She headed out to the patio—which was nothing more than a concrete slab—without waiting for an answer. There were two stacks of plates on either side of the bench, and a heavy knurled bar resting in the racks, all of it covered in a layer of rust.

"Do I get a demonstration?" she asked.

He ducked his head sheepishly. "No."

"Come on. Please." She gave him her best Puss in Boots eyes. "I want to watch."

He shook his head in capitulation and stooped to pick up one of the forty-five pound plates. Penny helped him load the other end of the bar, and he lay down on the bench. She studied his form as he set up under the bar. Hands shoulder-width apart, feet flat on the ground, good back arch. Once he unracked the weight, she forgot about his form and became distracted by his biceps. It didn't appear to be an especially challenging weight for him, but it was enough to make his muscles do amazing things before her eyes. She lifted a hand to her mouth to make sure she wasn't drooling.

After he'd done a few reps he glanced over at her. "Happy now?"

"Yes. Very." She moved to the head of the bench and helped him rack the bar. "Is one-thirty-five your usual work weight?"

He looked surprised—either that she could do plate math or that she knew what a work weight was. "No, it's just for showing off in front of girls. I usually work up to two-oh-five."

She eyed the rusty old rack, frowning. "You bench out here by yourself without a spotter or safeties?"

"Sometimes I get one of my roommates to spot me when they're home."

"And when they're not?"

"Then I figure my neighbors will hear the screams and call 911." He got to his feet and gestured to the bench. "Your turn."

Penny blinked. "What?"

"You got to drool over me," he said as he slid the forty-fives off the bar. "Now it's my turn to enjoy an exhibition."

She backed away from the bench. "Uh uh. No way."

"Yes way. Fair's fair. How much weight do you want?"

She looked down at her dress and leather-soled ballet flats. The residue from the floor would give her shoes a little more traction, but it still wasn't ideal. "Just the bar."

He raised a skeptical eyebrow. "I'll bet you can bench more than the bar. How much?"

"Um." Penny bit her lip. "Give me the twenty-fives, I guess."

"Ninety-five?" He looked impressed again.

Her personal record was one-fifteen, but she figured she could manage ninety-five pounds without a warm-up. Maybe. Hopefully.

Caleb loaded the weight for her and gestured to the bench again. "All yours."

Penny's stomach churned with stage fright as she got under the bar. She'd never lifted in front of a man before. Her weight class was women only, and she liked it that way. She always felt a little like an imposter when she exercised. Like a fat kid pretending to be an athlete. Bench pressing in front of someone as fit as Caleb was a terrifying prospect.

"You got this," he said, taking a position at the head of the bench to help her unrack. "Ready?"

The bench was too high for her to get her feet flat on the ground, she didn't have chalk, and she was wearing a dress, but sure. She nodded and Caleb gave her a wolfish grin. "What?" she said, staring up his nostrils.

"I've got a great view of your boobs from this position."

"And I've got a great view of your crotch." It was only inches away from her face, close enough that his shorts were brushing the top of her head. "Let's get this over with," she said, trying not to let his proximity distract her.

He lifted the bar out of the rack and waited until she had it in position over her chest before letting go and stepping back.

Penny took a breath, braced her abdomen, and lowered the bar down to her diaphragm and back up again. That wasn't so bad. Her arms only felt a little shaky. She took another breath and did it again. It felt even smoother the second time. She did it three more times, and then Caleb put his hands on the bar and helped her guide it into the rack.

She sat up, feeling a little dizzy. "Happy now?"

"Yes," he said, looking a little dizzy himself. His pupils had gone wide and dark with naked lust. "That was unbelievably hot." He pulled her off the bench and into his arms. "Can I come watch your next weight class?"

"Nope. No boys allowed." She slid her hands under his tank top and over the bare skin of his back.

"That's a tragedy," he said and kissed her. His mouth tasted salty and he smelled like coffee and sea air.

She closed her eyes and melted into him as his tongue slid into her mouth. A seagull called out overhead, and with the sun warming her skin Penny could almost imagine they were at the beach—the sound of the surf crashing around them, soft sand between their bare toes.

We should go to the beach sometime, she thought. Then she remembered they only had two more weekends left together and kissed him harder to push away the sadness.

"Where's your bedroom?" she said when they finally came up for air, and he led her back into the house and through the messy living room, down a grubby hall with some truly appalling carpet, and into a small bedroom.

The carpet in there wasn't much better, but it at least looked as though it had been recently vacuumed, and there were no dirty dishes or old pizza boxes sitting out, which put his room head and shoulders above the rest of the house. There was a cheap desk covered with books and a double bed with a faded plaid bedspread, but other than that the room had no personality what-soever. No pictures on the walls, no decorations of any kind, nothing that wasn't purely functional. It made her think of a jail cell.

"Sorry it's not nicer," he said, looking around the room with an expression of disgust.

She reached for him and kissed him. "You're here. That's all I need."

He closed the door, winding his arms around her, and they fell into each other.

Chapter Nineteen

*A*n hour later, Penny lay curled against Caleb on his sad, lumpy mattress in his sad, drab room in his sad, gross house. *What kind of life is this?* she wondered as she listened to his breathing slow and deepen. There was nothing joyful or beautiful in this place to brighten his life. He didn't even seem to have friends to distract him. It was like he was living in exile in a self-imposed prison. Doing nothing but working and exercising and saving his money until he was sprung from his incarceration.

Now that she'd seen how dreary his life was, it was easy to understand why seeing her had been the brightest part of his days. It wasn't that she was all that special, it was that everything else was so awful in comparison. He must be counting the days until he could leave this place and start his new life.

He let out a soft snore and she smiled, marveling that he managed to be sexy even while snoring and drooling a little out of one side of his mouth. Moving carefully, so as not to disturb him, she unwound herself from the heavy arm draped over her and slipped out of bed. She padded over to his closet and slid open the louvered door. Inside, all the shirts she'd gazed at lustfully over the months hung on cheap wire hangers. She ran her fingers over them until she found her favorite, the red plaid flannel he'd been wearing the day he dumped iced coffee all over Kenneth. She pulled it off the hanger and put it on. It fit her surprisingly well— one of the many benefits of sleeping with a man who lifted weights. Kenneth's puny shirts hadn't even fit her arms, much less her bust.

She wandered over to Caleb's desk as she buttoned up the borrowed shirt. There was no chair, so she sat on the edge of the mattress as she peered at the stacks of books covering the surface of the desk. The nearest stack was all from the library— mostly science fiction with a couple of thrillers scattered in. There was a pile of imposing biology and anatomy textbooks at the back that had gathered a fine layer of dust. The rest of the books were more eclectic, their spines creased and the corners well-worn as if they'd been read over and over again. She studied them, hoping for some kind of window into Caleb's soul. His tastes ran the gamut from Edgar Allen Poe and Fritz Leiber to Michael Chabon, Margaret Atwood, and John Le Carré. It was difficult to draw any conclusions other than he had good taste in literature.

A single framed picture perched at the back of the desk, partially hidden behind all the books. It was the only photo in the entire room. A group of smiling kids beamed out of the frame from the shore of a lake somewhere. She picked it up to study it more closely, searching the faces to see if one of them was Caleb. She found him standing off to one side. A teenager by the looks of it, but several years older than the other kids.

"Hey," Caleb said behind her, his voice husky and sleep-roughened. "What are you doing?"

Penny turned toward him, clutching the photo against her chest. "Snooping,"

"Ah." He propped himself up on one elbow. His hair was all lopsided and sticking up, and he looked just as sexy as when he'd been snoring. "Find anything interesting?"

"Not really. You're so secretive, I was hoping for something juicier."

He actually had the nerve to look affronted. "I'm not secretive."

"Yes! You are! I barely know anything about you, you never talk about yourself—or anyone else for that matter—and wrangling an invitation to your house was like extracting a tooth from a grumpy bear."

"I thought it was pretty obvious why I didn't want to invite you over here."

"Okay, fine. But the rest of it still stands."

He stretched out his arm and ran his fingers along her thigh, dipping them under the hem of the shirt she'd borrowed from him. "What do you want to know?"

Refusing to be distracted by his wandering fingers, she held out the photo. "Tell me about this."

He sat up with a sigh and took it from her, adjusting the pillow behind his back. "That's Camp Northbrook. I was a counselor there for three summers in high school."

"Why is it the only picture you have in your room?"

He shrugged and handed it back to her. "I don't know. The others are all back at my parents' place."

"See, that's what I mean," Penny said. "You don't want to talk about things."

"I don't know what you want to hear."

"I just want to understand you." She thrust the picture back at him. "This photo is the only one you didn't leave behind. There must be something special about it."

He stared at the photo with an inscrutable expression. "I guess it's one of the last places I remember being really happy."

She scooched closer and crossed her legs underneath her. "Why?"

"We moved a lot, so I never really made close friends at school or felt like I fit in. But at camp, everyone was just there for the summer, so everyone was new. It's a camp for special needs kids, and most of them were really excited to be there. Seeing how much harder they worked to do things most of us take for granted really gives you a sense of perspective. I guess they showed me what kind of man I wanted to be—which was something my father never did."

"That's why you're going to med school." The realization raised a lump in the back of Penny's throat. "It's not because of your father, it's because of them. Because you want to be able to help them."

"I guess. I never thought of it like that, but maybe." He shoved the photo back at her. "Is that what you wanted to hear?"

"Yes." She leaned over and kissed him softly on the lips. "That wasn't too terrible, was it?"

His hand smoothed over her curls. She hadn't straightened her hair in a week. "Not *too* terrible, no."

"Wonder of wonders. Caleb Mayhew talked about himself and didn't die. And now I feel like I finally know something real about you." She set the photo back on the desk and selected a Neil Gaiman hardback from the top of a stack. "Tell me about this next."

He regarded it dubiously. "You want a book report?"

"No, I want to know what you like about it. I assume you like it, since it's one of only a dozen books you seem to own."

"I have crates of books at home. I just didn't want to lug them all around with me."

"So why do you lug around this one?" She flipped it open and a piece of paper that had been tucked between the pages fluttered to the floor. "Oops." She stooped to pick it up. It was a letter from the University of Mississippi billing office about the tuition deposit deadline. "You haven't paid your bill yet?"

He leaned over and snatched it out of her hand. "I will."

"The letter says it's already overdue."

He sat up on the edge of the bed, covering himself with the

sheets, and shoved the letter in his desk drawer. "There's a grace period."

"Which ends in a week."

"You read all that in the half-second you were looking at it?"

"I'm a fast reader." Penny frowned. "Is the money a problem?"

"No, I've got the money." His face was turned away from her, so she couldn't read his expression. Not that she'd have been able to read it anyway.

"Why haven't you paid your bill?"

"Laziness. I'll get to it." He shot her an exasperated look. "Would you like to see my electric bill next, or can we talk about something more interesting?"

"You haven't started packing yet."

"So? I've got two and a half weeks."

"I'd have started packing a month in advance." Two months in advance, even.

He cracked a faint smile. "Yeah, but we both know you're a freak about things like that. And I don't have that much stuff. It'll take me two hours, tops."

"Still."

He sat back on the bed and pulled her into his arms, tucking her head under his chin. "Tell me something about you now."

"Like what?"

"Tell me about your family." His fingertips stroked a path down her arm, and she let her eyes fall closed.

"My family are really boring."

"Boring families are nice. Do you like them?"

"Yes. They drive me crazy sometimes, but they're my family. I love them."

"Liking them and loving them aren't the same thing."

"No, it's not." She gave his arm an affectionate squeeze. "But I like them too."

"You're close?"

"I'm really close to my parents. My brothers and sisters…" She thought about her brother who only seemed to care about football, and her sisters who only ever talked about their kids and their husbands. "We don't have as much in common."

"What's your dad like?" Caleb's voice had grown soft, and it rumbled pleasantly under her ear.

"Quiet. Kind. Nerdy. His favorite TV show is *Jeopardy*, and he looks forward to his *Times* Sunday crossword all week. When I'm home we do it together."

Homesickness burned at the back of her throat as she pictured her dad bent over the kitchen table with his reading glasses on, chewing the cap of his ballpoint pen while her mother cooked breakfast.

Penny FaceTimed with her mother almost every week, but her father didn't like to talk on the phone. Occasionally, he'd wander through the room when her mother was talking to her and say hi, but video calls made him even more uncomfortable than the phone. Instead, he sent Penny long weekly emails touching on a range of topics, including politics, the antics of their neighbors, the latest documentary he'd watched on TV, and any new bird sightings he'd made on his morning walks.

Caleb smoothed a hand over her hair and she burrowed deeper into his arms. "He tells lots of dad jokes," she said, smiling faintly. "He's really big into the dad jokes."

"What's he do for a living?"

"He's a chemical engineer too."

"You wanted to be like him."

"I wanted to be like both my parents, but a chemical engineering major seemed more lucrative than English. Also, I didn't want to have to write all those papers."

"You said your mom's a teacher, right?"

"High school English and German."

"*Ich spreche ein bisschen Deutsch*," he said in an impressive German accent.

Penny looked up, surprised. "You speak German?"

He shrugged. "Just enough to get me in trouble. We lived in Germany when I was in middle school."

"My mom would love you. She'd talk to you in nothing but German." Between this and his taste in books, she'd be calling him "son" within ten minutes of meeting him.

Except her mother would never meet him. Penny hadn't even told her parents he existed. What was the point, when he'd be out of her life soon? No sense getting her mother's hopes up, only to crush them again. She wouldn't approve of what Penny was doing, anyway. She'd think she was setting herself up to get hurt. Which was exactly what she was doing.

Penny's throat squeezed again and Caleb kissed the top of her head. "Your parents sound nice."

"They are."

"You must miss them."

"It was hard moving here, so far away from them."

"Why did you?"

She shook her head. "It's your turn again." He'd finally struck on something she didn't want to talk about.

"Penelope." He put a finger under her jaw and tilted her face toward his. "Why did you move out here? If you telework anyway, why move so far away from your family?"

She lowered her eyes, embarrassed. "For a man."

"What happened?"

"I thought I was in love. So when he wanted to move here to pursue acting, I followed him—stupidly, as it turned out. He moved out here ahead of me while I was still waiting for my tele-work application to be approved. I was so excited. It was supposed to be the start of our new lives together. But when I got out here a couple months later, I found out he'd started seeing someone else. An actress, of course." Penny still couldn't believe that Brendon had let her move out here instead of breaking up with her before she disrupted her entire life for him. Even that one small consider-ation had been too much for him. "He dumped me a month after I got here." She felt Caleb go still, and flinched in anticipation of his pity. "Don't feel sorry for me. I hate it when people feel sorry for me."

"I don't." He lifted her chin again and regarded her steadily. "I feel sorry for that asshole who didn't know how lucky he was to have you." There wasn't a trace of pity in his soft brown eyes. Only affection.

"Now you're just sucking up."

"I'm serious. Any guy who'd cheat on you must not be working with a fully charged battery. Including that loser Kenneth."

Penny sighed and laid her head down on his chest. "Unfortunately, cheating boyfriends are a recurring theme in my life."

"So why didn't you move back home?" Caleb asked, changing the subject.

"Stubbornness." Her fingers toyed with the light dusting of hair on his chest. "Running back to Virginia with my tail between my legs would have been admitting to everyone I'd made a mistake. I wanted to prove I could make it on my own in a new city."

Penny had promised herself she'd give it two years. That was long enough that she wouldn't look like a quitter. After two years in Los Angeles, she could consider applying for a supervisory position back in DC. Or maybe even transfer to Dallas. There was a satellite office there now that was always looking for Chem-Es. She could start over in a new city of her own choosing this time.

"Do you still regret moving here?"

"Not so much. It's better now that I've made friends."

"But you still miss your family."

She nodded against his chest. "Every day."

He tightened his arm around her, and she nuzzled her face into his throat. When he held her like this she didn't feel homesick at all. She felt like she was exactly where she belonged.

"I couldn't wait to get away from my family," Caleb said

quietly. "I know this place is a dump, but the fact that it's not on an army post and my dad is a hundred and sixty miles away makes it feel like a resort."

Penny lifted her head and touched his cheek. "I guess that's why you don't have any pictures of your family."

His jaw tightened. "I do have one, actually. I just don't have it sitting out." He shifted her off him and got up. She was afraid she'd upset him until he started rifling through a drawer in the desk. He pulled out another framed photo and handed it to her.

It was from Caleb's high school graduation. He wore a serious expression with his navy blue gown and National Honor Society collar. His two younger brothers flanked him in ties, looking miserable. Caleb's father stood a little to one side in his uniform, glowering at the camera. The only one smiling was Caleb's mother, standing rigidly at the other end of the photo. She was small-boned and petite, with perfectly coiffed hair. None of his family were touching or standing close. They were lined up like grim little soldiers, their postures ramrod straight and their hands at their sides.

"Your dad does look a little like Colonel Kurtz," she said.

"You said you hadn't seen *Apocalypse Now*."

"I looked it up on Wikipedia."

Caleb took the photo from her and stared at it. His lips compressed into a taut line. "My dad's not quiet or kind like yours."

She slid her fingers into his hand and bit down on her lip to keep herself from asking anything more.

His fingers curled around hers. "He likes to give orders and expects everyone to follow. All that matters is what he wants. If you don't live up to his expectations, he blows up."

"He was abusive." It wasn't a question. Whether or not his father had laid a hand on him, it was clear Caleb had been left with deep scars.

There was a long silence, during which the only sound was his uneven breathing. She stroked her thumb over his knuckles, trying to soothe some of the tension away.

"Yes," he said finally. He shook his head like he was trying to shake off the memories. "It could have been worse though. Lots of people have it worse."

Very gently, Penny took the photo from him and studied it more closely. "You don't look anything like your father."

Caleb grimaced. "That's not what my mother says."

"You look more like a young Zac Efron in this photo. And Zac Efron could never play Colonel Kurtz. He's got much too sweet of a face."

She was rewarded with a faint smile. "Is that your roundabout way of trying to compliment me?"

"It's not roundabout. Zac Efron is an international heartthrob."

"Is that an official title? Is there some sort of nomination process or a panel of judges that bestow international heartthrob status?"

She leaned forward and gave him a slow, lingering kiss. His hands came up to cup her face, holding her gingerly. Like she might shatter if he held on too tightly.

Orange afternoon light slanted in through the blinds, picking up the highlights in Caleb's hair and bathing his skin in a golden glow. He was so beautiful she couldn't believe he was real.

He was a hero from a Greek myth come to life and somehow she had made him hers—but only for a little while. Their story wasn't a fairy tale, or even one of Shakespeare's comedies where the couple winds up together in the end. They were a tragedy. Maybe not as tragic as Hamlet, where everybody dies, or Oedipus, who kicked off a whole cycle of misery and disaster. But they were tragic enough.

Penny knew, as certainly as she knew the sun would set in the west, that she was going to be shattered when Caleb left. And she had no one to blame but herself.

Chapter Twenty

*T*hey didn't go back to Caleb's house anymore by mutual agreement. Now that Penny had seen it for herself, she could understand why he preferred to spend his time at her apartment.

When they weren't having sex like it was going out of style, they watched a lot of television together. For someone who didn't own a TV or even have an internet connection at his house, Caleb seemed to like television an awful lot.

His things started collecting at Penny's apartment. His toothbrush and deodorant moved into her bathroom. A gargantuan tub of protein powder squatted on her kitchen counter. The second of his hoodies joined the first in her closet, along with several of his shirts. Then on Thursday, he brought his laundry over to use the machines in her building, and now those clothes lived in her bedroom as well. His shirts and jeans hung on her hangers, his underwear and socks occupied the basket which became a semi-permanent fixture in the corner of the room, and his dirty clothes mingled with hers in her hamper.

They seemed to be failing miserably at the no-strings thing.

Not that Penny was complaining—but she'd had serious, long-term relationships that hadn't moved this fast. Caleb had effectively moved in with her, and the ease and speed with which they'd integrated their lives rattled her whenever she stopped to think about it.

So she chose not to think about it. As a strategy, denial was working pretty well for her.

Penny continued to be astonished by how much she and Caleb had in common. Besides having enough physical chemistry to power the next SpaceX launch, they'd read a lot of the same books, laughed in all the same places at the TV shows they watched, and shared the same political views. She wasn't just wildly attracted to his body; she actually *liked* him.

Plus, Caleb know how to cook and cared about eating healthy. In her previous relationships, balancing her food preferences with her boyfriends' unhealthy ones had been a perilous minefield that frequently resulted in Penny settling for a dry chicken breast or wilted salad at whatever burger joint or wing place she'd been wheedled into patronizing. But meals with Caleb were an entirely different proposition. Rather than undermining her good habits, he reinforced them.

She'd sworn never to cook for a man again, but cooking *with* a man was different. They compared favorite recipes, planned and shopped for meals together, and prepared the food side-by-side in her small—but immaculately clean—kitchen. Caleb didn't just pull his own weight in the kitchen; his proficiency even surpassed hers in some areas. A stint working in the kitchen at Applebee's had left him with some impressive sous-chefing skills. The man diced onions with a dexterity that was downright sexual.

Penny loved to watch his hands as he worked. The gentle precision with which he held the knife handle as the blade flashed left her lightheaded and drooling. More than once they'd had to put their meal prep on hold while she dragged him into the bedroom.

At present, he was pounding a trio of chicken breasts into submission with a meat tenderizer—which was also weirdly a turn-on—while Penny sliced tomatoes for the caprese salad. The fabric of his plaid shirt pulled tight across his broad shoulders as he worked, and he had the sleeves rolled and pushed up to his elbows. The sight of his forearms tensing as he hammered the meat presented an unfair distraction. Instead of paying attention to where her blade was going, she was ogling the man in her kitchen.

"Fudge nuggets!" Penny exclaimed as the knife cut into her index finger. "Son of a biscuit."

"Did you cut yourself?" Caleb asked, abandoning his tenderizer to rush to her side. "How bad?"

"It's fine," she said, squeezing her injured finger to stanch the bleeding.

"Let me see."

She pulled her hand back, cradling it against her chest. "You've been handling raw chicken."

"Come on, then." He nudged her toward the sink with his elbow and washed his hands thoroughly with antibacterial soap before reaching for her. "Put it under the water and let's see how bad it is."

It wasn't too bad, but it was right next to the fingernail and hurt like the dickens. Caleb's fingertips gingerly prodded the area around the wound as he examined it, and once again Penny was impressed by how gentle his big, rough hands could be.

"No stitches necessary." He shut off the water and tore off a paper towel that he pressed against her finger. "Hold this in place while I get you a Band-Aid."

While he headed off to the bathroom in search of first aid supplies, Penny tried to remember the last time someone other than her mother had fussed over her like this, and came up blank. It felt nice to be the one taken care of for a change.

Caleb came back and peeled the blood-soaked paper towel away from her finger, frowning in concentration as he tended her injury. As she watched him, an unfamiliar sensation unfolded in her chest. It expanded, filling up all the empty spaces, and making her feel lighter than air.

I love him.

She'd thought she'd been in love before, but she'd never felt anything like this for any man she'd dated. She'd exchanged *I love yous* and pictured weddings and children down the road, but she'd never once felt this sort of desperate, possessive urgency. This certainty. This pain.

"You all right?" Caleb asked, peering at her with worried eyes. "You look a little dazed. You're not phobic about blood, are you?"

She shook her head, too shaken to form words.

"There," he said softly, kissing her finger once he'd finished wrapping the bandage around it. "All better."

"My big, strong hero." She leaned forward to kiss him, her lips lingering on his. Savoring every breath while she still could.

He wrapped his arms around her, drawing her close. "You sure you're okay?" He pulled back to look at her with a frown. "You're shaking."

"I guess I scared myself a little." She tried to give him a reassuring smile.

His eyes crinkled with concern and he reached up to trace a finger over her lips. "You should be more careful."

She wound her arms around his waist and rested her cheek against his chest. "I know."

SUNDAY WAS MOTHER'S DAY, and Caleb had gone back to his house to work out while Penny was at the nursing home. The administrators had planned a party for the residents, and Penny brought cupcakes decorated with pink buttercream roses. Despite the attempt at cheer, it was a melancholy occasion for the mothers whose children hadn't visited, and others who were remembering mothers who had long since passed.

As soon as it was over, Penny FaceTimed her mother from the parking lot of the nursing home.

"Happy Mother's Day!" she said when her mother's face appeared on the screen. Margaret Popplestone was round and soft with short brown hair mostly gone to gray and Penny's hazel eyes. Her hair was done and she was wearing makeup, but she'd already changed out of her church clothes and into an old T-shirt—one Penny got her five years ago that said *I'm silently correcting your grammar.* "How was brunch?"

Penny's siblings had taken Margaret out to a Mother's Day brunch buffet after church, like they always did. This was the second year in a row Penny had missed it.

Her mother's face moved out of frame for a moment as she pulled her legs up under her on the couch. "Dana's baby is teething and Cassie's oldest dropped her father's iPhone into the fountain at the restaurant." The smile that lit her face was absolutely sincere. "It was lovely."

"I'm sorry I wasn't there," Penny said.

"Your presence was missed, as always. Have I mentioned lately how proud I am of you for sticking it out in Los Angeles on your own?"

"Not in the last seven days, no." Penny lowered the phone to rest it on the steering wheel. The angle was dreadful—she probably had four chins from this perspective—but it was too uncomfortable to hold it higher for any length of time.

"Well, I am." Margaret leaned out of frame again and reappeared with a bundle of knitting. "You took a bad situation and you made lemonade out of it."

Penny made a wry face. "That's me. Out here on the West Coast, swimming in sour water."

Her mother glanced up from the knitting she was arranging over her lap. It looked like it might be a sweater, or possibly a blanket. "Oh, dear. Someone's got a case of the mopes. What brought this on?"

"Nothing."

"Don't lie to your mother." She directed her patented disapproving teacher look at the camera. "Especially on Mother's Day. You earn triple demerits for that."

Penny shook her head. "I didn't call you to complain about my life. Tell me what's going on with you."

"You already know what's going on with me. It's the same things that are always going on. Now tell me what's got my baby down in the dumps."

"A boy," Penny admitted with a sigh.

Margaret nodded as she arranged the stitches on her needles. "Are you still upset about Kenneth?"

"No, definitely not. I'm *way* over him. This is someone new."

"Oh!" Her mother's eyes lifted in excitement. "A *new* boy! Do tell."

"Technically, I've known him for a while. I just got to know him recently."

"Who is he? What's his name?"

"Caleb. He's a barista at that coffee shop by my house."

"Interesting," her mother said, looking back down at her knitting.

"He's not *just* a barista," Penny said in response to her unspoken critique.

"I wasn't judging." She was a little, but Penny let it go.

"He's about to start medical school. You'd like him, actually."

Margaret had never liked a single one of Penny's boyfriends—which, in fairness, had turned out to be justified in every case. She'd never come right out and said so, of course, but Penny could always tell. When her mother disliked someone, she became even more polite than usual. Thank goodness she'd never had a chance to meet Kenneth, or she might have smothered him to death with good manners.

Margaret lifted an eyebrow. "A younger man, eh?"

"He took a gap year, but yeah. A little younger."

"So what's the problem with this young doctor-in-the-making? Why does he have you feeling sad?"

"He's moving away. In less than two weeks."

Her mother's lips pursed. "Hmmm. How far away?"

Penny was glad Margaret was knitting. It was easier to talk about it when she didn't have to look her directly in the eye. "Mississippi."

"Oh no. That's fairly dire."

"It's where he's going to med school." Penny bit her lip. "He told me up front that we only had a month before he left and it would be better not to get involved."

"And?"

"And I thought I could handle it. I thought I could spend time with him without getting attached."

Her mother looked into the camera, her head tilted to one side. "Oh, Penny. My sweet girl, you get attached to disposable food storage containers."

"I liked him, Mom. He's gorgeous—like seriously, unbelievably gorgeous—and really sweet once you get to know him. And he actually liked me back. I just wanted..." She looked down at her lap, too embarrassed to say the words aloud.

"You wanted to feel liked by a cute boy," her mother supplied for her. "Particularly after Kenneth bruised your self-esteem, I'd imagine. That's all right. It's what rebound relationships were invented for."

Penny clenched the steering wheel with the hand that wasn't holding the phone. "That's what I thought at first, but it's not like that with Caleb. It's not like anything I've ever felt before."

Margaret's sharp eyes shifted to study the digital image of Penny's face on her screen. "You love him."

"Yes." Penny's shoulders sagged. "I didn't mean to, it just happened."

Her mother smiled faintly. "That's usually how love works."

"And now he's leaving and I can't do anything about it."

"No." Her mother's tone was somber and compassionate. "You can't."

"I never should have let myself get close to him. It was a huge mistake." Penny's fingers were getting pins and needles from squeezing the steering wheel so hard. She pried them off and shook out her hand to get the blood flowing again.

Her mother clucked sympathetically. "Sometimes you have to follow where your heart leads you."

"Even if it's headed straight to heartbreak town?"

Margaret shrugged. "A little heartbreak builds character."

"You mean scar tissue."

"Po-tay-to, po-tah-to," her mother said lightly. "No one's ever died of heartbreak, is my point."

"Romeo and Juliet did."

Margaret's lip curled as she let out a derisive snort. "Romeo and Juliet died from being insufferable idiots. They'd have been much better off if they'd built up a little more scar tissue."

Penny smiled despite herself. Her mother had always hated that particular one of Shakespeare's plays—and the fact that it was a required part of the district's curriculum. "So what you're saying is it's actually a good thing I've fallen in love with a man I'm going to lose in twelve days."

Her mother's expression softened, causing a knot of homesickness to form in the pit of Penny's stomach. "Love is never a bad thing, sweetheart."

Penny shook her head to cover her emotions. "As if there were ever any doubts where I get my optimism from."

"Pfft. I'm a realist, thank you very much," Margaret said. "I'm not trying to sugarcoat this: it's going to hurt like the devil. But you've got a sensible head and a strong heart. You'll come through it tougher than you went into it."

"And tough's supposed to be an improvement?" Penny asked uncertainly.

"For a sweet soul like yours? Tough is a critical survival skill."

"WHAT ABOUT A GOING-AWAY PARTY?" Penny asked Caleb
that night as they were eating dinner. She was great at planning
parties, and it would give her something to focus on besides his
imminent departure. A way of building up her armor.

His face twisted into a scowl as he stabbed at his turkey meat-
loaf. "Hell no."

"Why not?"

"I hate being the center of attention. Besides, who would even
come? It's not like anyone's going to miss me."

"*I'm* going to miss you," Penny said.

Caleb looked up and their eyes locked across the table for a
moment before he looked down at his plate again. "Besides you."

"Roxanne will miss you."

"Only until she hires my replacement."

"Malik and Elyse, then."

"They'll miss that I'm usually the one to take the trash out to
the dumpster."

"Your roommates?"

He snorted. "Yeah, nope."

"Your regular customers will miss you. Charlotte, and Anita
with the baby, and that lady who brings her dog. Not to mention
everyone in my knitting group."

Caleb wasn't buying it. "They'll all forget about me as soon as
I'm gone. The only person besides you who might care is George,
and he's leaving too. Stop trying to make a party happen."

"But—"

"I'm serious," he said, starting to sound annoyed. "No party.
Promise me."

"Fine." So much for Operation Distraction. She turned her
attention back to her mashed sweet potatoes, trying not to pout,
but pouting a little anyway.

"Hey," Caleb said softly, and she looked up to find his expression had gentled. "It's a sweet thought and I appreciate the offer. I just don't want a party. Okay?"

Penny nodded, her sullenness fading into understanding. "Okay."

After dinner, they did the dishes together and watched another couple episodes of *Brooklyn Nine-Nine*—only thirteen left before they finished—until snuggling in front of the TV turned into making out in front of the TV, which eventually turned heated enough that they retired to the bedroom.

It was their usual routine, one they'd fallen into as easily and naturally as breathing. Penny could barely even remember how she'd spent her evenings before Caleb. It was like she'd been holding a spot open for him in her life, and he'd come along and slotted himself into it. A perfect fit.

Hours later, when they both should have been asleep, Penny lay on her side staring at the digital clock on her nightstand. Watching the minutes tick away into hours, which would turn into days, which would be gone before she knew it.

She felt Caleb shift in bed behind her, and then his hand glided over her hip. "Why aren't you asleep?" he asked, his voice low and raspy.

"I don't know."

His hand trailed along her arm and played with her fingers. "Are you okay?"

"Yes," she lied.

"Really? Because you've seemed sort of…" He hesitated like he was searching for the right word, finally settling on, "sad."

She *was* sad. Ever since the realization she loved him, it felt like a weight had settled on her chest. One that grew heavier every day. "I'm fine," she said, trying to force lightness into her voice. It wouldn't do any good to ruin their remaining time together by dwelling on how little time they had.

"Penelope." He nuzzled his nose against the back of her neck. "You can talk to me."

She squeezed her eyes shut and let out a breath. "I know I promised I wouldn't get attached, but..." Her courage failed her before she could go any further. Bringing the word *love* into the conversation was like going nuclear. It would change everything, and she didn't want anything to change.

"Easier said than done?" he supplied softly.

"Something like that."

There was a long pause—lengthy enough that she had time to fear she'd admitted too much. Then his arm tightened around her, pulling her against the curve of his body. "I'm sorry."

"I don't want you to be sorry." She understood now why he'd tried to hold himself back. He'd been right; she wasn't equipped for a no-strings fling—at least not with him. They'd clicked in a way she'd never imagined possible, and it had left her wanting a lot more than the simple good time she'd offered him.

But if she could go back and make the choice over again, knowing what she knew now, she wouldn't change a thing. It wasn't even worth considering. She'd pay any price for these stolen, impermanent moments.

Caleb propped himself up on one elbow and turned her over onto her back. His eyes glinted warmly in the darkness above her as he brushed a strand of curly hair from her temple. "I wish I could—"

"Don't." She shook her head and his fingers stroked over her face to cup her cheek. "I wouldn't trade a second of the time we've had together." *No matter how much it's going to hurt.* "No regrets, okay?"

He bent to kiss her, with such gentle intensity it left her shaking in his arms.

"No regrets."

Chapter Twenty-One

"What's that?"

Caleb stood behind Penny at the counter, bracing a tub of dirty dishes against his hip as he peered at the laptop in front of her. The document on the screen was headed with the words "Party Supplies" centered and in bold.

"It's not for you," Penny said, adding streamers to her list before glancing up at him.

His mouth had compressed into a flat line of displeasure. "I told you I didn't want a party."

The shop bell rang as Charlotte came in, and Elyse moved to the register, pocketing her phone.

"And I heard you," Penny said quietly. "I'm planning a going-away party for George."

She'd had the idea this morning. George was out of the hospital finally and Mike was taking the week to pack up his things before driving him up to San Jose on Saturday. When she'd called Mike this morning to propose a going-away party, he'd enthusiastically agreed to the idea.

She thought maybe George's party could stand in as a send-off for Caleb as well. She wouldn't do anything to call attention to

Caleb, but at least it would give everyone a chance to see him before he left. It was the perfect solution.

"Oh," Caleb said, sounding less than thrilled. He carried the tub around the counter and turned his back on her to rinse the dishes at the sink, but she could still see the tension in his jerky movements.

"Is that okay with you?" she asked.

His shoulders lifted in a shrug. "Sure. Do whatever you want."

"Thanks for your permission," she said, irritated by his irritation. Was she not allowed to plan parties for anyone else either? Did he hate all parties on general principle or something? What had parties ever done to him?

"Whatcha doing?" Charlotte asked, pausing beside Penny and nodding at her laptop. "You don't usually do work in here."

"Oh, it's not work. I'm planning a going-away party for George."

"Great idea!"

"That's what I thought," Penny said, raising her voice so Caleb would be able to hear her over the running water. He continued slotting cups into the dishwasher rack without giving her the satisfaction of a reaction.

Charlotte asked how George was doing, and Penny filled her in on his situation. Penny's eyes kept flicking to Caleb's back as they continued chatting about Charlotte's degree program, until Elyse brought her extra-large quad-shot latte over.

"Brain fuel," Charlotte said with a grin. "Time to hit the books." She carried her heavy backpack and coffee over to the couch and settled in to study. Caleb was still at the sink with his back turned.

"Hey, Elyse," Penny said, and the college student looked up from her phone, dark eyebrows raised above her large eyes. "Do you think Roxanne would let me throw a going-away party for George here one night this week?"

"Probably," Elyse said. "You can ask her."

"When's she scheduled to come in next?"

Elyse walked over to the clipboard hanging over the counter and squinted at it. "Today at three."

Perfect. Penny had knitting tonight, so she'd be able to talk to Roxanne about the party then.

Caleb picked up the rack of dirty dishes and disappeared into the back. Penny chewed on her lip as she watched the swinging door flap in his wake. After a moment's deliberation, she got up and followed him.

She'd never seen the kitchen area before, although she'd caught glimpses of it through the round window in the swinging door. The small space was dominated by a behemoth industrial fridge hulking beside a stainless steel food prep counter, and an entire wall of metal shelves full of beverage supplies.

Caleb looked up from loading the dishwasher, startled at her appearance. "What are you doing back here?"

"I'm talking to you about the party."

He shut the dishwasher and stood upright, sliding his hands into his back pockets.

"Are you mad about it?" Penny asked, moving closer to him.

His brows drew together as he shook his head. "It's fine."

He was wearing her favorite plaid shirt today, and she reached up and ran her hands over his chest. "It doesn't seem fine."

"I'm sorry." He wound his arms around her and pulled her into a hug, pressing his lips against her temple.

"What's wrong?" Penny asked as she rested her cheek against his chest. His heartbeat fluttered in her ear.

"I'm just being selfish." She could feel him struggling to get the words out as he drew a long, slow breath. Opening up didn't come naturally to him, but he'd been getting better at it. "I don't want to share you. We've only got so much time left, and I don't want to spend it with a bunch of people I barely know instead of with you."

Penny felt her heart turn over. "Oh." She hadn't even considered that. She'd just wanted something else to focus on besides the fact that Caleb was leaving soon.

His hands rubbed circles over her back. "It's dumb."

"It's not. I won't do the party."

He pulled back and shook his head, frowning. "No. George should have a party. It's the right thing to do."

She peered into his face, trying to discern the truth. "Are you sure?"

He kissed the tip of her nose. "I'm sure. Don't mind me, I'm just being a moody jackass today."

"I'll keep it short. George won't be up for a long party anyway. Just an hour or two to send him off in style."

"He'll love it." He kissed her lightly on the lips. "Now you better get back out there before Elyse starts to wonder what we're up to." He let go of her and took a step back.

She studied his inscrutable features. "Are you *sure* you're okay?"

His dark eyes met hers. "Everything's fine. Go plan your party."

Penny walked out of the kitchen and sat back down at her laptop, trying to ignore both the trickle of unease in the pit of her stomach and Elyse's curious look.

"WHAT IS WRONG WITH YOU?" Esther asked, elbowing Penny in the arm.

"Ow," Penny said, looking up from the half-knit hat in her hands. "What?"

"You're all spaced-out tonight."

"No, I'm not."

Jinny set down her needles and reached for one of the butterscotch toffee cookies Penny had brought. "She's right. You've barely said a word. It's not like you."

"Plus you're not knitting," Vilma pointed out. "You're just staring at your needles and frowning."

Penny sighed and turned over the hat she'd started as a going-away present for George. "I think I hate this color. It's ugly, right?" It was a variegated green that had seemed nice in the yarn store, but now that it was knit up, looked a little like vomit.

"It's certainly an interesting choice," Vilma said diplomatically.

"It's damn ugly." Cynthia shook her head as she set her wineglass down. "I didn't want to say anything if you liked it, but it's bad."

"Right?" Penny sighed, plucking at the ugly hat. "I can't give this to George. I should frog it and start over, shouldn't I?"

Cynthia shot her a look as she picked up her knitting. "You sure that's all that's bothering you?"

Olivia's eyes met Penny's across the table, but she kept silent. Penny still hadn't told the rest of the group about Caleb. At this point, she figured she might as well wait until he was gone. They'd made enough of a fuss over the fact that she'd started wearing her hair curly—she wasn't in the mood to put her relationship with Caleb under the microscope too.

Penny wrinkled her nose at the ugly hat in her lap. "I'm fine. I'm just annoyed I wasted time and money on this stupid yarn."

She'd talked to Roxanne before knitting and they'd settled on Thursday afternoon for George's party. Which meant Penny only had three nights to finish knitting his present. And now she'd have to start over and lose all of tonight's progress.

"I've got a skein of Malabrigo on me." Olivia dug around in her project bag until she came up with a hank of beautiful hand-dyed charcoal gray wool, which she held out to Penny. "You can use it if you want."

Penny accepted the soft yarn, squishing it between her fingers in appreciation. "Weren't you going to use it?"

Olivia shrugged. "You can have it. I'll be working on this shawl forever anyway." She smoothed out the shawl she was knitting for her next cosplay: a steampunk version of Agatha Christie's Miss Marple. "I always seem to get myself into knitting projects that take half an eternity."

"Thank you," Penny said, casting a grateful smile at her friend. "I'll pay you back."

"Whatever."

As Penny pulled the ugly hat off her needles and wound the crinkled yarn back into a ball, the conversation drifted to other topics. She made a concentrated effort to speak up more the rest of the night, not wanting to give them any more reason to think something was amiss.

She had to get better at pretending things were fine. She didn't want to spend her last few days with Caleb sulking and feeling sorry for herself.

When the group broke up for the night an hour later, Olivia fell into step beside her. "I feel like I haven't seen much of you lately."

"I'm sorry," Penny said guiltily. She'd been a terrible friend lately, spending all her time with Caleb.

Olivia pushed the door open and they stepped out into the cool night air. The moon hung low and round in the sky, casting everything in a bluish-silver light. "We should make some time to hang out."

"Yeah." Penny cast her eyes at the parking lot. Caleb was sitting in his car, waiting to give her a ride home. He didn't like her walking alone at night, even just the few blocks back to her apartment. "Definitely."

Olivia followed Penny's gaze to where Caleb sat behind the steering wheel of his ten-year-old Camry. He was looking down at his lap, his face lit by the glow from his phone's screen.

"When does Caleb leave?"

"A week from Thursday."

Olivia nodded. "Are you going to be okay with that?"

Penny looked down at her feet and shook her head. "Definitely not."

She felt Olivia squeeze her arm. "I'll be here when you need me."

It helped to know someone would be.

ONLY NINE MORE NIGHTS UNTIL *I lose him*, Penny thought as Caleb moved inside her Tuesday night. She clung to him, trying to commit every detail to memory. All too soon, her memories would be all she had.

It was going to break her. She knew that. She'd had the best of intentions going in, but she hadn't accounted for how strong her feelings for him would be.

She hadn't expected to fall in love.

If only she could believe he felt the same about her. That she'd stolen a piece of his heart the way he'd stolen a piece of hers.

But she could already feel him pulling away from her. He'd been quieter the last two days. Moodier. More distant. Not physically—if anything, his physical appetite seemed to have increased, as if he were trying to squeeze in as much sex as possible before he left. But he was more subdued. Like he was getting ready to let her go.

Just when she'd finally broken through his walls, he'd started putting them back up again.

Penny squeezed her eyes shut and tried to pretend there was nothing in the world but the two of them, together. That nothing could ever come between them. When they were together like this, she could imagine his body was telling her things his lips never would. That he was giving her everything he had, every piece of his heart, just like she'd given hers.

When he choked out her name in a rough groan, she tried to hear in it all the things she longed to hear from him but never would. The things she'd told herself she didn't need to hear him say.

She slid her hands into his hair and pulled his lips to hers, feeling his breath hitch as he sagged against her, defenseless and contented for one perfect moment. If only she could freeze time and live inside this moment forever. Like a genie in a bottle.

If genies were real, Caleb would be Penny's wish. He'd be all three of her wishes.

I wish I could be with him forever, she'd say. *I wish we could stay together. I wish we could have our happily ever after.*

Chapter Twenty-Two

*P*enny woke with a disoriented jolt. She reached out blindly for Caleb, but the bed beside her was cold and empty.

He's gone.

Panic sliced through her as she struggled to push through the lingering fog of sleep. She hadn't even gotten to say goodbye. How could this day have come so fast?

She forced her eyes open to a flood of relief when a familiar silhouette came into focus in the inky darkness by the window. He hadn't left after all.

Yet.

But he would. Soon.

How had she gotten so accustomed to having him around that his absence from her bed was enough to wake her? How would she cope when he really was gone? She was careening toward catastrophe like a roller coaster screaming down a slope, but it was too late to turn back now. Momentum had taken over. There was no stopping it.

She spoke his name and the silhouette shifted as he turned to face her.

"I didn't mean to wake you." The outline of his hair stood up in tousled spikes against the blinds, as if he'd been running his hands through it.

"What's wrong?"

"Can't sleep."

She held out her hand, and he came and took it, sliding into the bed beside her. His skin felt cool against hers, and she wrapped herself around him, trying to transfer her warmth to his body. "Why can't you sleep?"

He tucked her head under his chin. When he spoke, the vibrations tickled her nose. "I don't know."

She could feel the lie in his tense shoulders as she ran her hands over his back. "Tell me."

He was quiet for a long time before he answered. "Do you ever feel like you're about make a huge mistake?"

"Only all the time."

He nodded against her and didn't say anything.

"Is this about med school?" she asked.

Another long pause. When he finally spoke, his voice was so quiet she could barely hear him. "I don't want to go."

Penny's heart leapt into her throat. Every molecule of her body wanted to tell him to stay—to beg him, actually. But she couldn't do that. This was his chosen career. His life. His heart's desire. He'd worked tirelessly for years to get here, sacrificed his own happiness. She cared about him too much to let him throw it away.

Her arms tightened around him, trying to hold on to him even as her words told him to go. "It's just nerves. It's perfectly normal to feel that way."

"I guess."

She pulled away from him and reached for his face. Her fingertips skimmed over the bristle on his jaw as she pulled his head down to hers. In the darkness, she could only make out the barest outlines of his features, but she didn't need to see the lines around his eyes and mouth to know they were there. Their noses bumped, and then their foreheads. She slid her fingers into his hair, holding him there.

"You're going to be an amazing doctor. You're smart, compassionate, and cool under pressure. You've got this. You're going to rock it."

She felt his forehead scrunch against hers as he squeezed his eyes shut. "If I could stay..." He faltered, and her chest clenched.

"If I could stay, would you want me to?"

Tears burned in her eyes. "You can't stay. There's no point in thinking about it." It hurt too much already. Allowing herself to imagine there was any other possibility would only make it worse. "You have to go. It's your future."

He drew in a shaky breath, and she brushed her lips against his. His palm caressed her cheek, angling her head for a deeper kiss. His kisses were addictive. Penny had never done drugs in her life, but she imagined this must be what it felt like. This desperate, burning need for something. This agony at the prospect of giving it up.

"What if..." She hesitated, swallowing around the burning in the back of her throat.

Caleb's nose nudged against her cheek. "What?"

"We could try the long-distance thing. We could make it work."

He went still. "You really think so?"

"Sure we can." She didn't know how, but it was worth a try, at least. It was better than giving up. "That is...if you want to?"

A millennium passed in the moment before he answered. Civilizations rose and fell, and Penny died a thousand tiny deaths before he finally said, "Yeah. Okay." It lacked the enthusiasm she'd been hoping for, but at least he hadn't said no.

Even if he was just humoring her to spare her feelings, she counted it as a win. It was a sliver of hope to cling to. Because the one thing she was certain of was that she couldn't let him go.

"So this weekend..." Penny said as she sipped her lavender latte on Thursday morning, exactly one week before Caleb was due to leave. "I was thinking maybe we could actually leave my apartment for a change. Maybe have a picnic at the beach or something."

It was their last weekend together, and she wanted to do something special. They'd never actually been on anything resembling a date. She'd always assumed he couldn't afford to eat out, and it was easier for her to eat healthy at home, so they'd just fallen into the habit of staying in.

There was also the fact that Caleb had never actually suggested they go out. She ascribed it to the nontraditional way their relationship had started out. In the beginning, it was only supposed to be a booty call. Which then turned into a series of booty calls. Which somehow morphed into them bypassing the usual courtship rituals and moving straight to de facto living together.

But now that they were in this for the long haul, she wanted to go back and have some of those experiences with him before he left. Before it was too late.

Caleb leaned his hip against the counter and frowned—not exactly the reaction she'd been hoping for. "I'd love that, except..."

"Except what?"

"I won't be here this weekend."

Penny's stomach dropped into her shoes. "What? Why?"

"I have to go to see my parents." His fingers gripped the edge of the countertop, turning his knuckles white.

"Oh." She couldn't exactly begrudge him that. He was about to move two thousand miles away. Of course his parents would want to see him before he left.

He could have mentioned it before now though. Here she was, planning for their last weekend together when they'd already had their last weekend together. If she'd known, she would have tried to make it special. She would have tried to memorize every second.

He started to reach across the counter and halted halfway, his hand clenching into a fist. "I'm sorry."

She forced a smile. "Don't be. You need to see your parents."

"I really do."

"I understand."

His jaw clenched. "But you're still mad."

"I'm not mad. I'm just disappointed. I thought we'd have this last weekend together."

He pulled his hand back, gripping the edge of the counter again. "Trust me, I'd much rather spend it with you than with my parents."

"I know." She tried to shake off her disappointment so she wouldn't make him feel any worse than he obviously did. "When are you leaving?"

"Tomorrow after work."

Tonight was George's party. Was this Caleb's way of punishing her for planning a party before he left?

No, that was ridiculous. He was going to see his parents. There was no reason to ascribe ulterior motives to it.

"I'll be back Monday afternoon."

"Monday." So she wouldn't even see him at work Monday morning. And Monday night she had knitting. That only left them Tuesday and Wednesday, and then he'd be gone.

Their time was running out too quickly. There were only a few grains of sand left in the hourglass, and they were slipping away too fast.

"Hey," he said softly, his eyes locking on hers. "It's going to be okay."

"Sure." She gazed into the gold-edged depths, trying to believe him. "I know."

George's party was a low-key, if crowded affair. Antidote was still open for normal business, but Penny had spread the word to the regular morning customers, so the usual Thursday night crowd had swelled by a dozen or so additional bodies.

As Penny's gaze fell on Caleb standing alone in the hall by the bathrooms, guilt rattled its rusty chains like Marley's ghost. Not only had she forced him to spend one of his last nights here in a crowd of people, but she'd forced him to come to his workplace on a night he had off. He looked exactly as thrilled about it as could be expected.

At least George seemed to be enjoying himself. He sat on the couch at the back, surrounded by a small crowd of avid listeners as he told them stories about his "good old days" in the movie industry. Penny had decorated the back corner with balloons and streamers and a hand-painted banner that said "We'll Miss You." She'd taken up a collection to buy him a plant for his new apartment, and Roxanne and Reema had given him five pounds of Antidote's special order coffee beans. He'd loved the hat Penny had knit him so much he'd put it on immediately, and it still perched on his head as he presided over his audience like a king on a throne.

The cheerful animation that lit up his face was totally worth it. That was what Penny tried to tell herself, anyway, as her gaze flicked to Caleb again. She edged away from the group gathered around George and made her way over to Caleb, pulling him farther back into the hall.

"You're miserable, aren't you?"

He lowered his eyes to the iced coffee in his hand. "I'm fine."

"You're standing off by yourself scowling."

"Sorry if I'm not as eager to please everyone as you."

Penny's mouth fell open. "What's that supposed to mean?" She'd come over here to make nice, but if he was going to be snippy with her she'd save her sympathy.

"Nothing," he mumbled with all the eloquence of a surly teenager.

"Right. I guess I'll just go back to the party, then."

"Hang on." He reached out to snag her arm and she halted, looking at him expectantly. He blew out a breath. "I'm sorry. That was shitty."

"Apology accepted." She moved closer and hugged his arm. "Why don't you come try to have some fun?"

He shook his head. "I'm gonna take off."

"Already?" It hadn't even been an hour.

"I'm not very good company tonight."

That was a heck of an understatement, but it didn't mean she wanted him to leave. "I'm sorry about the party. Please just stay a little longer."

"It's not about the party."

She felt like it was at least a *little* about the party. "Then what is it?"

He grimaced at his shoes. "I'm stressed about seeing my parents tomorrow. I always get like this before I go home."

Nuts. Now she felt genuinely bad. She leaned up to kiss his cheek. "Let's go, then. I'll come with you."

He turned his head and brushed his lips against hers. "You should stay."

"It's okay. I don't mind leaving the party."

"Yes you do. You planned it. I know you want to stay until it's over and help clean up after."

The corners of her mouth curved. "I do a little. But not if you're not here. I'd rather be with you."

"Not tonight." He looked down at her hands where they held on to his arm. "I'm going to sleep at my place."

"What? No!" Her fingers dug into his sleeve. "Please don't do that."

"I've got to pack some stuff up to take home anyway." He met her gaze, his expression as inscrutable as it had ever been. "We'll talk when I get back."

What did *that* mean?

She let go of him, in a state of shock. The din of people in the cafe faded to white noise, which combined with the rushing of her pulse in her ears.

"Don't look at me like that." He reached for her, his hand cradling the back of her head as he kissed her brow. "Everything's fine."

"Is it?" It didn't seem fine. *He* didn't seem fine, and instead of turning to her for support, he was pushing her away.

He stroked an errant curl off her cheek. "It will be." He kissed her slowly and deeply, in a way that felt too much like goodbye for Penny's comfort. "I'll see you here tomorrow morning before I go, all right? At the usual time."

All she could do was nod.

She watched him make his way over to George and lean over to speak in the old man's ear. George said something back, and then Caleb nodded and stuck out his hand. George wasn't having any of that handshake nonsense though. He pulled Caleb down into a one-armed hug, giving him a fatherly pounding on the back.

When Caleb stood upright, his expression was clouded by emotion. He ducked his head and pushed his way through the small crowd, tossing the remnants of his iced coffee in the trash as he walked out the door without so much as a backward glance.

PENNY'S CHEST felt tight Friday morning as she watched Caleb brush coffee grounds off the counter around the espresso machine. After their night apart, his pull on her seemed to have increased tenfold. As she stared at his flexing arms, she remembered what it felt like to have those arms wrapped around her, and it was all she could do to suppress a dreamy sigh of the sort uttered by actresses in Hallmark movies.

The invisible force he exerted on her felt like the beginning of a tsunami. A slow, merciless surge that would keep intensifying until it had destroyed everything it touched, and then recede again, leaving chaos in its wake.

Stop being so melodramatic. She shook her head and raised her latte to her lips, breathing in the lavender scent.

Caleb had been slightly more subdued than usual when she came in this morning, but not alarmingly so. He'd even mustered a smile for her, which he didn't often do at work.

Now, as he leaned under the counter to retrieve his half-drunk iced coffee from the fridge, she noted the signs of strain in the heavy lines around his eyes and mouth.

"Did you sleep last night?" she asked when he came closer.

He paused in front of her, resting his drink against the edge of the counter as he made a wry face. "Not much."

Penny hadn't slept well either. Her bed had felt cold and uncomfortable without him. She was going to have to teach herself how to sleep alone again.

Her fingers traced the rim of her saucer. "How long a drive is it?"

"Two and a half hours, give or take."

"You're not going to fall asleep on the road, are you?"

The corners of his mouth quirked. "I'll be fine. Don't worry."

"I think you know there's no stopping me from worrying." She tried to keep her voice light, but it came out sounding strained.

His expression clouded as he gazed at her. She wanted to touch him to reassure both him and herself, but she knew she shouldn't. Not here when he was working. He stood barely three feet away from her, but the distance between them felt much greater.

She almost reached for him anyway. Malik was in the back, and even if someone saw, what difference would it make at this point? Caleb would be done with this job in just a few days.

Before she could make up her mind, a new customer came in.

Caleb pushed his drink toward Penny for safekeeping and went to the register.

He spent the next fifteen minutes making and delivering drinks to a steady trickle of customers. Every once in a while, he'd pass by for a sip of his iced coffee and give Penny a soft smile before going back to serving customers. It never got busy enough to be actually busy; it was just busy enough to keep him away from her.

Penny watched the minutes tick by until it was time for her to go home and get back to work. Caleb shot a glance her way as soon as she stood up and hoisted her purse over her shoulder.

"Malik, I'm going on break for a minute," he said over his shoulder, dropping the rag in his hand and moving around the counter to follow Penny out the door. When they were far enough down the sidewalk that they were out of sight of the windows, she stopped and turned to face him.

Her legs felt wobbly, and there was nothing for her to hold on to for support except Caleb.

He stepped forward and took her face in both hands, rubbing his nose against hers. His breath warmed her lips when he spoke. "I'll miss you."

"I'll miss you too." Her eyes burned as she blinked up at him. It was taking every ounce of willpower she had not to cry.

His thumb brushed over her cheekbone. "It's only three days."

"I know." Only three days this time. But when he came back they'd only have another three days left together before he left for good. And then how long would it be before she saw him again? Weeks? Months? Forever?

His fingertips slid into her hair as he pulled her into a kiss. The first touch of his lips was tender, but it quickly became fervent and demanding, like he was trying to give her something to remember him by. Before she was ready, the kiss dissolved into a series of light, gentle pecks, so fragile and bittersweet it made her heart ache.

"Penny, I—" He hesitated, and she tensed in breathless anticipation. "I'll see you Monday."

She nodded. "Call me when you get there. So I know you're okay."

"You got it." He pressed a final, chaste kiss to her lips and let go of her.

She gave him one last long look, trying to memorize every detail as she waited for her breath to come back. When she was certain her legs could carry her without failing, she turned her back on him and walked off down the sidewalk.

If it was this hard to let him go for just a few days, what was she going to do when he left her for real?

Chapter Twenty-Three

Caleb called Friday night as promised to let Penny know he'd arrived safely.

"Are you surviving?" she asked, wishing it was a video call so she could see his face. Something told her he wouldn't be on board for that though.

"Yeah, so far." His voice sounded even flatter than usual.

"If it gets bad, you know you can call me, right? Any time, day or night, and I'll answer the phone."

"Sure."

Penny pressed the phone to her ear, as if that would somehow make her feel closer to him. "If it gets too bad, I will get in my car and drive there myself to rescue you. I make a great buffer, just so you know. Parents love me, and I can basically talk forever about anything."

"Thanks, but I can handle my parents on my own."

He sounded distant and vaguely impatient—like he was in a hurry to get off the phone—so she let him go after a few minutes.

The conversation did nothing to assuage her separation anxiety. She spent the rest of the night worrying about him and wondering what he'd meant when he said they'd talk Monday.

Was he planning to break up with her? Had he changed his mind about keeping their relationship going long-distance?

A little voice in the back of her head, the one that was always trying to make things easier for everyone else, whispered that she should let him off the hook. It was probably what he wanted. He was just humoring her with the long-distance thing, trying not to hurt her feelings. No way did he intend to go through with it after he moved.

She was creating another Brendon situation. By trying to hold on to Caleb, she was setting herself up to be cheated on again. Better to accept reality and let him go like she'd agreed to in the first place.

Penny spent a long night tossing and turning in her empty bed. Even after she finally dropped off around three a.m., a series of stressful dreams in which she was falling off a high, narrow bridge caused her to jerk herself repeatedly awake.

When her alarm went off at eight the next morning, it was almost a relief, even though she felt like she hadn't gotten any sleep at all. She rolled over and grabbed her phone off the night-stand to text Caleb.

How's it going so far?

She lay in bed staring at her phone for ten minutes before she gave up on getting an answer and got out of bed to change for yoga. *No more moping.* She needed to get out of the house, get some exercise, and spend some time around other people.

Despite her best efforts, it was hard not to let her dismal mood get the better of her.

"You seem down," Melody observed over coffee after class. "Is everything okay?"

Penny's shoulders sagged as she picked at the sleeve on her cardboard cup. "Remember the guy I wanted to seduce? The one who's moving away soon?"

"The booty call?" Lacey said, scooting closer with her triple-shot mocha.

Penny nodded. "We've been sort of seeing each other the last couple weeks."

Tessa's eyebrows shot up. "*Casually sleeping together* seeing each other? Or *seeing each other* seeing each other?"

"It started out as the first one but turned into the second."

Melody pushed her glasses up and peered at Penny. "Is it serious?"

"Yes." Penny frowned into her plain nonfat latte. "I didn't mean for it to be. It just happened."

"And he's still moving away?" Melody asked.

"He's going to med school in Mississippi. He leaves Thursday." Penny slipped her phone out of her purse and checked her messages for the third time since they'd sat down. Still no response to her text to Caleb this morning.

Lacey winced. "Ouch."

"We decided to do the long-distance thing." Penny shoved her phone back into her purse glumly. "Or try to, at least."

"Oh." Melody's lips formed a perfect O as she exchanged a look with Lacey across the table.

"How long's med school take?" Lacey asked.

"Four years," Tessa answered like she was delivering a death sentence.

"Plus a year-long internship followed by another four years of residency," Melody added.

"Yikes," Lacey said sympathetically.

Yikes was right. When you laid it all out like that, the situation sounded hopeless. What did their endgame even look like? Was Penny supposed to follow Caleb to Mississippi at some point? With her job, she could theoretically live anywhere, but was she willing to move to Mississippi for someone she'd spent less than a month with, and who would be so busy with school he'd hardly have time to spend with her anyway? She supposed she could wait until he'd graduated and hope he was able to get an internship in Los Angeles or some other city she liked better, but that was four years away. And she'd watched enough *ER* and *Grey's Anatomy* to know she wasn't likely to see much of him during his residency either.

It was beyond hopeless. There was no way they'd ever be able to make this work. Maybe if they had a strong, established relationship going in, they might have a chance. But they barely knew each other. There were too many odds stacked against them.

After yoga, Penny went home and changed for her escort shift at Planned Parenthood. At least the protestors aggressively reciting bible verses and chanting Hail Marys kept her from getting too far inside her own head and spiraling into self-pity. Until she got home. Then it was just her and her insecurities alone together in an empty apartment.

And still no text from Caleb.

Fortunately, her two-night sleep deficit finally caught up with her, and she dozed off reading in bed before nine. At ten thirty, she was jolted out of a deep sleep by the blip of her text alert. She'd fallen asleep with her phone in the bed with her, and it took a few fumbling, bleary seconds before she was able to locate it in the blankets.

Caleb had finally responded.

It sucks here. I miss you.

Penny typed her reply as fast as her fingers would obey.

I'm sorry. I miss you too. I'm awake if you want to talk.

She fell asleep again clutching her phone as she waited for a response that never came.

SHE DIDN'T HEAR from Caleb again until Monday afternoon.

When the call came through at three thirty-five, Penny dragged her attention away from the action outline she'd been typing up and stared at his photo on her phone screen as a flood of mixed feelings rushed through her.

She'd cried herself to sleep last night, her delayed breakdown triggered by the lavender-scented sachet in her lingerie drawer, of all things. This morning she'd woken feeling like a wound that had scabbed over, and she wasn't eager to tear it open again.

She honestly didn't know what she wanted to say to him at this point—or what she wanted him to say to her. She'd half convinced herself a clean break would be in both their best interests. Maybe they should even go ahead and call it quits now, when she'd started to build up a little armor. Letting Caleb back into her life for three days, only to lose him again, seemed like gratuitous self-flagellation.

It took her until the third ring to work up the courage to answer.

"Hey," he said, sounding uncharacteristically cheerful. "I'm about an hour out."

"Okay." She chewed on her lower lip. "Are you coming over here?"

"I brought some stuff back with me. I've got to unload it at my place first."

She twisted a strand of hair around her finger. "How was your visit with your parents?"

His voice turned hard. "I don't want to talk about it."

Of course he didn't. He never wanted to talk about anything.

"Listen," he said more gently, "I was thinking maybe tonight we could go out. On a date."

Seventy-two hours ago, Penny would have jumped at an offer like that. Part of her still wanted to. But she was trying to listen to her self-preservation instincts, and they were buzzing a furious warning right now.

She squeezed the phone. "We don't do dates."

"I thought we could try it for once."

"I've got knitting tonight."

"I thought maybe you could skip it."

After he'd disappeared for three days with no notice and

almost no communication? Now he expected her to drop her plans at the last minute for him?

The old Penny would have agreed in a heartbeat, without even thinking about it. But that wasn't her anymore. She was through rearranging her life to suit men who weren't willing to rearrange theirs for her. If he wanted to see her, it would have to be on her terms.

"I can't do that," she told him.

"You mean you won't." The hurt in his tone made her flinch. It took all her willpower not to change her mind.

"You can come over after." It was a compromise. A fair one.

"Fine." The word sounded like it had been dragged over broken glass. "I'll see you after, then." He hung up without another word.

They were going to break up tonight.

The certainty settled over her like a blanket of snow: icy cold, weighty, and numbing.

FOR POSSIBLY THE first time ever, Penny was the first to arrive at knitting. Unfortunately, she was also empty-handed.

"I'm sorry I didn't bake any treats today," she said when the others joined her at the couch she'd been holding for them.

Vilma set her wineglass down and lowered herself into an armchair, casting a concerned look in Penny's direction. "That's all right, honey. You know you're not obligated to bring us treats every week."

"Yeah," Jinny said as she bent over her knitting bag. "We like you even when you don't bake us cookies."

"How was your weekend?" Olivia asked Penny cautiously. She left unspoken her real question, which was how Penny's relationship with Caleb was.

"Crappy," Penny replied, and everyone stopped what they were doing to stare at her.

"Whoa," Esther said.

Jinny's mouth fell open. "I've literally never heard you swear before."

Penny felt like this was an exaggeration. Surely she'd sworn at least once around them. And it wasn't like crappy was even a real swear word; you could say it on TV. It wasn't like she'd dropped an F-bomb or anything. Although in her current mood, she just might.

Olivia dropped her laptop bag and purse to the floor. "What happened?"

Penny glanced up at her, then down again. "Caleb went home to see his parents this weekend at the last minute and I'm being a petulant baby about it." She clutched her knitting bag in her lap the way she used to clutch her favorite teddy bear as a child.

Olivia silently handed Penny her wineglass and sat down beside her.

Cynthia took the seat on Penny's other side. "Who's Caleb?"

"Someone I've sort of been seeing," Penny mumbled into her wineglass.

"Whoa," Esther said again.

"The same Caleb who works here?" Vilma asked, eyebrows lifting in surprise.

"Wait." Jinny's eyes widened. *"Hottie Barista* Caleb?"

Penny felt her cheeks flush and took another gulp of wine.

"You've been seeing Hottie Barista?" Esther asked. "Since when?"

"A few weeks," Penny said.

Esther's eyes narrowed as they shifted to Olivia. "You knew, didn't you?" Olivia shrugged and leaned back on the couch.

"I think you should back up and start from the beginning," Vilma said as she took out her knitting.

"Yes!" Jinny leaned forward in her chair excitedly. "How did you and Hottie Barista become a thing? I want *all* the gory details."

Penny filled them in on the entire Caleb saga. The news that he was moving away was met with a chorus of disappointed *oh*s and sympathetic clucks. When she'd finished recounting their phone call a few hours ago, Cynthia wordlessly passed Penny her own wine to replace Penny's now-empty glass.

"Why didn't you tell us all this was going on?" Vilma asked.

Penny stared down into Cynthia's glass of pinot noir. "I guess because I knew I was making a mistake, and I was afraid you'd talk sense into me. I didn't want to be sensible. For once in my life I wanted to be insensible." She looked up at the faces of her friends, relieved to have it out in the open. "Go ahead, tell me how crazy stupid I was."

"You weren't *crazy* stupid," Esther said. "You were just a regular amount of stupid."

"What she means," Jinny said, punching Esther in the arm as she shot her a reproving look, "is that any of us probably would have done the same thing."

"It's true," Vilma said. "I am a happily married woman and that boy is young enough to be my son, but even I would have had to think twice about it."

Cynthia barked a laugh. "Vilma, you dirty old woman."

Vilma shrugged as her knitting needles clicked a staccato rhythm. "I'm forty-seven. I'm not dead."

"Amen." Cynthia nodded her head. "That Caleb is straight smokin'." She directed a look of approval at Penny. "When life presents an opportunity like that, you have to go for it."

"Was the sex good?" Jinny grinned as her eyebrows waggled suggestively. "I'll bet it was good."

"*So* good." Penny's face heated at the memory, and she pressed a hand to her cheek. "But it wasn't just about the sex. I mean, it *was*, but it definitely isn't anymore. I really like him. I think I even love him."

"Wow." Olivia's eyes widened. Penny hadn't told her that part yet.

"Wow is right," Penny said, handing Cynthia back her wineglass.

Esther sat back in her chair, frowning. "Do you think he loves you back?"

"I don't know." It was a question Penny had been asking herself. "He can be so closed off sometimes. There are these moments when he's so sweet and tender, I think it's possible maybe he does. But then other times it feels like he's putting up a wall between us."

"Maybe he's just protecting himself," Jinny said. "Maybe he loves you, and he's just as afraid of losing you as you are of him."

Esther shifted in her chair. "Not to be Debbie Downer—"

"Here it comes." Jinny rolled her eyes. "The eternal pessimist's take."

Esther shot her a sideways glare. "I think it needs to be said: there is a possibility he's just using you for a good time. I don't need to tell you that men can sometimes be scum." The Esther of a year ago would have happily declared *all* men to be scum. That she was even allowing the existence of *some* decent men in the world was a sign of how much her relationship with Jonathan had improved her outlook.

Penny didn't think Caleb was scum. She might doubt the depth of his feelings for her, but she didn't doubt that he had *some* feelings. Even if he was just having a good time, it didn't make him scum. That was the arrangement she'd freely entered into. It wasn't his fault if he was adhering to it and Penny wasn't.

She shook her head, groaning. "It doesn't matter anyway, because he's still leaving on Thursday."

"It matters," Cynthia said quietly. "Love always matters."

Penny folded forward to cradle her head in her hands. "What am I going to do, you guys? I can't hold on to him, but I don't think I can let him go either."

Cynthia laid a warm hand on her back. "It'll be okay."

"How?" Penny whined, rubbing her temples.

"You'll know what to do when the time comes," Vilma said with enough confidence that Penny could almost believe it.

At least she wouldn't be alone. That was some consolation.

Olivia's hand clamped down on Penny's knee.

"Penny," Cynthia hissed.

She heard Malik's voice cut through the din in the coffee shop: "Yo, Caleb. What's up, man?"

Penny shot upright so fast she made herself dizzy.

Caleb was *here*. Walking straight toward her. He stopped behind Esther's chair, casting an uneasy glance at the circle of women before his eyes found Penny's. "Hey."

Penny swallowed, her chest constricting painfully under the weight of his gaze. "Hi."

He shoved his hands deep in his pockets. "I know you said to come over later, but I couldn't wait. Can we talk?"

Chapter Twenty-Four

*C*aleb tilted his head in the direction of the back hall, and Penny got to her feet. Her chest grew tighter as she followed him down the hall and past the restrooms. The pounding of her heartbeat marked time with her footsteps, heavy and portentous.

He opened the door to the office and gestured her inside.

The scent of coffee beans overwhelmed her senses as he stepped in behind her and shut the door. Memories of the last time they were in this cramped space assaulted her. Their scorching second kiss. How she'd thrown caution to the wind and shamelessly propositioned him. It had started with the kiss in the hospital, but this room was where she'd thrown down the gauntlet that had led them here—right back to this same place.

As Caleb's eyes roved over her face, she saw the same emotions she'd seen that day three weeks ago: naked longing tinged with regret.

He cleared his throat. "Penny, I…"

She watched his chest rise and fall, waiting for him to say whatever it was he'd come here to say. She wouldn't be throwing herself at him today. The confidence that had emboldened her last time had drained away, replaced by a sense of resignation.

Deep furrows sprouted across his forehead. "I don't want to lose you."

That was something, anyway. A nice consolation prize.

Her shoulders sagged as she exhaled an unsteady breath. "I don't want to lose you either."

"Then ask me to stay."

Her lips parted in surprise. She stared. "What?"

His eyes were unwavering and clear. "Ask me to stay."

A painful knot twisted in her stomach. "I can't." No matter how much she might want to, she could never do that to him.

"Yes, you can."

She shook her head. "You have to go."

"What if I didn't?"

"What are you talking about?"

He took a step toward her. "If there was a way I could stay, would you want me to?"

She opened her mouth, then closed it again, not sure what to say to that. Afraid to let herself hope there was a chance. "How?"

"It doesn't matter."

"It does matter. This is your life we're talking about. Your career."

Impatience flared across his face. "Just answer the question. Hypothetically, would you want me to stay?"

Tears burned in her eyes, and she looked down to hide them from him. "Of course I would."

His hand closed on hers. "I'm not going to medical school."

The room tilted around her as she jerked her head up. *"What?"*

A heart-stopping smile lit his face. "I don't want to go, so I'm not."

He actually sounded serious. Penny yanked her hand out of his grasp. "You can't do that. That's crazy."

His smile slipped. "It's done. That's why I went home this weekend. To tell my parents I wasn't going."

"Wait. *That's* why you went home?" Her head spun as she tried to grasp what he was telling her. "When did you decide all this?"

His gaze dropped to the floor and he shifted his feet. "I've been thinking about it for a long time. But I made up my mind last week."

"*Last week?* Why didn't you tell me?"

The look he gave her was accusing. "I told you I was having regrets."

"I thought it was just last-minute nerves."

"I was hoping you'd tell me to stay. But you didn't." The hurt in his eyes broke her heart in two.

She reached for his hand again, twining her fingers around his. "Of course I didn't—I couldn't do that to you. You think I didn't want to?" Her voice shook with emotion. She cradled his hand in both of hers and brought it to her lips. "It would have been selfish to try to talk you out of your dream."

Caleb lifted his other hand to her face, skimming his fingertips over her cheek. "It was never my dream. I wanted to be talked out of it."

"I didn't know that!" she said, ashamed that she'd misread him so badly. "Even if I had, I don't think that I would have done it. I can't be responsible for something like that. It has to be your choice." She squeezed his hand to disguise the trembling in her own. "Please tell me you're not doing this for me."

"I'm doing it for *me*." He swiped his thumb under her lashes to catch the moisture collecting there. "I never wanted to be a doctor. I was only doing it to please my father. I would have been miserable."

She wanted to believe him. *So* much. But she was terrified he was making a terrible mistake for the wrong reasons. She couldn't be the person who kept him from going to medical school after he'd worked so hard to get there.

She sucked in a shaking breath. "What if I told you I didn't want to see you anymore?"

He flinched, but his eyes remained locked on hers, and his voice was steady when he spoke. "I'd be crushed, but it wouldn't change my decision to stay. I'm not meant for med school."

Penny's vision swam, blurring his beautiful face, and she let out a choking sob. "You're really staying?"

His arms closed around her, dragging her into the sheltering warmth of his body. His lips met hers in a tender caress that quickly intensified into a fierce, heated, shattering kiss that left her gasping and lightheaded.

"I'm really staying," he murmured against her lips.

She pulled back and punched him in the arm. Hard.

"Ow! What the hell?"

"Why didn't you talk to me? You could have told me before you went to your parents!"

Caleb rubbed his arm where she'd landed her blow. "Honestly? I wasn't a hundred percent sure I'd be able to stand up to my father. I didn't want to say anything in case I caved under the pressure."

She threw herself back into his arms. "I thought you wanted to break up with me. I had no idea you were thinking of this."

"I'm sorry." He lifted her chin and pressed his forehead against hers.

"*I'm* sorry that you had to face your father alone." She gripped him tighter and shoved her face into his neck, breathing in the comforting, spicy-coffee scent of his skin. "I wish I could have been there for you."

"You were. I just kept thinking about you, and you gave me strength."

"I'm so glad you're staying," she said to his rough cheek. "You have no idea. I tried so hard not to get attached, but I failed miserably. I'm terrible at this."

He smoothed his hand over her hair. "Me too."

"How did your dad take it?" she asked, and felt him stiffen.

"Exactly as badly as I imagined."

She pulled back to study him. "Are you okay?" His eyes skated away from hers, and she reached up to touch his cheek. "Tell me."

"He said I wasn't his son anymore and I wasn't welcome in his house."

"Oh my God. He didn't mean it, did he?" It horrified her to imagine a parent could be so cold to their child. Especially when that child was as wonderful as Caleb.

He took a shaky breath. "It's not the first time he's said something like that. It'll probably blow over eventually." His jaw tightened. "Maybe. I don't even care. It's my life. If he's not willing to let me live it the way I want to, I don't need him."

"He's your father."

"Not much of one."

"What about your mother?"

"She didn't say anything. She never does."

Penny pressed her palm against Caleb's cheek and kissed the corner of his mouth. "I'm so sorry."

His eyes closed. "It doesn't matter."

"It does. They're your family."

He shook his head. "I don't want to talk about them right now." She opened her mouth to argue but he cut her off. "I will talk about it, I promise. I just don't want to think about them right *now*." He touched a curl at her temple. "I only want to think about you."

Penny pressed her mouth against his and felt some of his tension melt away as their tongues tangled in a tender, slow kiss.

"Penelope." His voice was rough with emotion. "I have to tell you something."

She stilled. "What?"

"I love you."

"Oh." She exhaled a relieved laugh. "I love you too."

A heartrending smile lit his eyes. "You do?"

"Yes!" She clasped his face and kissed him again and again, bursting with happiness. "I've been trying to hide it, because I didn't want to freak you out."

Caleb gazed intently at her mouth as his fingertips skimmed her lower lip. "I've loved you for months. I loved you even before —when you used to come in here and try to talk to me."

"I still don't understand why you wouldn't talk to me." She nipped his earlobe in gentle retribution.

"I was afraid to let myself get close to you, because I knew I couldn't have you."

All this time, she'd been trying so hard not to get too attached to him—it had never occurred to her that he might already be attached to her. "You were trying to protect yourself. And then I basically forced myself on you and tried to treat you like a cheap fling. It must have been awful."

His smile turned into a smirk. "It wasn't all bad."

Their mouths met again in a series of greedy, exuberant kisses as they floated on an engulfing wave of bliss. She was intensely aware of him—his temperature, his density, the gravity of his emotions, the potential energy sparking off his skin.

"Not to cut short this romantic moment," he murmured huskily in her ear, "but we should probably go."

Penny's consciousness lurched back to their present location, and the fact that it provided only the illusion of privacy. "Right. Someone might walk in."

He brushed a kiss against her jaw. "I was thinking more that we should go let your friends know you're all right before they storm in here and string me up by my balls."

"They wouldn't do that." She paused, smiling. "Unless you deserved it."

"I'll have to try not to deserve it, then."

She took his face in her hands, gazing into the amber depths of his eyes. "Are *you* all right?"

"As long as I have you, everything else will be okay."

She believed him. No misgivings. No regrets.

"You have me," she said. "For as long as you want me."

His perfectly proportioned face broke into a double-rainbow smile. "How about forever?"

She grinned back at him, feeling lighter than air. "Forever sounds perfect."

Epilogue

SEVERAL MONTHS LATER

"*W*ould you rather have a cake that's velvety and moist or one that's light and airy?"

At the sound of her voice, Caleb looks up from the pathophysiology textbook he's reading at the dining table. He's back in school to get a degree in occupational therapy—a career that appeals to him far more than being an MD ever did.

Penny leans against the kitchen counter, looking beautiful in sweatpants with her curly hair pulled into a loose bun. It's his birthday today, and she's baking him a cake. He can't even remember the last time he had a cake on his birthday. Elementary school, maybe, when they were living in San Antonio.

He considers her question and finds he has no preference, other than the fact that he likes the sound of the word *velvety* on her lips.

"Both?" he ventures.

It's the wrong answer, he discovers when she lets out an adorable little huff of vexation. "They're mutually exclusive," Penny says, absently waving a measuring cup as she speaks. "Creaming the butter and sugar together creates air bubbles that are expanded by gases from the leavening agents, producing a taller, light-textured cake. Alternatively, you can use the two-stage method to blend the butter and dry ingredients together, which allows the fats to coat the proteins, preventing gluten development for a tender, melt-in-your-mouth cake."

Somewhere in the middle of this impromptu lesson on the chemistry of cake baking, Caleb decides he's going to marry this woman.

The sudden intensity of his resolve leaves him a little breathless.

He's loved her for a long time. For months, he loved her from afar, silently and without hope. He learned to live with the ache of it the way you live with a broken rib: trying not to breathe too deep or move too fast.

But now, improbably, she is standing in the kitchen of the apartment they share, it is his birthday, and he doesn't have to pretend anymore. He is going to spend the rest of his life with her.

Penny lifts her eyebrows, obviously waiting for him to speak.

His mouth opens. "Huh?" he says eloquently.

She shakes her head fondly, and a strand of hair breaks loose and falls across her forehead. "Did you hear anything I said?"

"I got distracted somewhere in the middle."

She brushes the flyaway curl out of her face with the back of her hand. "Where exactly did I lose you?"

"When you said the word creaming."

He watches the blush spread up from her chest and into her cheeks. He adores that blush. Making it appear is one of his top five joys in life.

Penny's full, pink lips press together as her eyes sparkle with amusement. "You're incorrigible."

"Not me," he says. "I'm as corrigible as they come."

He's never proposed before, although he and his last girlfriend had negotiated an informal understanding. She would follow him when he went to medical school, and in return, one day, he would make her a doctor's wife. It wasn't something he wanted so much as something that was expected. Marriage, like medical school, felt like an obligation. A trap that was closing around him.

It was a relief when Heather called things off just after Christmas. He's not sure he would have had the courage to do it himself —but he should have.

He'd already taken notice of Penny by then. He noticed her on his very first day of work at Antidote. How could he not? With her sunny demeanor and warm, friendly manner, the whole place seemed to get a thousand watts lighter as soon as she walked into it.

Everything about her was bright: her red hair, her floral dresses, her brightly colored lips and nails. He'd been living in the black and white part of *The Wizard of Oz*, and Penny was in full Technicolor. But his fate was truly sealed the moment she smiled. The first time he saw her lush lips curve, pinking the apples of her cheeks and making her hazel eyes shine, he was a goner.

He never used to be someone to believe in love at first sight, but he has no other explanation for it. Something in her spoke to something in him, from the very moment she walked into his life.

But he had a girlfriend. A plan that had already been laid out for him. Commitments.

He tried to ignore the unsettling new feelings Penny awoke in him. He tried to ignore *her*, because it was too difficult to do anything else. She represented all the things in his life he wanted but couldn't have. Passion. Self-determination. Hope.

He started volunteering to work doubles on Mondays when he knew she came for her knitting club, so he'd be able to see her twice in one day. He couldn't help himself. The dopamine rush he got around her was the only time he felt alive.

Now he gets to feel that rush every minute of every day. How did he ever get so lucky?

He watches Penny now as she turns her attention back to her baking, frowning over her food scale. "I feel like a chocolate cake should err on the side of density," she decides as she reaches for the cocoa powder.

She insisted on baking a cake for his birthday. He told her it wasn't necessary, but secretly he's pleased. It feels like he's had to take care of himself his whole life, so he's still getting used to having someone in his life who wants to take care of him. He will never, ever take it for granted.

His parents aren't exactly shining role models for marriage and family. Caleb grew up watching his father suck the joy out of every life around him while his mother performed her role with the glassy-eyed cheerfulness of a marionette. He and his brothers were raised in an emotional wasteland where empathy was nonexistent, weakness was met with cruelty, and affection was a sham. His two brothers leaned in, adopting The Colonel's twisted ideas of masculinity and honor as they clamored for paternal approval.

Caleb never took to the indoctrination. Whether because he was the eldest, or because he'd just been born that way, he was more sensitive than his brothers, and more stubborn—to his father's perpetual disappointment. To protect himself, Caleb grew extra-thick armor and retreated so far behind his walls that he forgot the way out.

Until Penny walked into his life and dismantled them brick by brick.

It's still a little scary, letting himself be vulnerable. He's a work in progress. But he's learning, slowly, that he can expose his underbelly without being punished. That there is comfort and kindness in the world and that—improbably—he is deserving of it. That *this* is what unconditional love is like.

He wants the whole package now: marriage, kids, pets, a house with a white picket fence, and family vacations to Disney World. Whatever will make Penny happy, he wants to give it to her.

She looks up at him, and a little line appears between her brows. "What do you think about adding Guinness to the batter?"

"I think that sounds amazing."

She takes a can out of the fridge and pops the top. When she's done measuring out the quantity she needs, she waves the half-empty can at him. "You want to finish it?"

He's supposed to be studying, but what the hell? It's his birthday, and his best friend is baking him a cake.

He gets up from the table and wanders into their small kitchen to accept the beer. Takes a long drink as he leans back against the counter, watching Penny combine the last of the ingredients.

She fits the bowl into the stand mixer and flips it on. A loud mechanical whir fills the air. When she's sure it's mixing to her satisfaction, she turns back around and regards him from the opposite end of the kitchen. Her eyes narrow. "What?"

"What?" His fingers clench around the beer can and the metal lets out a small *pop*.

"You keep looking at me funny."

His defenses are so worn down, he's forgotten how to put his game face on. He takes another drink of beer. "Funny how?"

"Like you have a secret." Her eyes narrow farther.

He sets the beer down and goes to stand in front of her, crowding her against the counter. "Not me." He kisses the tip of her nose as his hands settle on her hips. "I'm an open book." It's a small lie, but one he hopes he can be forgiven for.

He tries not to think about what ifs. If George hadn't had a heart attack in that place on that day, leaving Caleb an emotional wreck, he wouldn't have played his hand by kissing Penny in that stairwell. She never would have known he had feelings for her. He would have gone to Mississippi and never seen her again.

He'd be living there right now, suffering through the misery of medical school for a father who would never give him the approval he craved. How long would he have lasted? Would he have knuckled under out of sheer stubbornness and lived out the rest of his life as a doctor? Or would he have crumbled under the pressure and washed out, earning even more of his father's disgust?

He reaches up to touch Penny's cheek. "Do you know you're the most beautiful woman I've ever known?"

She waves the compliment away, giving his shoulder a gentle shove. "Aw, go on."

"You are."

"No, I mean it. Go on." The smile she flashes him is twinkly-eyed and teasing. "Keep complimenting me."

His fingers trace the curve of her jaw. "You're smart, you're caring, you're excellent in bed—"

"I was kidding." Another exquisite blush streaks across her pale skin. "You don't really have to keep giving me compliments."

Too bad. He plans to spend the rest of his life complimenting her. "You do know you're the best thing that's ever happened to me, right?"

She gives his thumb a gentle bite, then follows it up with a kiss. "Right back atcha." Her eyes flick to the clock on the microwave and she twists in his grasp to shut off the mixer.

Caleb leans around her and dips a greedy finger in the chocolate batter.

"That has raw eggs in it!"

He grins and pops it in his mouth. It tastes heavenly.

She shakes her head at him. "Don't blame me when you come down with salmonella." When he goes in for another scoop she swats his hand. "Don't fill up on cake batter or you won't have room for dinner."

They're going out for a nice dinner tonight at a steakhouse. Candlelight, wine, the whole shebang. Then back home to eat cake before they fall into bed. Their bed. It's Caleb's idea of a perfect night.

Briefly, he toys with the idea of proposing over dinner tonight, right between the cocktails and the entree. Now that he's made his decision, he wants to move on it. But he also wants to do this right. Choose his moment. Give her a ring. Make the moment special. She deserves that much, and it requires thought and careful planning.

That's okay. He can wait. He's not going anywhere.

Her eyes sharpen and narrow. "You're doing it again."

"Doing what?"

"Looking at me funny. Do I have something on my face?"

"I don't know. Let me check." He takes her face in his hand, studying her carefully, and smears a streak of chocolate batter across her cheek.

Her expression melts into indulgent amusement. "Very funny."

The thought drifts across his mind that on their wedding day, they will recreate a scene very much like this, and she will look at him in exactly this same way. He smiles. "There's something there all right. Let me just—" He bends down and licks the cake batter from her face.

"Nice." Her nose wrinkles. "Thanks. That's very helpful."

"You know me. Always trying to help." He drags his thumb across her soft lips. "Hang on. I think there's a little more right..." He lowers his head until his lips are just barely touching hers. "Here."

Her eyes fall closed when he kisses her. The kitchen smells like chocolate, and the preheated oven envelops them in warmth as she sinks into his arms.

She is it for him. The love of his life. He can't believe he almost let her go.

Her hand grips the front of his shirt as she pushes her face into his neck. Sighs. "I'm so happy right now."

He slides one hand down her back while the other traps her hand against his heart. "Me too."

Happy birthday to him.

Acknowledgments

Profuse thanks are due to everyone who was good to me while I was tearing my hair out trying to finish this book. But most especially I need to thank:

Alison, for lending her professional and scientific expertise.

Bethany, Mer, Joanna, and Lisa, for their encouragement, enthusiasm, and beta reading skills.

My editor, Julia, who is awesome at her job.

Danielle, for talking to me about bras a lot.

Tammy, for going to coffee shops with me and giving me ideas to steal.

And last, but definitely not least, to Dave and James, for all the support they've given me.

About the Author

SUSANNAH NIX lives in Texas with her husband, two ornery cats, and a flatulent pit bull. When she's not writing, she enjoys reading, cooking, knitting, watching stupid amounts of television, and getting distracted by Tumblr. She is also a powerlifter who can deadlift as much as Captain America weighs.

www.susannahnix.com